The Café At Kate's

Caroline Rebisz

ISBN: 979-8-3730-3099-1

DEDICATION

For Danuta and Beth.

CONTENTS

	Acknowledgments	i
1	Rose Cottage	Pg 1#
2	The King's Head Pub	Pg 11#
3	The Café at Kate's	Pg 17#
4	The Caravan in the Woods	Pg 26#
5	Salisbury District Hospital	Pg 31#
6	The Café at Kate's	Pg 37#
7	Laurel House	Pg 44#
8	Green Farm Cottages	Pg 49#
9	Laurel House	Pg 52#
10	Laurel House	Pg 56#
11	Rose Cottage	Pg 63#
12	Southampton Airport	Pg 70#
13	Rose Cottage	Pg 75#
14	Green Farm Cottages	Pg 82#
15	The Café at Kate's	Pg 87#
16	West Quay, Southampton	Pg 92#
17	The Manor House	Pg 97#
18	Laurel House	Pg 101#
19	The Manor House	Pg 105#
20	The King's Head Pub	Pg 112#

21	The Caravan in the Woods	Pg 118#
22	Rose Cottage	Pg 123#
23	The Manor House	Pg 127#
24	Rose Cottage	Pg 135#
25	The Café at Kate's	Pg 140#
26	The Café at Kate's	Pg 146#
27	The Rectory	Pg 156#
28	The Café at Kate's	Pg 161#
29	The Gundog Pub	Pg 165#
30	Rose Cottage	Pg 171#
31	The King's Head Pub	Pg 176#
32	The Village Hall	Pg 182#
33	Rose Cottage	Pg 189#
34	The King's Head Pub	Pg 198#
35	Rose Cottage	Pg 202#
36	Rose Cottage	Pg 207#
37	Poole Harbour	Pg 211#
38	Antonio's Restaurant	Pg 217#
39	Epilogue	Pg 225#
	Afterword	Pg 228#
	About The Author	Pg 230#

ACKNOWLEDGMENTS

I am indebted to those who support my ambitions. My husband is my firm supporter, giving me the space to be creative and applauding my sales dashboard, even if it's the tenth time I've looked at it in a day. My daughter, Dr Beth Rebisz, is my BETA reader. Her impartial advice and guidance is invaluable. My mother, Pamela, took on the task of proofreading this book. Thank you, Mum. Finally to my daughter, Danuta and my son-in-law, Andrew, for their support and encouragement.

CHAPTER ONE
ROSE COTTAGE

Jenni stretched out her back, kneading the knots which had formed around her neck muscles. She ached all over, but in a good way.

Jenni was exhausted. Her work this evening was not finished. Tomorrow was the big day. The Café at Kate's would open for the first time. All her plans had aligned perfectly and she was sure she was ready to go. It had been a hard slog over the last few months, but the excitement about tomorrow had been the motivation which kept her going.

Yes. She was ready.

Well, almost.

There was still the small matter of a coffee and walnut cake to frost and twenty-four cinnamon buns to bake. Jenni had been hard at it all afternoon. There had been times during the day when she decided she had taken on more than she could cope with. But that was just her self-doubts trying to pour water on the fire of enthusiasm for her new project. Deep down, she was confident everything would be perfect.

Well, hopefully. There we go. The self-doubt kicking in again!

The café was the brainchild of Jenni and her new best friend, Kate Penrose. Kate ran the local village store, which was imaginatively called Kate's. Not the most original name, but it worked. Its reputation was known far and wide, not just in the village of Sixpenny Bissett. People came from the surrounding villages, confident of finding fresh produce. The cheery, welcoming nature of its owner was an added bonus.

Despite Jenni putting up the finance for the revamp of the café area, the two women had agreed to call the new venture, The Café at Kate's. It would avoid confusion and would piggyback off the reputation of the shop. The two friends would run the General Store and Café separately, on the advice of Jenni's businessman son, George, but in practical terms they would work together to help each other out. Both of them needed the other, if they were going to make this a success and, most importantly, save the store. Over the last twelve months, the store had been hardly breaking even, despite its reputation for service and quality. It needed some diversification and the café was the answer, hopefully.

Jenni had moved to the village of Sixpenny Bissett nine months ago. It was a fresh start for her after losing her beloved husband, Reggie, in a car accident. She had struggled for months to adjust to widowhood in her native Birmingham; the constant reminders of her new status got too much. Escaping to the countryside allowed Jenni to reinvent herself, without seeing those concerned faces of sympathy and understanding.

Life in Sixpenny Bissett had not been a resounding success so far, but at least Jenni felt settled and had embraced country living with aplomb. She had even replaced her heels for wellies, something her Brummie friends would be horrified to hear. Jenni liked most of the villagers, with a couple of notable exceptions, and was excited to be sharing her new venture with her friends, the following morning.

"Mum." Jimmy interrupted her quiet reflections as he strode purposedly into the kitchen. "What time is dinner?"

Bloody hell. Jenni could cry.

Why could her son not see how busy she was? All he was worried about was his stomach. At no point during the day had Jimmy or Charlie even offered a hand. They had swanned into the kitchen on occasions to boil a kettle. She had been made to feel grateful that a hot brew had come her way as the two houseguests looked after themselves. Jenni didn't mind her son and his girlfriend living with her, but she did resent their lack of understanding of the pressures, ahead of the grand opening.

If truth be told, Jenni did resent Jimmy and Charlie living with her. It had messed up her plans no end. Her new life in the country had been hijacked with their arrival. But what could she do? As a mother, she could only support her son at his time of trouble. She couldn't turn him away.

Looking at the huge kitchen wall clock, Jenni noticed it was 7pm already. The afternoon had vanished under the weight of flour and butter as she creamed them together to create her magic. Whilst she was tired, that could not prevent her excitement of a job well done, especially as she surveyed the delicious cakes lined up on the breakfast bar.

"Jimmy, you and Charlie will have to fend for yourselves tonight. Can you not see? I am up against it to get these cakes finished and the Aga is full to the brim now. Why don't you pop down to The King's Head and grab some food? There's nothing coming your way from here this evening so if you are hungry, then that's your only option." She sighed with frustration.

The look on her son's face was a picture to behold. Shock that his mother was rejecting his pleas for sustenance; confusion at the thought of having to go out for food; and fear of having to tell his girlfriend that the answer to her demands for his mother to provide them with dinner was greeted with a resounding NO.

"Bloody hell, Mum, I hope it's not going to be like this every night. This crazy café idea. I just knew it was going to mess things up."

Jenni could have burst with fury at the selfishness of her boy. How dare he? What a little sod? All these years of caring for him and indulging his every want and that's the sort of attitude she was rewarded with.

Perhaps she had just answered her own question there. She had indulged him. Too much. And look at what that had led to.

Jenni decided the least she could do was to put a lid on her anger, as she rounded on Jimmy. She was not known for blowing a gasket, even though her younger son was pushing his luck with his attitude. Her voice was icy but controlled. "Don't forget that I am doing you a favour, putting up you and your girlfriend. That wasn't part of my plan. This was meant to be my new life in the country and I certainly didn't want to be sharing it with two whining twenty somethings." The emphasis on 'my' was pronounced.

Jimmy looked crestfallen. Despite acting like a spoilt teenager, he was fully aware of his responsibilities, even if he was trying to kick against them right now. Growing up was not much fun, in his opinion.

Jimmy had made such a mess of his life recently. Without his mother's support, he would have to rely on Charlie's family for a home and that was not going to happen anytime soon. Firstly, they probably wouldn't have them to stay even if they asked and secondly, Jimmy was scared stiff of Charlie's father. It just wasn't an option. His mum was his only supporter right now. He couldn't afford to annoy her. Mum trumped Charlie all day long.

"Sorry, Mum." A spot of contrition might help, he thought. "Is there anything I can do to help you?"

Jenni's anger dissolved as she glanced at her favourite son. She couldn't stay angry with him for long, especially when he put that stupid hangdog expression on his face. She enveloped him in one of her infamous 'Mumma cuddles'. Wrapping her arms around him, she squeezed him affectionally as his head flopped to rest on her shoulder. Luckily, Jenni was a tall woman, the perfect size for her gangly son.

Jimmy was never too old for one of her cuddles. Life, as an adult was so difficult. Taking responsibility was not something Jimmy had grasped fully, especially as Jenni was quick to run to his aid. Jenni knew she had been far too soft on her younger son since he returned from Australia. She loved having him home. Unfortunately, the fly in the ointment, was Charlie Wright. Having that lazy girl living with them was certainly not helping Jenni's mood. They came as a BOGOF. If one came with the other; she was stuck with them both.

"Don't you worry, Jimmy darling." Jenni was reaching for her handbag. "Look, take this and go and grab a meal for you both at the pub." She wafted a couple of £20 notes in his face. "I will be here for another hour at least. If I get finished, I will join you, but don't worry if I don't."

As she watched her son slope off with his shoulders drooped, Jenni sighed. Her son was not happy. That was clear to see. The upcoming responsibility of fatherhood was resting heavily on his shoulders. He didn't appear to be excited about the baby's arrival and had reluctantly involved himself in shopping for baby equipment. His heart clearly wasn't in it. Or perhaps it was a future with Charlie which was dragging down his mood. She was a difficult girl and rarely showed any affection towards Jenni's son. It appeared the feelings between them were mutually sour.

But they had made their bed and would have to lie in it. Jenni could actually hear her own mother, in her head, as she used her matriarchal favourite saying. Perhaps far too apt. One stupid drunken mistake had a ripple effect through the two young people's lives. They each blamed the other for their unhappiness. It was probably not surprising that the relationship was strained to breaking point.

Once Jimmy and Charlie had left for the pub, Jenni visibly relaxed.

It seemed she was constantly on edge since Charlie had moved in. Jenni hadn't really agreed to the stroppy girl joining their household. She had been pushed into a corner; one her better judgement would not allow her to wriggle out of. Charlie refused to stay with her parents who seemed to hold some pretty medieval ideas on marriage and babies. Charlie and Jimmy had steadfastly refused the former idea, which went against everything Charlie's parents believed in. Jenni, being Jenni, was too much of a push over. She had agreed that they could stay with her temporarily.

Unfortunately that temporary nature was extending day by day.

Jenni didn't think she was being unreasonable, but Charlie was lazy. She would leave her dinner plate on the side, expecting someone else to put it in the dishwasher. The dishwasher fairy unfortunately never appeared. Surprisingly! Jimmy and Charlie's bedroom was a tip, which hurt Jenni. Most of the clutter was Charlie's, although her son could create a mess wherever he was in the house. Jenni's beautiful home did not deserve to be treated with so little respect. Charlie never offered to help with any of the chores and seemed to spend all her time on her phone or watching daytime TV.

Once the baby was born, there would be changes. Jenni had let things go for too long now, hoping that their conscience might have kicked in. But neither of them seemed to notice the trail of destruction they left behind, in every room, or the frustration it instilled in Jenni.

She felt like an invisible woman in her own home.

Things had to change. Jenni had decided. She hadn't spoken to Jimmy about it yet, but there was a serious case of reality checking coming his way. As a father, he would have to pick up responsibility for his partner and the new-born. Jenni was no longer going to hold his hand.

He had to step up.

The last of the cinnamon buns were coming out of the Aga. They looked and smelled amazing. Jenni wafted the smell towards her nose with her fingers enjoying the rich, warming flavours. Surrounded by the fruits of her labour, Jenni was filled with renewed excitement for the week ahead. She had worked so hard to prepare for opening day and was determined to make it flourish.

Not just for her, but for Kate too.

Kate had made no secret of the fact that the success of the café would be the catalyst to keeping the village store in business. She was relying on Jenni to bring in the extra custom needed to revitalise Kate's General Store. The two friends were secretly confident that their venture would be a resounding success. If enthusiasm counted for anything, they would be a roaring success. No doubt about it.

As if she could read her best friend's mind, Kate stuck her head round the kitchen door. "Mind if I come in?"

She was already in. That was Kate's way. If you didn't want her to interrupt anything important or secretive, lock your door. Jenni smiled; happy memories of young Henrique came to mind.

Over recent months, the two women had become inseparable, bosom buddies, who were completely relaxed in each other's company, popping in to see each other whenever they wanted. Poor old Jeremy, Kate's husband, saw less and less of his wife as the plans for the café developed.

The friends never really needed an excuse to sneak off to the pub for a bottle of wine. And the café was the perfect excuse. Their bond included keeping each other's secrets. Jenni had intimate knowledge of the Penrose finances and the impact Kate's General Store was having on the family.

In return, Kate was the ear Jenni bent when she'd had enough of Charlie and Jimmy's antics. Kate had made it clear to her bestie that the two of them were taking advantage of Jenni's kind nature and that she really should set some ground rules now or bear the consequences after the baby was born. It was this particular discussion which they failed to agree on. Jenni was keen to wait until the baby was home from hospital. Then she would make changes. The couple would be flush with the emotion of a new life so it would be perfect timing for some challenging rules to be laid down.

Jenni might be a push over when it came to her son, but she would only take so much.

"Blimey, Jenni. You have been busy." Kate surveyed the goodies displayed across the breakfast bar. "I hope people are hungry tomorrow. You have enough to feed the whole village."

Jenni laughed as she strolled over to the fridge to find a bottle of Chardonnay. Pouring two generous glasses, she passed one to Kate and took a satisfying sip herself.

"I know I have gone a bit over the top, but some of this will go in the chest freezer. God knows how I am going to keep up, physically, if I bake every night. My plan is to bulk bake at the weekends and freeze." Jenni was arranging the cakes into two sections, as if to explain her thinking. "Give it a week and I may have a better idea of sale volumes. I just don't know what to expect yet."

Kate could see the nervousness in Jenni's expression. Jenni was investing some serious money in the venture and Kate would hate to see things fail. Reaching across, Kate rubbed Jenni's arm reassuringly.

"Don't you worry, my lovely. I can feel it in my waters. You are going to smash it."

"Oh thanks, matey." The expression on Jenni's face relaxed as her beautiful smile shone through. When Jenni smiled, people noticed. It was a thing of wonder. "I'm super excited for tomorrow and a tiny bit nervous too. But day one is bound to be good as everyone will want to come and support. Or at least have a nose. It's the week after that I am worried about. What if no-one comes back after opening week?"

"Oh shut up, you silly sausage." Kate smiled as she spoke, not wishing her friend to be offended. "It will take time to build your reputation. And you will. I have every confidence in you and more importantly, so has Jeremy."

Jeremy had said a special prayer for Jenni at Parish Communion that morning. He had an ulterior motive too. He needed the café to be a success to help the General Store survive. It had been his persuasive arguments which had pushed his wife into taking on the store some years back and he had watched her buckling under the worry and strain of trying to make it profitable. The café had to be a success. It didn't bear thinking about the alternative.

"I honestly don't know what I would have done without you and Jeremy cheering me on," sighed Jenni. "I just don't get the same sort of support from Jimmy or Charlie. Nearest thing I get to cheering from them is when I put food on the table."

Kate didn't want to say, 'I told you so'. She had made her feelings clear on the subject of selfish Jimmy and his lazy girlfriend. No, now was not the time.

"What about the beautiful Henrique? Has he been supportive?" Kate winked.

Henrique was the Spanish gardener who serviced most of the village. He saved an extra special service for Jenni. It was a secret, but one that Kate knew all about. In detail. Not that she was jealous, of course. Well, not much.

"I haven't seen much of him in the last few weeks. Been too busy. But I'm sure he will be a frequent visitor. He is quite partial to cake."

Kate laughed. "That's not all he's partial too. Bet its hard getting a bit of alone time with the kids around."

Jenni and Henrique had an arrangement. Since Jimmy had moved back home, it had become more difficult for them to meet up secretly. Jenni was adamant that the rest of the village could not find out about her secret relationship. It was just sex and bloody good sex at that. But it was a secret which only Kate was privy to. Jimmy might suspect something, but there was no way he would ever ask his mother the question. He would be mortified with the answer. So whenever the fancy took them, Jenni and Henrique would meet at the caravan in the woods for a steamy session.

Jenni maintained a fairly clinical approach to their relationship. She enjoyed the sex and loved Henrique's company, but it was not a 'grown up' thing. It was a fantasy she was living out. It was daring and exciting, but that was it.

Unfortunately, Henrique did not feel the same way. He had a crush on Jenni which wasn't going away. He had tried, but the woman enticed him in, again and again. He kept promising himself he would put an end to it. He knew Jenni didn't feel the same way about him. But he couldn't stop seeing her. He told himself he could handle it, but each time they slept together he fell a little bit deeper in love with the older woman.

"I think I might knock it on the head, Kate," said her friend. "I really haven't got the time anyway, especially now with the café and the baby coming."

Kate nodded her head. Her obvious agreement to her friend's resolution didn't match her face, which was smirking. "Of course you will, Jenni. Just like you told me the last five times we discussed Henrique."

Her laughter was good natured. Kate had enjoyed hearing about the saucy liaison and was secretly quite jealous. The idea of having a young stud in one's bed was tempting, even for a vicar's wife. And good luck to Jenni. She deserved a bit of fun now that she had the terrible twosome living with her. Those kids, not that you could call them kids. They were old enough to stand on their own two feet.

But that was another matter entirely.

"Anyway, Jenni, how can I help? Do you want me to put cling film over these so they stay fresh for the morning?"

The two women were soon engrossed in preparations for the launch day.

All thoughts of the sexy Spaniard were soon forgotten.

CHAPTER TWO
THE KING'S HEAD PUB

The pub was unusually quiet. Sunday evening was unpopular with the residents of Sixpenny Bissett, or so it seemed.

As they studied the menus, Jimmy was in a reflective mood.

He didn't know what he had done to deserve his mother. She was one in a million. At least the cash she had pushed his way would win over Charlie. His girlfriend seemed to be moaning constantly about money, at the moment. Jimmy had a decent amount in savings, which his dad had left for him when he died, but he was reluctant to spend that on Charlie. If she thought he was some sort of cash cow she could get that idea firmly out of her head. If it wasn't for the baby, she would be well gone.

He didn't want a serious relationship right now, especially not with her.

Jimmy had made such a mess of his life recently. It hurt him deeply when his mum was angry with him. Childlike in his behaviour, he only wanted to please her. What didn't help was her constantly reminding him about how disappointed she was with him. It was bad enough that he felt guilty for spoiling her plans for the future, without her constantly reminding him of his failings. Anyway it wasn't all his fault. He didn't plan on getting Charlie pregnant. She never told him she wasn't on the pill.

How was he supposed to know?

Unfortunately, he was now caught between the demands of the two women in his life. His mother, who was a saint in everyone's eyes. She stoically put up with the upheaval in her life due to his early return from travelling. And his girlfriend, if you could even call her that. There wasn't much friendship involved.

His mother hadn't expected him to come home so soon.

He hadn't expected to come home so soon.

And certainly not with a pregnant girlfriend in tow.

Charlie was not the easiest of girlfriends. In fact, he didn't really like her much. She was having his baby; that was the extent of their connection. He didn't love her and she certainly didn't love him. Sometimes, he was sure she hated him. Charlie was only here because living with Jimmy was preferable to her own parents. They had been livid with her for messing up her life spectacularly. Charlie could not bear listening to her parents moans and, other than a quick trip back home to tell them about her pregnancy, she had seen nothing more of them since.

That didn't stop her moaning in his ear, at every opportunity, about how hard done by she felt.

God knows what would happen when the baby was born. He didn't want the kid. Would he be shackled to Charlie because of an adventurous sperm? Trust him to have exceptional swimmers.

He had met Charlie in Argentina. She was doing a solo trip, similar to him, and they had been thrown together on the cattle ranch where they briefly worked. Initially, they had a great laugh together. Charlie was 'one of the lads' and could drink most of the other workers under the table. She was tall and leggy, and whilst nothing much to look at in Jimmy's opinion, had the most gorgeous body, which had definitely benefited from exposure to the sun. She was golden, with such a healthy glow to her skin.

Charlie had been so alive.

Jimmy had been dragged into her exciting sphere and was dazzled by her confidence and bravado. Like a moth to the flame, he got too close and inevitably got burnt. After one particularly liquid evening, they had ended up in bed together and the rest was history.

Charlie had decided to join Jimmy on the next leg of his journey and by the time they were in Australia, she suspected she was pregnant. She hadn't told him of her fears until it had been too late to get rid of it. The last stage of their travelling had been in the outback of Australia. Perhaps if they had been living nearer a city, he could have got the whole thing sorted.

He couldn't forgive Charlie for hiding the truth from him until it was too late. And now he was stuck. Why she had been determined to keep the baby was beyond him. Her attitude since they had arrived home had been one of complete disinterest in the baby. Why she hadn't just got rid of it in Aussieland, continued to baffle Jimmy.

Her selfish decision had left him at the mercy of his mum and his moody bitch of a girlfriend.

Jimmy didn't feel responsible for the current situation. He was the victim. No wonder Charlie was such a brat in his company. She could see through his arrogance. It takes two to tango. Unfortunately, Jimmy had an unrealistic view that Charlie should be dancing solo.

"What are you going to have?" Charlie hit him over the head with the menu, bringing him back to reality with a thump.

"Owww, fuck off," snarled Jimmy.

He really wasn't in the mood for her playacting. In company, Charlie tried to make out that they were a happy, young couple, excitedly awaiting the birth of their baby. How wrong could their audiences' perception be.

"Seriously, Jimmy. What are you having? Will the cash cover the full roast dinner?" Charlie certainly had no reservations about taking money from Jenni. She would use Jenni and her cash without any qualms.

"Yeah." Jimmy got up intending to put the order in. "I'm having the beef. You? Drink?"

"Soda and lime." Charlie pulled out her phone and started to scroll.

That bloody phone was permanently attached to her hand, thought Jimmy. God knows who she is talking to as she doesn't have any friends, he decided meanly. Strolling over to the bar, he noticed Henrique was on duty. Jimmy liked the Spaniard and quite often challenged him to a game of darts over a beer. Being the only two young men in the village naturally thrust them together.

Thank goodness Jimmy didn't know what else they shared in common.

"Evening, mate." Jimmy flashed Henrique a smile as he slapped the menu down on the bar. "Can we have two roast beefs, a pint of cider and a tonic water please, Henrique."

"Evening, Jimmy. I guess your mum is not cooking tonight then. Will she be joining you?"

Henrique was dying to see Jenni, even if it was only in company. He had missed her over recent weeks as preparations for the café and the demands of Jimmy and his girlfriend had kept her away from the caravan. He was suffering from withdrawal symptoms and was desperate to coax Jenni back into bed soon.

"O-M-G, Henrique. Our house is like a bloody bakery. Cakes everywhere. Mum has been cooking all day and couldn't even spare some food for us. Kicked out to the pub. She said she will pop down later, but I doubt it. There's nothing to eat at home unless you want cake and, even then, she wouldn't let me taste anything." Jimmy rested his head in his fist on the bar. "This café will be the death of me." He groaned as if to emphasise the impact on his normal diet.

Henrique liked Jimmy but he really could be one spoilt brat. The Spaniard knew how hard Jenni worked to get ready for the opening day tomorrow and without any real support from Jimmy or Charlie. Granted Jimmy was now working, but surely Charlie could help out, he thought.

"Your mum must be exhausted. I tell you what, why don't I plate up a roast for her too and you could pop it home for her? That will definitely get you back into her good book." He prided himself with his knowledge of English colloquialisms, even if he didn't get it spot on all the time.

"Brilliant idea, but just one problem," sighed Jimmy. "Mum only gave me enough cash for me and Charlie so, sorry, no can do."

Henrique wanted to slap his mate for the sheer selfishness of that remark. Jenni really doesn't deserve a son like that, he decided. "Leave it with me, Jimmy. I will sort it, on the house." The reality would be that he would be paying, but it was the least he could do for Jenni. "Give me five minutes and your mum's food will be ready."

Henrique was determined that the two selfish adults could wait while Jenni got priority in the food stakes. Jimmy slouched his way back to his seat, looking like the weight of the world was wedged heavily on his shoulders. Charlie raised her head from her phone as he scrapped the chair across the floor.

"Bloody hell, Jimmy. Pick the fucking chair up. Don't scrape it. That went right through my head. You know I have a fucking headache. 'Der Brain'."

Jimmy was not a violent man but there were times when he felt he could literally slap Charlie. She was a right bitch and spent every moment they were together moaning. Thank goodness he had a job now and didn't have to suffer her presence during the day

Jimmy had a labouring job working for Alaistair Middleton. It was hard, psychical work, but paid a decent wage and got him out of the house. Somehow, he would have to pay for the baby and the huge list of equipment Charlie was preparing to buy. Alaistair was a good bloke and wasn't on Jimmy's case all the time. He left him to do whatever he had assigned for the day and would pick him up and bring him home after work. He couldn't really ask for a better boss at the moment.

But Jimmy had plans. He really wanted to work at Richard Samuel's boatyard. The idea of designing and building boats had caught his interest. He had asked Jenni to put in a good word, but she hadn't yet. Secretly, Jimmy decided it was Richard who his mother had been shagging the night he returned home unexpectedly. He couldn't prove it, but obviously something had gone wrong as Jenni avoided Richard like the plague. His request might have to wait until that particular frost had melted.

Charlie interrupted his thoughts yet again. "You cretin. This is tonic. I wanted lime and soda. Go and get me another one."

"Get it yourself, you stupid bitch. I have had enough of your nagging for one day. You are seriously worse than my mother."

Charlie's laughter was cruel and nasty. "Your bloody mother is the stupid bitch not me. All those pigging rules drive me mad. Why can't she just chill out."

Jimmy was seething with anger. Oh, it was okay for him to moan about his mother but there was no way he would take it from Charlie "Shut the fuck up. If you don't like the rules then why don't you bugger off back to your parents. See what it's like there. My mum doesn't have to put you up and you could start by helping out a bit more rather than sit on your fat arse all day."

That shut her up.

Charlie looked totally shocked at his outburst and, for once, was silent. Her head dropped back into her phone and a rosy hue coloured her cheeks. Jimmy sat back in his chair, picking up his cider. He sipped on the appley nectar as he stared at his girlfriend. He felt a bit guilty for being that nasty with her, but unfortunately Charlie brought the worst out in him. In fact, he felt quite proud of himself for growing some balls for a change.

His musing was interrupted by Henrique, with a large plate enveloped in tin foil. The heat wafting from the parcel indicated that it had just come out of the oven.

"Here you go, Jimmy. Get that back to your mum and I will have yours and Charlie's food ready when you are back. Give your mother my best, please."

Henrique grinned, hoping that Jenni would know the gift was from him and not her lackadaisical son. The pink heart-shaped napkin he had hidden in the foil may well give him away. Anything to grab her attention right now. And also to show that Jenni was appreciated, even if her disaster of a son didn't show her the respect due.

CHAPTER THREE
THE CAFÉ AT KATE'S

Jenni glanced across at Kate, who was setting up behind the counter of the store. Jenni smiled, that beaming smile which lit up her face with joy and excitement.

It was Monday morning and the first day of business for the Café at Kate's. All her planning was about to be put into practise.

Jenni and Kate had been in the shop for over an hour now, preparing. The coffee machine was warming up nicely. All the beautiful cups and saucers were laid out on the shelves behind the counter, gleaming in the early morning sunlight. On display were the cinnamon buns and two large cakes. One was a traditional Victoria sponge, a firm favourite, alongside a coffee and walnut cake. They were displayed, magnificently, in the glass cabinet under the counter, ensuring they would catch the eyes of anyone entering the shop or pausing for a coffee.

Their tempting calories would be hard to resist, Jenni hoped. Quietly in her mind, she thanked Alastair for suggesting the glass display cabinet. It was certainly a draw. The crystal cake stands were another fabulous investment, showing off her wares.

Jenni stepped back to inspect the counter. She was bursting with pride. Everything was set for the day ahead. Her nervousness that the business would flop had flown out the window. Today was not a day for negativity. It was the start of something special. A new venture with her best buddy. How could they fail? Jenni had put her heart and soul into the café and she was determined to make it an enormous success. Knowing that she had the unswerving support of Kate Penrose was the extra boost, if she needed it.

Jimmy and Charlie had still been fast asleep when she left this morning. What a surprise!

Tiptoeing down the stairs, she had fed Freddie the cat, who had obliged with an early morning cuddle. It had taken her a few trips to transport her valuable produce up the road to the store, where Kate was waiting. Her friend had agreed to unlock early, giving Jenni plenty of time to prepare. The store always opened at 8am and Jenni had agreed to mirror the opening times initially, until she had a better feel for her customer habits.

Fortunately, the quietness of the previous evening had been the bonus she had desperately needed to calm her pre-launch nerves.

It had been worth the money to send the kids out for dinner. The arrival of a heaped plate of roast beef had also been most welcome. Despite Jimmy bragging that it was his idea to think about his mother's needs, when he dropped the savoury delights home, Jenni was sure there was another at work. Henrique often took the Sunday evening shift and the pink heart napkin was a giveaway that her young lover was at work. She let her son make a fool of himself as he strutted around the kitchen, preening himself like a peacock.

How she wished he was as thoughtful as the action he was falsely owning.

"Right, Jenni, are you ready?" Kate was beside her, draping an arm across her shoulder in a companionable fashion.

"Ready as I'll ever be," smiled Jenni. Giving her new bestie a squeeze, she raised the counter flap and stepped behind. Raising her arms out as if to show off her goods, she continued. "Does it look alright?"

"Beautiful. I seriously could eat everything." Kate tapped her waistline. "Not sure us opening a café will help my figure." She laughed to herself as she reached the front door, drawing the bolts and flinging the door wide. "Morning, General."

The first customer this momentous day was Herbert Smythe-Jones, chair of the Parish Council and owner of The Manor House.

Everyone called Herbert, The General. It was a term of endearment and an acknowledgement of his service to his country. Herbert was extremely fond of Jenni. She reminded him of his beloved wife, who had died some years before. Since Jenni had arrived in Sixpenny Bissett, Herbert had come to accept that Jenni was not future wife material. He adored her, but she could only see him as the father she no longer had in her life.

Herbert had gradually come to accept they wanted different things from their relationship. With this acceptance came a deeper friendship than either of them had expected. He was quite happy to play the father role. It worked both ways. Herbert didn't get to see his own children as often as he would have liked. The busy nature of modern life would test their time. Having Jenni to nurture and support, was the company he had never expected to find in his later years.

From her perspective, Jenni adored Herbert and they would often be found spending a relaxing dinner together. When Jenni needed a 'grown up' conversation, The General was always her first choice. He became her sounding board when she was struggling with Jimmy and Charlie. She had worked through the financial figures for the café with Herbert and he had been instrumental in supporting her to set up the necessary banking and taxation formalities. It was apt that he would be the first to show his support this morning.

Herbert strolled into the café, nodding his head enthusiastically at the changes made to the building. His approval wasn't sought by Jenni but meant the world to her.

Jenni and Kate had revamped part of the original store to set up the eatery. It was a section of the shop which hadn't been fully utilised before and, with the help of local builder Alaistair Middleton, the improvements allowed customers to walk between both shop and café with ease. It would allow the two women to benefit from cross-selling their services.

"Good morning, Jenni my dear. This looks splendid. Well done. You have made such a lovely job of the décor." Herbert looked around, noticing the blackboard which displayed the prices, written in Jenni's beautiful hand. Everything was just spot on, in his opinion. "I think I will treat myself to a cappuccino and a slice of the coffee cake, please."

"Coming up," smiled Jenni. "My first ever customer and I am so happy it is you, Herbert. It means a lot to me." The feeling was genuine. She couldn't ask for a more perfect start to her life in business.

Herbert visibly puffed out his chest with pride at that remark. She really was the most adorable friend any gentleman could ask for.

The brand new coffee machine was getting its first official outing. Fortunately, Jenni had been practising over the weekend and had finally mastered its intricacies. The role of a barista was not easy and Jenni was determined to add some flare to her beverages to ensure repeat custom. As the first cappuccino took shape, her confidence surged. Slicing a generous piece of coffee and walnut cake, she placed both on a small wooden tray and accompanied Herbert of one of the round tables, set in the window area.

"Is this table ok, Herbert?" Jenni still could not bring herself to call her mentor The General. He was Herbert to her and always would be.

"Lovely thank you, Jenni."

The General settled down to savour his cake. It might be just after 8am which was, by any reckoning, a tad early for such luxury, but it was important to him to show his support. As one of the leaders of the village community, where he led, others would follow.

And, indeed, he was followed.

Paula St John arrived minutes after Jenni had finished serving Herbert. Paula was another friend who had become close to Jenni in the last few months. Despite the nefarious efforts of her estranged husband to sexually assault Jenni at last year's Christmas party, the two women had bonded in their shared disgust of his actions. Paula had kicked her ex-husband out of the matrimonial home and was currently going through a fairly messy divorce. Peter St John was trying his hardest to stop his wife from obtaining her freedom. He was lost without her and really hadn't expected Paula to make a stand against his lechery.

For the first time in his life, Peter was not getting his own way. And he was frightened. His dread of being alone, without the steadying hand of his wife, was the reason for his fight against the divorce.

If only she could see how sorry he was. And he was sorry. Sorry he got caught.

"Morning, Jenni. Wow, this is so impressive. Well done." Paula's stomach was rumbling as she stared at the sweet offerings. "I can't stop as I have a job down in Bournemouth this week. Can I get a coffee to go?"

"Of course." Jenni was glad that she had invested in some take-away materials. Kate had insisted that it wouldn't be necessary, but Jenni's experience of living in a city for years had enlightened her decision. She had also invested in some reusable coffee cups which she hoped might be of interest to those environmentally friendly customers.

Paula had noticed Jenni's eyes moving towards the brightly coloured cups. "Oh, aren't they beautiful. Could I buy the orange one, Jenni, and then you can pop my coffee in that. Also let me have one of those gorgeous smelling buns. I will save that for later."

Jenni was buzzing at this point. Her first two customers in and she had already taken more cash than she had expected. Hopefully two satisfied customer who might spread the word.

Any worries about her decision to go into business were disappearing as fast as her cakes were selling. Over the course of the morning she had a regular stream of customers. Many of the visitors were people she had never met before. Unknown to her, she had a number of secretive local advocates who had been spreading the word over recent weeks.

The valley newsletter publication had been carrying a message from the chair of the Parish Council, Herbert Smythe-Jones, asking the wider community to support both the café and village shop as a vital resource to the surrounding area. Most valley residents understood the need for local facilities and were more than happy to help. Keeping that custom going after day one was the biggest challenge and one that Jenni was fully aware of. She had built that risk into her business model and had planned to supplement her quieter days with some private catering work.

By lunchtime Jenni had even had to pop home, quickly, to pick up another

Victoria Sponge cake. Sales were steady and Jenni had given up counting the number of cups she had washed up between customers. She had hardly had time to rest her feet all morning and was glad of the comfortable trainers she had opted for rather than heels. Jenni was sure today was unique as people tried her out, but she was fully aware of the need to create a great first impression.

She would need that repeat business if the café was to be a success.

"Hi, Mum." Jimmy interrupted her musings. He and Alastair were covered in plaster, liberally scattered over their hair, evidence of their morning's work. Jenni grimaced as she imagined the mess they would make to the dainty tablecloths covering her seated tables.

Luckily, Alastair seemed to read her mind.

"Don't worry, Jenni, we are not going to destroy your beautiful surroundings with two hairy arsed builders cluttering up your pristine establishment." He laughed. "We are just grabbing a sandwich from Kate's and if you can do us two teas and two portions of that wonderful looking coffee and walnut cake, please. Builders' tea for me and I'm sure you know how young Jimmy takes his."

Jenni heaved a sigh of relief. It was never good to turn a customer away, but the two of them looked a right mess. As she made the teas, her mind jumped ahead to the idea of setting up some seating in the courtyard outside. It would be ideal on sunny days and allow some of the many workmen, who currently frequented the pub for lunch, to consider her services as an alternative.

After lunch, both the shop and café quieten down and Kate wandered over, taking a seat. Jenni had set the area out with small, white, wooden tables and chairs allowing groups of two to sit together. These tables could easily be pushed together if a larger party were to arrive. That would be vital for groups like the knitting club, who she hoped might make a regular weekly booking.

Each table was exquisitely decorated with an embroidered white and peach tablecloth with matching sugar pots. Her attention to the intricate details was carefully thought through. Each item matched the colour code for the café, but with individual designs to give it a more eclectic feel.

"Coffee?"

"Please," said Kate. "Don't know about you but I have been rushed off my feet all day. Not that I'm complaining. I literally ran out of milk by lunchtime so I know business has been booming."

Jenni answered with a beaming smile and a flat white. "Luckily, I have enough milk to sort you out, my lovely."

Jenni took a seat opposite and stretched out her ankles. Reaching upwards, she stretched her arms towards the ceiling, feeling the gentle crack of muscle and sinew. It had been a long, hard morning and she had loved every minute of it.

"Well, darling Jenni. I think you have played a blinder today. Of course, there will be those who have popped in today for a nosey at something new, but I think I can say without hesitation, we did it!" Kate offered her palm for a high five.

Jenni slapped her friend's palm in a celebratory fashion. "God knows how much money I have taken today, but it's much more than I expected, Kate. Everyone has been so very lovely."

Jenni felt quite emotional and wiped a tear from her eye. No more would she doubt her abilities. She could do this. And she could enjoy running the business too. She had found her niche and was determined to make it work.

"Thank goodness I baked like a woman possessed over the weekend," she sighed. "I honestly can't see myself working a full day in the café and then baking every night. I'm pooped."

Kate's mind was racing. "I have an idea. How about stocking some of my pastries and croissants in the mornings? There is a market for breakfast, especially for those heading off to the station. My delivery comes in packets but we could easily whip a few out each day onto your counter. Split the profit?" Kate winked.

All too often Kate had heard customers moan about not wanting a bag of four pastries for breakfast so it could work. They had a reasonable stream of customers heading up to Salisbury, or down to Bournemouth, from the one and only station in the valley, so why not cash in on the passing trade. If it proved successful, they could consider an even earlier opening to catch the commuters.

"Sounds like a plan, matey. I knew there was a reason we decided to work together on this venture. We will smash it."

Jenni sipped her coffee as she gazed with pride at her new dominion. She was so glad she had decided to add something extra to her life. She really couldn't see herself shuffling into early retirement and the last thing on her mind was the thought of being an unpaid babysitter to her future grandchild. Not that Charlie had shown any interest in finding a job.

As the two friends relaxed in each other's company they were interrupted by a most welcome customer. Henrique, the Spanish gardener, who looked after most of the village, slipped quietly through the store's door. Well, as quietly as anyone can with the tinkling bell hanging over the entrance. He made his way over to the café area, removing his grass-laden boots as he walked.

Jenni giggled. "Oh, Henrique, there is no need to take your boots off." She was on her feet, ready to serve.

"I don't want to get any muck on your beautifully clean floor," he smiled.

O-M-G thought Kate. He is the most attractive man ever. Lucky Jenni, getting to see him in all his glory. God knows why her friend was so determined to keep their relationship quiet. If it was her, she would be shouting it from the church steeple. Not that it would be very appropriate for the vicar's wife, of course.

Kate watched her best friend and the sex-bomb chatting at the counter. The body language between them was so obvious to any observer who was aware of their circumstances, but probably unseen to those not in the know. The little smiles and gestures between them were charged with sexual tension.

At times, their voices lowered to almost a whisper, allowing them an element of privacy. Unknown to Kate they were agreeing to meet after the celebrations planned on Friday. The pub was laying on a few drinks to toast and celebrate the new venture in the village.

Jenni believed she deserved a bit of time with Henrique as reward for her first week as an independent businesswoman. It had been far too long.

She had an itch and it needed scratching.

CHAPTER FOUR
THE CARAVAN IN THE WOODS

Jenni gasped as her lover hit the sweet spot.

Henrique was a considerate partner, ensuring that Jenni was satisfied before he finished. Reaching a peak, he collapsed on top of Jenni, breathing in the scent of her. Jenni wrapped her arms around his torso, reaching up to run her fingers through his hair. His curls, at the back of his head, were soft to the touch. She adored his body. He was the sexiest man she had ever known. Not that she had known many. He was only her second, if truth be told.

Jenni would not let herself feel guilty for her sexual relationship with Henrique. She could not think about how poor Reggie would have felt, seeing his wife wrapped around a boy young enough to be her son. She would not seek confirmation that what she was doing was right.

Jenni wanted to enjoy her time with the man and that was that. Perhaps she was being selfish. She wouldn't let herself think like that.

She kissed him, drinking in his taste as she explored with her tongue. In all the years since Reggie had died, she could not have imagined finding someone like Henrique. He enjoyed her company and made no demands of her. She could seek him out when she wanted to feel the release of a sexual encounter and then they could revert back to friendship afterwards. There was no embarrassment between them when they met outside of the bedroom. Unfortunately though, Jenni did not realise that he was in love with her. It was transactional sex on her part and she just assumed that he felt the same way.

Henrique could not tell her how he felt.

He was confused enough about his feelings. There could be no future for them. He could not see himself moving in Jenni's world. It would not be acceptable. But he loved their encounters, whether they be hurried like today, or last all night long. Since Jimmy had moved back home, meeting for any extended period of time had become challenging for the couple.

They grabbed any opportunity when it came along and tonight was one such.

Jenni had gone to the event at The King's Head pub with Kate and Jeremy Penrose. She had left Jimmy and Charlie in front of the TV. Charlie was moaning about backache and, for once, Jimmy seemed to be taking his responsibilities seriously. The celebrations were only scheduled to last for a couple of hours, a fact she withheld from her son. Thus giving Jenni time to rush over to the caravan and enjoy some furtive time with her young lover.

The chill of the summer evening was seeping in through the doorway, as Jenni pulled a blanket around her naked body. They were in the sitting room area of the caravan, having not made it to the bed. Their desire to have each other had taken over. Henrique pulled on his boxers as he shut the door and turned on the electric fire.

His consideration for her welfare was another reason she adored the Spaniard. Perhaps it was the way he had been brought up, to respect others, but in this, he was so different to her wayward son. Despite his youth, he had a maturity which allowed him to move in different circles to Jimmy. And feel comfortable in those circles. Unfortunately, the prejudices of the wealthy villagers wouldn't accept him as an equal. A fact which irritated Jenni in the extreme.

It never seemed to bother Henrique. He accepted his position in life with his usual Hispanic flair for understatement. He was happy in the shadows, invaluable to the community who took immense pride in their gardens, but invisible when it came to social activities, unless he was behind the bar at The King's Head, of course.

"Glass of wine, Jenni?" He had the bottle in hand and was drawing the cork before she could answer.

"I really shouldn't," sighed Jenni. "But seeing as you have opened it now, it would be rude not to."

Henrique smiled, confused with her English expressions. Whilst his language skills were improving day by day, he still struggled with some of the colloquial sayings Jenni used. Those words, spoken in her soft Brummie accent, added to his confusion at times.

Jenni had been an excellent coach, supporting his knowledge of the English language, especially as she shared her extensive library with him. Henrique loved to read and found delving into the delights of the classics was helping his vocabulary grow. He saw his future in the UK and hoped that one day he could set down some firmer roots, perhaps buying a small cottage somewhere in the valley.

His girlfriend, Jacinta, had plans to move over to be with him, something he had been resisting. She just assumed that marriage and babies would be their future together. The last thing he needed right now was playing happy families with Jacinta. He suspected her true motives for wanting to move to the UK were centred in a growing suspicion about his fidelity. A suspicion grounded in truth.

Jenni and Henrique sat cuddled up on the sofa bed, sipping the full-bodied wine. His fingers drew circles around her shoulders, gently moving to touch her ear lobes and stroking down her neck.

Jenni's mind was elsewhere, not paying due attention to his fingers. She was in reflective mood. It had been a long week. Her feet could bear testament to that. But it had been a successful week, which confirmed to her that she had made the right decision about her future. She had loved the busy times in the café and had taken advantage of the lulls between customers to plan out the following day.

A steady stream of customers had visited over the week. Some would probably become regulars, she was thinking particularly about The General, Paula and Alaistair. They had seemed to have established a routine with her already. Added to her friends, there were new faces from other villages who had returned after the rush of launch day.

Yesterday four businessmen arrived and, surprisingly, asked to use a small area of the café to hold an impromptu informal meeting. They had spent a good wedge of cash, which had made the inconvenience of losing a couple of tables for an hour well worthwhile. Alan, the organiser, seemed extremely impressed and had said they would be back.

Everything had exceeded her expectations for the first week.

She could not have planned it any better.

Jenni had managed to keep up with the baking and had started to get into a good routine. She had always been a morning person and by rising at 7am, she could knock out some muffins or a cake and have that cooked and decorated before the shop opened. Leaving the clearing up for Charlie, when she woke around midday, added some additional enjoyment for Jenni. After leaving an absolute chaotic mess on Tuesday morning, she was shocked and surprised to find the kitchen pristine on her return. Perhaps the girl had picked up on the vibes she had been sending her way.

Unfortunately, Jenni was not to know that it was Jimmy who had cleared up before his day of labouring. Charlie definitely had her son under the proverbial thumb.

Her thoughts were interrupted by the trill of her mobile. Glancing at the screen she could see it was Jimmy.

"Sorry, Henrique, I'd better get this. Hello, Jimmy, everything ok?"

She could hear the desperation in his voice instantly. "Mum, where the fuck have you been? I've been trying to ring you for ages."

"Jimmy, please tone down your language. This is literally the first time my phone has rung tonight."

Mobile signal in the village was notoriously patchy. All too often residents saw this as an advantage. The pace of life in the valley was slow. A snail's pace. What need was there to be in constant communication with others?

Jimmy continued. "I even came down the pub and you weren't there. Where the hell are you?"

Jenni's frustration at the line of questioning peaked. "Jimmy, why are you calling? Is there a problem?" Sometimes her son's inability to manage his own life drove her to distraction.

"Mum, its Charlie. I think she's about to have the baby. What the fuck do I do?"

Jenni groaned. "Have you spoken to the hospital?"

"Charlie did. They said to come in asap. But Charlie won't go without you. Says I will be useless in the delivery room and she wants you."

For once Charlie was probably quite right. However, she was shocked that the girl wanted her there for the birth. Up until now, there had been little conversation between the two women. They shared an interest in Jimmy and that was the extent of their relationship to date.

"Okay, I'm on my way but you will have to drive. I'm over the limit." Jenni was struggling into her underwear as she spoke. Ever the gentleman, Henrique reached behind her to fasten her bra, sending kisses down her spine. She shivered with anticipation and disappointment, knowing it would end far too abruptly. "Make sure Charlie has her overnight bag packed and I will be back in 10 minutes."

Jenni turned to face Henrique. "Sorry, duty calls. Looks like I'm about to become a grandmother. Fancy making love to a granny next time?" She giggled, thinking about the ridiculousness of their current situation.

Within minutes she was fully dressed and struggling into her ankle boots. Kissing Henrique on both cheeks, she left, running, as fast as it was safe to do, through the woods. As she ran, the enormity of what was about to happen started to hit her.

She was about to become a grandmother.

And she was going to be present at the birth.

"Oh my dear Lord," she shouted to the world. "I'm going to be a bloody granny."

CHAPTER FIVE
SALISBURY DISTRICT HOSPTAL
BEATRICE LABOUR WARD

"Now, Charlie, when the next contraction comes, I want you to push down as hard as you can into your bottom."

Lindsay, their midwife, held Charlie's hand and squeezed it gently. She had a soft Scottish accent, which was soothing and authoritative at the same time. She could tell the young woman was struggling after an hour of pushing. This baby was taking it's time making an entrance. Lindsay glanced across at Jenni, nodding her head.

"Now, Jenni, I want you to take Charlie's hand and encourage her as she pushes. We will have this baby out in no time at all."

In the organised chaos of the delivery room, Jenni watched her son's girlfriend as she worked hard to give birth. A new-found respect for the woman had formed in Jenni's mind as she had watched Charlie manage her precious task without moaning and complaining. She had borne the pain in silence, which was frankly uncanny. Jenni's experience of Charlie's behaviour to date had not been so positive. She was quick to moan and share her dislike of anything. In the last few hours, she had taken the suffering of childbirth in her stride, without the faintest mutter of argument.

Jimmy, on the other hand, was next to useless. He had spent the last couple of hours walking the corridors of the labour ward. In his normal fashion, he had most of the support staff running around after him, supplying him with cups of tea and even a sandwich, whilst poor Charlie couldn't have a drop in case an emergency caesarean was needed. Without Jenni to support the frightened young woman, Charlie would have been alone. Once again, Jenni questioned the values she had instilled in her youngest. So different to his father, who had been a rock throughout both of Jenni's deliveries.

After leaving Henrique, Jenni had arrived home to find Jimmy in a state of panic. He was rushing around the house like a headless chicken, whilst Charlie was calmness personified. She had packed her overnight case and was sitting patiently waiting for Jenni in the hallway. Jenni had to give her son a shake to bring him back down to earth, and ensure he was calm enough to drive the two women to the hospital. Throughout the journey, Charlie had remained still and quiet, despite the pain. No screaming and shouting from this mother. Jenni was suitably impressed with her stoicism. Early in the drive a huge contraction had taken over Charlie's body and she had reached for Jenni's hand, not letting go of it since.

The two women were united in the task of bringing the latest edition to the Sullivan family into the world. They had formed a new bond which surprised them both. Charlie would have been lost without the woman who had been her nemesis for the last few months but who was now an angel, easing her distress. For her part, Jenni wiped Charlie's forehead, squeezing her hand as she noticed the change in the heartbeat monitor. Another contraction was coming.

"You can do this, Charlie. One more big push." Jenni could feel her own body contracting as she relived her own birthing experience. She was fully aware that the time was drawing close. The head was incredibly close to crowning and soon they would meet the baby.

Charlie screamed as the contraction took over. Her fingernails dug into Jenni's hand. Jenni bit down on her lip, trying hard not to register the pain which stung her palm. Remembering her own experience when delivering a baby's head, she would forgive Charlie anything, knowing what the poor girl was about to suffer.

"Daddy, come over here," Lindsay called out with an authoritarian voice.

Jimmy had been curled up on a chair beside the bed, watching events with a look of shock and horror. He had not expected this whole birthing process to take so long. Unable to bear to look at the pain etched across his girlfriend's face, he had done the cowardly thing and left it all to his mother. He did not want to imagine what was going on down there. He didn't think he could bear to look.

"Now, Daddy, I want you to hold Charlie's legs. Give her something to push hard against. Can you see the baby's head now?"

Jimmy followed the midwife's glance and stared in wonder at the sight of wet, bloodied hair peeping through Charlie's vagina. All his reservations fled as he had his first glimpse of his child. The fact that he didn't even want to be a dad seemed irrelevant as he watched his baby struggling to enter the world.

A smile burst across his face as he looked at his mother.

"Mum, I can see the baby. Charlie, it's coming. You can do it."

That was the most encouragement Jimmy had displayed in the five hours since they arrived at the hospital. He was behaving like an excited child as he bounced up and down on his heels. Despite holding onto Charlie's foot to give her leverage, his head kept popping down between her legs as he provided both women with a running commentary on progress. If they weren't otherwise occupied, perhaps they might have smiled at the change in Jimmy's attitude. He was fascinated by the slow, inch by inch, journey of his child into the world .

Meanwhile, Charlie said nothing.

Only weak gasps escaped her lips as she rode the contraction. As she came down the other side, Lindsay asked her to pant, allowing the baby's head to crown completely. Charlie's grip remained strong on Jenni's hand and the poor girl's eyes were transfixed on Jenni's kind face. How hard it must be for her to not have her own mother with her. To have to rely on this woman, who has been on her case for the last few months. Always moaning at her.

Jenni felt a wave of guilt wash over her, buffeting her with shame. Once they are home, things will change, she resolved. Charlie will need her love and support and Jenni would need to find a way to give her that.

Unfortunately, she wouldn't get much love from Jimmy. It was clear that their relationship was doomed. The only thing keeping them together was this child.

What a sad state of affairs.

The final push. Charlie bore down with every last bit of energy. Jenni rubbed her shoulders as the young girl pushed, adding encouraging words. Finally there was a gush of embryotic fluid and the baby slithered out into Lindsay's safe hands.

At first, silence filled the room.

Two sets of eyes focused their stares on the midwife. Jenni was concerned. Surely the baby should be crying by now. Charlie had collapsed back on the bed and was staring at the ceiling. She failed to register any emotion, neither happiness, concern nor relief.

And then the most welcome noise. A cry. A full-bodied cry.

Lindsay smiled at Jimmy. She could see the relief written across his face. Often a baby took their time declaring their existence to the world. It was not unusual but could scare the new parents if the silence lasted too long. She had been rubbing baby's legs to stimulate the first breath.

"Daddy, tell Mummy the sex." Lindsay tied and cut the cord.

Poor Jimmy was frantically looking at the baby's body, initially mistaking the cord for another appendage. With little confidence he spluttered, "a girl. I think it's a girl."

"Charlie, can I lay baby on your chest?" asked Lindsay.

She looked with concern at the mother, who showed little or no interest in the wee child. It was not uncommon for a first-time mother to fail to instantly bond with their offspring. But this mother had been unusual throughout proceedings. She had been far too quiet and, if it hadn't been for the pain, wouldn't have displayed any emotion at all. Lindsay made a mental note to keep an eye on Charlie.

"You take it." A faint whisper and a nod to Jenni.

Lindsay passed the swaddled child over to Jenni. She was getting even more concerned about the mother now. This was very strange behaviour. That first skin on skin interaction was vital for both mother and child. Thank goodness the father and grandmother looked thrilled with their new addition. The little girl would have all the love she needed there. Lindsay was an expert in judging characters; a skill learnt over thirty odd years of midwifery.

Jenni wished she could bottle the emotions she felt when the little girl was placed in her arms. An overwhelming feeling of unconditional love. Her tiny rosebud mouth snuffled as it sought comfort. Piercing blue eyes stared at Jenni, examining the new world around her. Jenni opened the blanket and checked the baby's tiny fingers and toes. They were incredibly small, but perfectly formed. A tear squeezed its way out of Jenni's eyes as she bent her head to kiss her granddaughter.

"Jimmy, do you want to hold your daughter?"

Jenni offered the precious bundle to her son. Her heart contracted as she watched Jimmy holding the tiny baby. Tears flooded down his cheeks as Jimmy fell in love with his daughter. The baby he hadn't wanted, who had grabbed hold of his heart and would never let it go.

Jenni smiled as she watched this precious moment. Her baby with his own baby. The wonder on her son's face was beautiful to watch. It was as if Jimmy suddenly became a man at that moment. This child was totally dependent on him, whether he liked it or not.

Jenni dragged her attention away from the baby and focused on Charlie. She lay back on the bed with a blank expression on her face. She was oblivious to the midwife cleaning away the afterbirth and tidying Charlie up. She was a passenger in the most momentous day of her life. She did not register when Lindsay updated her on birth weight and her initial assessment of baby.

Charlie appeared to be totally disinterested.

"Charlie, sweetheart, are you ok?" Jenni gently stroked Charlie's sweaty hair away from her brow. "Your daughter is so beautiful. Thank you for such a wonderful gift. My first grandchild."

Charlie's eyes were glazed with tears. Silently, she cried as if her heart was breaking. Jenni did what comes naturally to her. She held the girl as she cried. Rocking her gently and rubbing her hand across her back.

"Oh, sweetheart," she whispered. "It's alright. I bet you are tired. You have done good work today, my lovely."

Charlie continued to cry, sobbing into Jenni's shoulder. Her body shook with a new pain. An emotional pain. After a few minutes, she pushed Jenni away, flopping back onto the pillows. Looking deeply into Jenni's eyes she made her wishes known, to the surprise of everyone in the room.

"Take it away please. I just want to be on my own and sleep." She rolled over onto her side, flinging her arm over her face.

Jenni looked at Lindsay, who had been listening intently to the conversation. It confirmed her concerns that mother was not in a good place. Perhaps a little time apart from the baby would help. Sleep is a natural healer for most troubles.

"Ok, Charlie, why don't you have a little sleep. I will take baby with Daddy into the next room. You just press the buzzer when you are ready. Then we can try feeding bubba."

Charlie remained tight-lipped. Pretending sleep, she ignored the midwife. She had no intention of feeding the kid. That was the last thing on her mind.

Quietly, Lindsay ushered Jimmy, Jenni, and the baby cot from the room. Fortunately, the labour ward was not busy at all tonight so she would leave father and baby in the next door delivery suite for an hour or two. If mother did not come round in that time, then perhaps, they would have to resort to a bottle.

Poor thing, she thought. Not the most auspicious start for the beautiful little girl.

Mother not interested at all.

CHAPTER SIX
THE CAFÉ AT KATE'S

Jenni was exhausted and elated in equal measure.

The store was about to open for business. Jenni had rushed in at the last minute and was trying to get the coffee machine up to speed before her first customers arrived. She was disappointed to see Kate wasn't working this morning, leaving Claire in charge. Jenni would have loved to tell Kate her news. Let's face it, today was one of those days where Jenni really wished she could have been the one having the morning off.

But that couldn't happen, especially as it was her first week in business. It just wouldn't do.

She had arrived home from the hospital about an hour ago, leaving Jimmy with the car. Grabbing a taxi, she had managed to snatch a catnap on the way back, but the journey really wasn't long enough to refresh her weariness. A quick jump in the shower and a fresh outfit was all she had time for, before the café needed to be opened. Poor little Freddie had been most put out that Jenni didn't have the time and energy to play his normal feeding time games. God knows what he will think of the new addition to the family, she thought.

As she sipped a black coffee, Jenni reflected on the events of last night. She could not help but be worried about Charlie. Something was not right at all. Jenni and Jimmy had sat beside the cot for hours, watching his daughter sleep. Jenni had to admit the baby was utterly adorable. Charlie had not even popped her head round the door to check on her new-born. The pethidine, which Lindsay had given Charlie late in labour, had passed into the baby too which had obviously led to her sleepiness.

It had given Jenni and Jimmy a chance to talk about Charlie.

Jimmy, who was not the most observant of lads, had noticed Charlie's unusual state of mind. They shared their fears that her early rejection of her daughter was a concern. It certainly didn't seem normal, even if she was exhausted and drained from the birth. Surely the delight of holding the baby in her arms would have sent all thoughts of pain and tiredness from her mind. It had certainly been the case for Jenni when she gave birth to George and then Jimmy, a few years later.

Lindsay had been checking in regularly on Charlie, but she continued to sleep or fain sleep. Jenni believed it was the latter. Thinking it would be what his girlfriend would want, Jimmy had taken it upon himself to ring her parents and tell them the news. His bubble was burst when the call diverted to answerphone. They never rang back. Charlie's mother and father didn't seem to share Jenni's excitement about the thought of becoming grandparents.

At around 3am, the baby woke and greeted them with her urgent calls for nourishment. Despite trying to encourage Charlie to take her daughter to her breast, the woman turned her head away. Her face was distressing to see. It spoke of heartbreak rather than the joy they expected. Reluctantly Jenni gave her granddaughter her first bottle. It should have been a moment of delight, but for Jenni it was one of anxiety. It was far too early for Charlie to get the 'baby blues'. That normally happened when the mother's milk came in, a few days after birth.

Charlie wouldn't be forced to hold the baby and it wouldn't have been right to do so. The new mother would have to come round in her own time.

As Jenni had cradled the infant in her arms, she wondered what the future held. Her parents were not the tight family unit they should be. So different to the family George and Jimmy, her own sons, were born into. She remembered the early days after George arrived. Those days of blissful love, when Reggie had smothered her with support and affection. She had been able to relax and build her whole daily life around her new son. Family and friends had been there to help out and admire the new arrival.

By contrast, Charlie was clearly struggling to show any feelings for her daughter. Her parents seemed disinterested in their new granddaughter. Jenni certainly struggled with that fact. She had felt she was too young to become a grandmother but, after her initial reservations, the excitement had built. The idea of welcoming a next generation to her family overcome any silly worries about being seen as old. Her only regret was that poor Reggie would never meet his first grandchild.

Jimmy was clearly in love with his daughter. That love might have to be enough for now. He was somewhat estranged from Charlie, seeming to struggle to understand why she was not in awe of the little human being they had created together. A few nights of rushed sex had created such a beautiful creature. Jimmy was the first to acknowledge that his feelings about the baby had been confused before. He resented Charlie getting pregnant and really wasn't ready to settle down to family life.

Now his entire world had shifted on its axis.

He was a father. He would be the best father ever. And he would try harder to make Charlie happy. Recognising that he had been an absolute shit to her over recent weeks made him feel ashamed. Once they were home from hospital, he was going to spend his time making things good with Charlie. He might not love his girlfriend, but she deserved better.

During the long night, Jimmy had spilled his heart out to his mother, like never before. She had seen a new, more mature side to her younger son. And she had resolved to treat him as an adult. For far too long she had cut him more slack than his older brother. He was her baby and she had struggled to see him as the man he had grown into. Perhaps, if she changed her attitude to Jimmy he would thrive and take on board his new responsibilities without her constant moaning.

Lost in her thoughts, Jenni did not see Henrique until he was right in front of her at the counter.

"Morning, beautiful. Any news?"

His smile lit up his face. He wasn't wearing his usual gardening outfit. A smart pair of tailored shorts and a polo shirt showed off his toned body. His unruly hair was slicked back, controlled with gel. Not for the first time, Jenni pondered the question 'what did he see in her?' He was the most beautiful man ever. He could have anyone he wanted. But he seemed to want her.

Why?

Coming back to reality, she found her voice. "A baby girl. Lily Rose." Jenni beamed with happiness. "7lb 8oz. A good size for a first baby."

"That is wonderful news, Jenni. How is Charlie feeling?"

"She's okay." Jenni lied, knowing that even though she shared a bed with this young man, she could not share all her secrets. "Hopefully, they will be home later this afternoon."

"Oh that's good. But Jenni, you look exhausted. Did you get any sleep at all?"

Jenni was so tired that she couldn't resent him for noticing the weary look on her face. She felt all of the 50 years she had lived right now. And it no doubt showed. All she wanted to do was to crawl back into bed for a couple of hours, but that was impossible.

"No sleep I'm afraid," she sighed. "Lily was born at 2am and by the time we had settled her and fed her, it was dawn. Charlie managed to sleep, but Jimmy and myself pulled an 'all-nighter'. Think we will all just collapse tonight. And at least I have the day off tomorrow."

"Oh that's a shame. I was hoping to make love to a grandmother tonight." He laughed, not unkindly. His sexy wink could not even raise a jot of lust from Jenni today. She seriously didn't have the energy.

"Shush," Jenni looked around quickly to check there was no-one in hearing range. She giggled as she continued furtively. "Honestly, I am knackered so tonight is just not going to work. But I will text you. Maybe later next week."

He blew her a kiss as he picked up his coffee and iced bun. "I'm off to London for the day. Meeting some old friends from university."

"Have a lovely day, Henrique." She shouted after him as he headed for the door.

It was strange, but she felt sad once he had gone. And a little bit jealous. This relationship with Henrique, if you could call it that, confused the hell out of her. Also, Jenni had been so excited to talk to someone about her news and losing his company left her alone with her elation. She was fit to burst with her news and wanted to scream it from the rafters so that everyone knew.

Jenni Sullivan had a beautiful baby granddaughter!

How she missed seeing Kate today. Why did it have to be her day off, just when Jenni had the best news in the world to share. As if she were a mind reader, her friend tapped on the café window, grabbing Jenni's attention. Delighted, Jenni motioned frantically for her to come in.

"Hey, Jenni. What's up?"

She could not contain her excitement. "Charlie had the baby last night."

"Oh My God. Tell me." Kate threw her arms around Jenni, as she leant over the counter depositing her huge boobs on its tiled top and planting a sloppy kiss on each cheek.

"Lily Rose. She is the most beautiful baby ever. Yes, I know I am biased, but she is gorgeous. Have you got time for a coffee and I will tell you all."

Kate looked at her watch. "Shit, I am supposed to be taking the kids swimming in half hour. Let me skip the coffee and you just jump to the gory details." She laughed as she settled her elbows on the counter, giving Jenni her undivided attention.

"Where to start?"

"The beginning is usually the best option," laughed Kate.

"Well, if you want to start at the beginning, I was actually enjoying myself at Henrique's caravan when a call came from my beloved son trying to find me. Seriously his timing couldn't have been worse. And Charlie refused to go to hospital without me. Can you believe that?"

Kate's face looked horrified. "Charlie wanted you at hospital? Seriously? I thought she couldn't stand you. No offence."

"None taken." Jenni had been honest with Kate about the mutual dislike between her and her son's stroppy girlfriend. "I was shocked just like you. Poor girl, I think she realised Jimmy would be no hope at all. So I was the least worst option."

"Wow, she must have been desperate" joked Kate. "So how was the old birth thing? I've never been the other end of it, if you know what I mean."

"Exactly. Me too. It was amazing. I really cannot put into words what it was like. And look at this." Jenni offered her hand which had small indentations where Charlie's nails had cut into Jenni's skin. "I've got the scars to prove it."

Kate took her hand and kissed it. A wet sloppy kiss. "Let Mumma kiss it better." She grinned. "But seriously, did it all go smoothly? Is Charlie ok?"

The expression on Jenni's face changed. She became thoughtful. Jenni was still concerned about Charlie's reaction after the delivery. It was far too strange for her liking.

"I'm really not sure, Kate. She hadn't even held Lily when I left this morning. She wouldn't let the midwife place her on her chest and insisted I should be the first person to hold Lily. It's just so sad to see. She looks like she doesn't want to know the baby."

"Oh dear. That doesn't sound good," said Kate. Her tone had changed from humorous to serious, picking up on her friend's concern. "Perhaps she will come round in time. It does sound unusual, but if she has carried that child for nine months, I can't see her resisting for too long."

"God, I hope you are right, mate. In the meantime little Lily has a doting father and a Nanny who is in love big time. She is so beautiful and perfect. I'm sure every Nan thinks their grandchild is beautiful, but mine definitely is. Here look, I got a couple of snaps on my phone." Jenni grabbed her mobile, which was charging behind the coffee machine, and swiped up her new screensaver. The first of many she will take of little Lily Rose Sullivan.

"Oh, darling, she is gorgeous. When are they home and can I pop round for a cuddle?" Kate was widening the picture on the screen so she could see every feature of the tiny human.

"Jimmy texted me a few minutes ago. Seems the doctor needs to sign off Lily as fit to go home then they will be on their way back. Leave it for tonight, but why not pop round tomorrow sometime. It will give Charlie a distraction too if there are others in the house."

"Of course. I'll pop round after morning service. Will you be joining me?"

"Do you know what, I think I will pass. I haven't slept all night so I'm knackered. Think I just want to sleep as long as I can tonight. But after church will be fine. I've got some baking to do, but with a new baby in the house, I might have to grab my chances when I can."

The thought of baking and dealing with a new-born was really bringing her change in circumstances into focus. She would have to juggle a number of balls over the coming weeks. But one thing she was sure of. Lily Rose, and all her needs, would have to fit into the current chaos which was Jenni's life. She was strong, determined, and confident that she would manage.

She had to.

Charlie and Jimmy looked lost as new parents. They would need direction and support and Jenni would need to help them. Perhaps Charlie's parents would get over their initial reservations of Jimmy as a son-in-law and get on board too. They may even go and spend some time with her parents in Kent, which would give Jenni a well-deserved break.

Look at her. Already trying to get rid of them before they were even home from hospital. Jenni was having an internal struggle. The needs of her beloved son and granddaughter and her own needs. She rarely put herself first, but over recent weeks she had been determined to prioritise her business and her life.

She was not ready to give either up just yet.

CHAPTER SEVEN
LAUREL HOUSE

Alaistair picked up the wine bottle and motioned to Paula. "Shall I open this one?"

Paula nodded as she blew on the serving spoon. Confident she wouldn't burn her lips she took a taste. Perfect. Not too much salt and just the right amount of garlic, she thought.

Alaistair was making himself at home in her kitchen, as he rummaged through the drawers for the corkscrew. He whistled a tune as he picked the capsule from the top of the bottle. Piercing the cork with the sharp point, he applied pressure, drilling the screw far into the bottle neck. The cork was released with a satisfying pop.

Over recent months, Wednesday evening had become a regular feature. Alaistair would join Paula for supper, whilst they put the world to rights. They enjoyed each other's company and they always had something to talk about. At the weekend, Alaistair would often take Paula out for dinner further afield. Neither of them were prepared to face the gossips. Any relationship, which might be budding, would not do so in the full glare of the village elders.

Wednesday used to be Peter and Alastair's evening. For years they had sat at the bar, in the same seats, at The King's Head pub. They would chat about the football or Peter's latest conquest. It was a habit they had nurtured. Since Peter had been thrown out of the matrimonial home, Alaistair had been avoiding his mate. At no stage had he thought about what impact his departure may have had on Peter. He saw it as the easiest solution. It was, unfortunately, the cowards way out.

Because Alastair had feelings for Paula.

It certainly wouldn't be appropriate to rub Peter's nose in it. And knowing Peter the way he did, he would not be surprised if the guy tried to destroy any chance of him and Paula finding happiness. Alaistair was certain Paula had feelings for him too and he was determined to take things at her pace. She had been distraught with the breakdown of her marriage so he was not going to jump right in with his size 9s and run before he could walk. Al smiled at his feet analogy. Pretty good.

"How's your appetite, Al?" Paula was about to spoon out the fluffy brown rice.

"Starved," laughed Alaistair.

To be fair, he was always hungry. Paula loved the fact that he had such a good appetite. She always made too much food. All these years she had never grasped portion control. But Al was like the food monster, hoovering up any remains. Tonight she had made her own chicken curry, a favourite of Al's.

"Great. Why don't you pop the wine on the table and I have this served up in a jiffy."

To the casual observer, Paula and Alaistair appeared to move around the kitchen like an old married couple. Swivelling around the island, with a secretive glance at each other, they found their positions at the kitchen table. Paula placed a heaped plate of rice in front of Alaistair and started to spoon rich curry on top. She seemed to know instinctively when enough was enough. He didn't have to say a word.

They ate in silence at first. Alaistair could never turn down one of Paula's curries. The flavours were built with a mixture of spices and always with a good heap of garlic. So much better than the local Indian restaurant, which Al had frequented on a regular basis after his first wife had left him.

The two friends shared life experiences and not only their love of decent food. Alaistair's first wife had left him for another woman. He had been damaged by her departure, not just because she took a good chunk of the family assets. The thought that she preferred life with a woman, rather than him, hurt Al deeply. He was paranoid that everyone was gossiping about his lack of prowess. People would assume that he must be the reason behind Ruby's venture into a totally different direction, sexually. He had suspected nothing at all before she had left. How blind could he be? How could he have not noticed her dissatisfaction with him as a man?

Paula, on the other hand, had been fully aware of her husband's infidelities. She had turned a blind eye to his misdemeanours. Until he tried it on with the newcomer, Jenni Sullivan. Right in front of her. That fateful night had been the catalyst. She had kicked Peter out. Jenni had done her a favour, without even realising it. Since Peter had left, Paula had felt like a new woman. She had won back her self-respect and confidence. Her upholstery business was going from strength to strength. Living alone wasn't the problem she thought it would be. She enjoyed her own company and now spent more time with friends, without worry what her errant husband might be up to.

Breaking the silence, Alastair brought up the thorny subject. "How are things going with the divorce, Paula? Peter still being difficult?"

"Funny you should mention that, Al." Paula looked thoughtful as she continued. "Something strange happened this week. Peter has stopped fighting."

"Meaning?"

Paula had leant heavily on Alaistair over the last few months. He had been her rock, supporting her in the early days after she kicked Peter out. Looking after both his friends, he had even persuaded local farmer, Thomas Hadley, to rent out the cottage adjoining Al's to Peter. Staying in the local B&B was not a long term option for Peter St John and, Al's thinking had been that if he helped to get Peter settled, he would go easy on Paula. It hadn't worked out as planned. Peter had continued to make his wife's life difficult. Disagreeing to every solution she had offered to divide their assets. She was trying her hardest to reduce the amount either of them would have to pay to solicitors.

"Well, it's rather strange. My solicitor rang me earlier. Peter has agreed to everything. Right out of the blue. So strange. Not sure why he has changed direction so suddenly. Have you seen him recently, Al?"

"Not much. I saw him out in the back garden at the weekend, but he wasn't really in a chatty mood. If I'm honest, he looked a mess."

Alaistair had tried to start a conversation with Peter but had only managed to extract a couple of grunts from his mate. He looked like he hadn't washed for days, his hair matted and greasy and his clothes dirty and unkempt. The complete opposite to the normal Peter. He had always been fastidious with his appearance. He had definitely let himself go.

"Perhaps I better check on him. Do you think? It is just not like Peter to change course so abruptly. I'm a bit worried." Paula's face showed her level of concern.

"You are too nice, Paula. That's your problem. I don't think he will thank you for your concern, but I can understand why you want to. Just try not to let him hurt you. Be cautious."

Alaistair did not trust Peter St John. This could be the latest ploy to win his wife back. He must not succeed, for Paula's sake. Alaistair was underestimating Paula's inner strength. She had no intention of letting her husband back into her life. However you cannot live with someone for that long and turn the emotional tap off just like that. She still cared about him even when she hated everything about him.

Alaistair didn't understand that. His anger at Ruby had festered for too long. He had found it incredibly hard to even speak to her after they parted. The idea of Paula and Peter remaining civil was one he struggled to comprehend.

"Anyway, changing the subject slightly to more positive things, have you seen the newest addition to the village?" asked Paula.

She had been itching to pop round and see Jenni's grandchild, but didn't want to interfere just yet, anticipating the demands on her friend's time. Jenni was juggling running a new business and the needs of a new baby within the family.

"I haven't yet. I gave Jimmy the week off." Alaistair had not been over the moon with Jimmy's timing. They had just started an extension and he had to find a temporary labourer to fill in for the new father. "I saw Jenni at lunchtime and she showed me some pictures. She does look cute, although all babies look cute don't they? Jenni looked tired though. Bless her."

"I might try and pop round at the weekend. I found the sweetest little outfit when I was in Southampton yesterday. I can't wait to give it to her."

Paula didn't have children of her own. She had been pregnant once but had lost the child. A devastating miscarriage which put an end to her motherhood ambitions. Al and Ruby had never had children either. It was something they had never really discussed. Perhaps if they had they might have seen the problem which was on the horizon, way before either of them was hurt.

After the friends had finished eating, the couple took their coffees into the lounge. Sitting on the deep, comfy sofa together, Al slung his arm across the back of the couch. Paula turned Netflix on and before long they found a film to watch. Subconsciously she shifted her weight towards Alaistair. Her head came to rest on his shoulder and Al tucked his arm around her. Gently he kissed the top of her head.

They were totally relaxed in each other's company. There was no need to push things too fast. Being friends meant everything to them both and the last thing either of them wanted was to ruin a good friendship by making the wrong move.

It would happen in its own good time.

CHAPTER EIGHT
NUMBER 2, GREEN FARM COTTAGES

Peter had hit rock bottom.

He had made such a mess of his life. Paula had been the one good thing in his world. She was his best friend, his golf buddy, his life partner. They had built a home together, despite the difficult start. They had been happy together.

And he had fucked it up.

Why the hell do we never really value what we have until we lose it?

He had spent years sailing far too close to the wind. Peter had an unhealthy obsession with women. It was impossible for him to be faithful. Well, that was his excuse. The sight of a sexy woman was a challenge to him. He loved the chase, probably more than the conquest. And he spent a great deal of time chasing. Once he had got them into bed, he was usually disappointed.

And he always went home to Paula.

She was the foundation he had built his adult life upon. She must have known what he was getting up to and she had turned a blind eye. She never questioned him. She had never seemed to be disappointed in him. In fact she never really noticed what he did when they weren't together. She never questioned his movements and likewise, he never challenged when she was late home. That was a rare occurrence, to be fair, but their marriage was not built on strict rules and regulations. It was free and easy.

Or so he had thought.

They had had a successful marriage. They had built a lovely home with all the trimmings of 21st century living. They worked hard and made enough money to keep themselves comfortable, well into retirement. Together they had reached the lofty pinnacle of being invited to join one of the most expensive golf courses in the valley. He had been captain of the men's team. She led the women. To the outside world they must have seemed the perfect couple.

And he had fucked it up.

What did he have to show for all his hard work now? A rented cottage across the road from his beautiful house. He had lost the will to fight for Paula. She wouldn't have him back now. It was all his own fault. He deserved everything that was coming his way. He could see the way Al looked at Paula. In time, his best mate would muscle in on his territory and there was nothing he could do to stop it.

He was not going to hang around to watch.

He had decided he was better off out of it. For good.

He had spoken to his mother earlier.

That was a joy.

Not.

The bitch had ripped him apart one more time. She loved to humiliate him so why not have their final conversation follow a similar path. Moaning about his character and what a failure he had been as a son and husband. She was still angry with him because Christmas was cancelled last year. All because he had tried it on with the newcomer when he was pissed out of his brains. His mother's attempt to play happy families had been thwarted by his stupidity. She would not miss him. Not one bit.

She would probably decide that this was the one courageous thing he had done in his life.

And perhaps it was.

Peter opened a fresh bottle of whiskey. It was a good one. No cheap rubbish for his last drink. Pouring a generous slug into his glass, he downed it in one. The fiery spirit burnt his throat as it travelled downwards. As it hit his empty stomach, his body greeted its healing qualities. Oh God, that felt good, he thought.

Beside the whiskey sat a full bottle of paracetamol. A tear pushed its way out of Peter's eye and started its lonely tract down his cheek. He wouldn't wipe it away. Let it remain as a reminder that he was still here.

For now.

Tipping the pills into his palm, he poured another slug of whiskey.

On the coffee table was a picture of him and Paula on their wedding day. Paula was heavy with the child which would die in her womb. They looked so happy then, not knowing what lay ahead. He saluted the picture with the whiskey glass, throwing the pills into his mouth. The gulp of spirit drew the pills down his throat. He coughed as they scraped his windpipe on their journey to oblivion.

He had decided. This was the only way to take the pain away.

There was no going back now.

"Goodbye my love."

He blew a kiss towards the picture and swallowed another handful of pills.

CHAPTER NINE
LAUREL HOUSE

The sound of the phone penetrated Paula's mind, slowly drawing her towards a state of wakefulness.

Looking around confused, she tried to locate the noise. Reaching across to her bedside table, she flicked on the lamp, trying hard to bring both her body and mind alert. It was her mobile trilling at full volume. Unusually, she had forgotten to put her phone on silent mode.

Something she would be thankful for later.

It was Peter's number. As she swiped right, she noticed it was 1am. What the hell is he doing ringing her at this time, was her initial thought?

"Peter, what's up?" Her voice probably sounded harsher than she expected, but the irritation at being woken from a deep sleep was at the forefront of her mind.

"Help me, Paula." His voice was croaky and hardly more than a whisper. "Please come quick."

"Peter, what's up?" She tried again, impatient now.

A groan. "I took some pills. I don't feel good." Silence. "I don't want to die, Paula."

His words ended with a childlike whimper. The sound of his voice frightened her. It just was so unlike Peter, her arrogant ex-husband.

"Oh shit, Peter. How many pills?"

Paula was struggling into her leggings as she spoke. Flicking the mobile to loudspeaker, she fumbled around in the semi gloom as she tried to get dressed. A cast off t-shirt lay beside the bed and she grabbed that, pulling it over her head. Panic hit a blow to her stomach as she realised she needed to keep Peter alert.

"Talk to me, Peter. Stay awake. I'm coming. Now, you must stay awake." She was shouting now as she tried to get through to him.

Charging down the stairs, she slipped into her trainers, not stopping to do the laces up. Grabbing her house keys and torch, she fled out of the front door, slamming it behind her. It wasn't far to Green Farm Cottages. She ran the whole way, stopping at Al's front door first. Using her fist she banged on his door repeatedly.

It didn't take long for Al to appear at the door. He was still dressed. He looked confused to find her on his doorstep at this time of night.

"Paula, what's the matter?"

"Al, quick, ring for an ambulance. I have Peter on my mobile. I need to keep him awake. He's taken pills."

"Oh shit," cried Al. He was pulling his work boots on, which had been dropped at the front door earlier. "Come on, let's go."

Paula was crying now, frightened to see what she might find next door. Her mind was racing ahead of her body, hoping they wouldn't be too late. Al grabbed his mobile and followed her round to his neighbour's house. The front door was locked so they dashed round to the back. As they ran, Al dialled 999. The back door was locked too but didn't take too much force for Al to break it down. He put his shoulder to the hinges and pushed.

A strange thought passed through his mind. These doors need looking at, if they can be forced that easily. I will have to speak to Thomas about security. Our minds play tricks on us in an emergency, finding ways to keep us grounded whilst adrenaline is kicking in.

Peter was lying on the floor in the lounge. His mobile was wedged under his cheek. A trail of saliva was pooling around his mouth, but there was no sign that he had been sick. It appeared that he was no longer conscious. The smell of alcohol hung like a miasma around his body. The offending whiskey bottle was almost empty and the remains of the bottle of paracetamol were strewn across the coffee table.

"Oh, Peter." Paula cried as she shook her husband's shoulders. "Wake up. Wake up right now. You have got to stay awake."

Her voice was full of authority, trying to reach into his subconscious. Perhaps his mind might realise the seriousness of the situation. Grabbing the remainder of the whiskey bottle, she sloshed the spirit into his face. He groaned and opened his eyes. His pupils were huge and his stare vacant.

"Paula," he muttered.

"Don't sleep. Peter, listen to me. You must stay awake. Stay with me." She screamed in his face, partly to keep him awake and partly to let out the huge wave of emotion which was taking over her senses.

Paula lifted his head into her lap as she stroked his hair away from his face. Speaking any sort of nonsense she sat with him for the next twenty minutes, waiting for the ambulance. Her determination kept him awake. Every time his eyes closed, she slapped him across the face, shocking him awake.

She was not letting him give up now.

Al stood in the doorway watching. Tears coursed down his face as he considered how terrible things must have become for Peter, to make him go this far. What sort of mate was he? He hadn't seen this coming. Or had he? Had he ignored the signs? Had his obsession with Paula made him ignore the plight of his oldest friend? He had let Peter down and the guilt knocked frustratedly at the base of his skull.

Before too long, two lovely paramedics arrived to take over Peter's care. Al reached out his hands to Paula as she struggled to her feet. She collapsed into his arms.

They cried together.

They cried for Peter.

They cried, worried that he might not make it, judging by the concerned looks on the paramedic's faces.

Tomorrow they would think to the future.

They would decide how they could support husband and best friend through his pain. But right now they took comfort in each other's arms. With death so close by, they gripped hold of life, knowing that they would do everything in their power to help Peter recover.

If he lived.

CHAPTER TEN
LAUREL HOUSE

"Oh, Paula, you poor love." Kate enveloped her in a motherly embrace as soon as she entered the house.

Kate and Jenni had popped round to see their friend as soon as they had closed the store for the evening. News about Peter's suicide attempt had found its way to them via Alaistair. Not in a gossipy way. He was sure that Paula could do with the support of her closest female friends and hoped that she would forgive him for breaking her confidence. He may be the one Paula had leant on last night, but he imagined a woman's comfort was overdue.

Paula squeezed Kate, drawing emotional strength from the embrace. She could feel some of the pressure lifting from her shoulders. It had been a long exhausting day of heartache and trauma and she was glad to have the support of these two women. She took Jenni's proffered hand and held on as she centred herself back into reality. The shock of the previous night's events and the hours spent by a hospital bed were taking their toll. She was shattered both physically and mentally.

"Thank you both for coming. Al is a love for telling you. I bet he is worried sick he has done the wrong thing, but I couldn't be alone tonight." Paula sighed, feeling the love wafting her way.

"Well, let me open this wine," Kate indicated the bottle of red in her free hand. "Then we can talk or just sit in silence and drink. Whatever you want, my lovely."

Three generous glasses of red were poured as the women settled themselves on the sofas. Despite the fact that Jenni knew she had a mounting list of tasks which needed completing when she finally made it back to Rose Cottage, some things are more important than the humdrum of her own life. Her friend needed their love and she wouldn't be anywhere else right now. Baking could wait until later.

Paula had started to cry again, silent tears slipping down her cheeks. "Why did he do it?" she asked. "How shit must things have got for him to try and kill himself?"

Kate took Paula's hand and stroked it gently. "Paula love, we can never know what goes on in another person's mind. We have no window into the soul and Peter's struggles wouldn't necessarily be apparent to anyone else. All we can do now is to support him when he comes out of hospital."

Kate's role as a vicar's wife provided her with the life experience to deal with such challenging emotional situations. Added to that, she had a natural propensity to listen and care about others. She was the perfect person to have around at such a time. Jenni often wondered who Kate reached out to when she had a problem.

"How is he?" asked Jenni tentatively.

"Alive." Paula paused as she thought about the heroic struggle the doctors had performed to bring him back from the edge. "I thought he was going to die on the way to the hospital, but somehow they got him there in time to save him."

Kate had her serious face on. "Paula, you have got to prepare yourself for a reaction. He might be angry that he was saved. I know that sounds horrible to contemplate, but it happens."

Paula nodded. "I know what you mean, but this is different. He rang me. That's why Al and I were able to get the ambulance to him in time. He told me he didn't want to die."

"Oh, darling," cried Jenni. "I cannot imagine what it must have felt like getting that call. I'm so sorry you had to go through that."

Paula took another sip of wine. It was helping to take the edge of her heightened emotions. Having company was just what she needed. What a lovely bloke Alaistair Middleton was, she reflected.

Her mind replayed the events of the previous night as she tried to pick the bones out of it. If she had to do things again, she was sure she wouldn't do things any differently. The wonderful paramedics had told her that her efforts to keep Peter awake would have contributed to his survival.

She was only hopeful that when Peter had time to contemplate events, he would not blame her for trying to save him. She could clearly recall his plaintive voice, pleading for her help. Surely that was not the action of someone determined to end it all. She had sat by his hospital bed for hours, but Peter hadn't woken. He slept peacefully. Paula would only agree to leave once the doctors had reassured her that he was out of danger

Unknown to her at the time, Peter was not asleep throughout. He had sensed his ex-wife's presence but was far too ashamed to face her. As his body fought to recover from the damage he had inflicted with the whiskey and pills, he realised the huge debt of gratitude he owed to Paula and Alastair for saving his life, when all was lost.

"What happens next?" asked Jenni.

She shared Kate's concern that Paula might take Peter back into her life which, in their opinion, would be disastrous. It wasn't their decision to make, luckily, and they would stand by her and support her choice, even if they thought it was crazy.

"I had a chat with the doctor before I left this afternoon. Peter will be referred for a psyche review as soon as he is well enough. I think they want to keep him in for a few days to make sure he won't do it again." Paula took a sip of wine. Despite her friends' best intentions, alcohol was not really helping this evening. She would have been happier with a coffee and a piece of Jenni's wonderful cake. She didn't want to seem ungrateful. "One thing I am certain of, I am not having him back."

Kate and Jenni shared a glance. They were surprised to hear Paula speak those words. And relieved that they wouldn't have to broach the subject.

Paula continued. She had spotted the nervous glance between her friends and understood its meaning. "I will not be made to feel guilty for what Peter tried to do. I am not his keeper. Does that sound incredibly hard?"

Kate shook her head vigorously. "No, no, no. Paula, you are not responsible for his actions. He chose to make his own mistakes in life and unfortunately, he is paying the price for them. But the last thing you should be doing is pretending all those mistakes have been washed away by his latest cry for help. It doesn't help you and it certainly won't help Peter in the longer term."

Paula sighed deeply. "Thank you, Kate. I needed to hear that. I don't want Peter as my husband anymore. Nearly losing him though, it has frightened me. You don't live with someone for over twenty years and switch the love off like a light switch. I still care deeply for him, but not as my life partner."

Jenni had been following the conversation intently. "Perhaps what has happened will help you two find a way to remain friends and confidantes going forward. Peter has looked a bit lost since you guys have split up and, whilst that is in no way your problem, perhaps you still need to have each other in your lives, but just in a different way. It sounds like Peter is going to have to do some serious thinking about why he behaves the way he does. He's not an evil person, clearly, and hopefully he can get help to understand why he reacts to women in the way he does. If he can get help perhaps he will be a better person and find a future that is right for him."

Paula and Kate were stunned into silence. Where did Jenni get her thoughtful perception from? She had only known Paula for six months and Peter even less so, but she seemed to have summed it up perfectly. Jenni smiled as she recognised their shock.

"Ladies, let's face it, at times it is easier for the outsider to see the issues clearer. I'm not suggesting I am some kind of psychologist, but there is definitely a problem with Peter and he needs help. This cry for help must be the catalyst for him to get that support. Maybe with some counselling he will be a completely different man."

"You are honestly spot on, Jenni. Good must come of this dreadful night. Then Peter may find love again and it won't be with me. This may not be the right time to say this but, here goes. I think I am in love with Al." Paula blushed.

"For fucks sake," Kate laughed. "You are probably the last person to realise that, Paula. It has been obvious to me and Jenni for months. And good luck to you both. I think you will make the perfect team."

Paula looked confused. "How the hell did you see that? I haven't even said anything to Al yet."

"He adores you," Jenni interjected. "You can see it in his eyes. They follow you when you are in a room with him. You two need to get it on. Don't waste any more time. If what has happened over the last few days is not a wakeup call, then I don't know what is. Grab him and hold on tight."

Paula knew there was one big obstacle in the way of happiness for her and Alaistair. Peter. "Yes, but what about Peter. He is Al's best mate and my ex-husband. And he has just tried to kill himself. How the hell can we carry on as if nothing has happened? People will think we are awful, rubbing Peter's nose in it when he is at his most vulnerable."

"Paula, screw the gossips." Kate was on her soapbox now. She was determined the likes of Anna Fletcher, the village's number one tittle-tattler, would not destroy her friend's chance of happiness. "You and Al were meant for each other. I am certain that between you, the relationship with Peter can be worked through. Peter doesn't need you guys as a crutch. He needs friends who will help him recover, but not to the detriment of their own happiness. We are all going to be here for the three of you so you are not alone."

"Thank you, Kate, Jenni. I honestly don't know what I have done to deserve such good mates. Now I just need to build up the courage to seduce Al." Paula laughed nervously. "Anyway, less of my troubles. How is that little granddaughter of yours, Jenni?"

Jenni's face lit up with joy. "She is adorable. Got a fine set of lungs on her as I can testify when she wants that 3am feed, but I could forgive her anything. I do wish my timing with setting up the café had been better. I could just sit at home and hold her all day, but at least with me being at work it is giving Jimmy and Charlie time to bond with little Lily."

"How is Charlie now?" asked Kate. Jenni had shared her concerns about Charlie's reaction to the new baby and she was hoping it was purely a temporary setback.

"I honestly don't know," sighed Jenni. "She is getting more involved at least, but she just doesn't seem interested in Lily. I remember when George was first born, I couldn't take my eyes off him. I used to love to lie with him in my arms and examine every inch of him. Embedding his image in my brain."

"Oh yes, the first baby is such a wonder to behold," added Kate.

Paula was at a loss with the conversation as she was never lucky enough to hold a live baby in her arms. When they lost theirs, the doctors would not allow her to see the badly formed foetus, which was probably a blessing in disguise.

"I think it's more than the baby blues. Charlie hasn't attempted to breast feed so little Lily Rose went on the bottle straight away. But it's more than that. Jimmy seems to be doing everything. He gets up in the night to feed her, he's changing nappies and bathing her. Charlie just watches on. When I get home in the evening, she's offering to make dinner while I hold the baby. Surely it should be the other way around."

"Have her parents been in touch yet? Perhaps she is finding it hard being at the 'outlaws' rather than her own parents." Kate winked at her colloquialism.

"Again, that's the strange thing. As far as I know they haven't been in touch. Your only daughter provides you with a granddaughter and nothing? They must be one messed up family, as far as I can see."

"Very strange," agreed Paula. Peter's mother was another weird one, but she couldn't imagine her ignoring a grandchild if they had been lucky enough to bring their baby to term.

"Well, hopefully when Jimmy goes back to work next week, Charlie may enjoy having the time alone to get to know Lily without an audience. You never know, she may just feel awkward in front of you and Jimmy. Self-conscious or something."

Kate was always on hand with the considered view. Let's hope she is right on this one, thought Jenni. She really didn't know what to do about Charlie and really hoped the situation sorted itself out. A little niggle had started at the back of her mind on the night of Lily's birth and that niggle was increasing in size and worry in the days that followed.

Every mother reacts to childbirth in quite different ways. Jenni was trying not to compare her own experience with Charlie's. Their circumstances were all too different, but something just didn't feel right. Perhaps Jenni should have a quiet word with the midwife when she came for her next visit? Or would Charlie just resent her interfering.

Either way Charlie needed her love and support. That was one thing she was sure about.

CHAPTER ELEVEN
ROSE COTTAGE

Jenni eased herself back into the tub, relishing the fragrant bubbles which caressed her body.

It was Sunday morning. Jenni had promised herself a slow start, which included this wonderful bath and a pampering session. Her eyebrows looked like two hairy caterpillars sizing each other up and she wasn't even going to confess to the state of her bikini line. Jenni gently moved her hands in the water, sloshing the foam across her breasts. The smell of her newest bubble bath was intoxicating, helping to relax both her body and mind.

Just what she desperately needed.

It had been a frantic two weeks since she launched the café business. Her feet hadn't properly touched the ground, but she didn't regret a thing. The café was settling into a routine already. Jenni had a good idea about the busy times during the week and was already establishing that once the initial excitement passed, she may well shut one day in the week, allowing her to balance work and life now Lily had arrived. She didn't want to miss out on Lily's early days whilst she built up her new business. Getting that balance right was going to be key.

And the business was going so well. The takings were vastly exceeding her projections and, even after paying rent to Kate and covering her contributions to the bills, the cut of the profits she could take, made the venture worthwhile. Even if she hadn't been making money, Jenni would not regret her decision. Whilst she was weary after a week working, she felt motivated and enthused by her new job. Jenni had got her mojo back and the value of that could not be measured in money.

And then there was Lily Rose.

Her granddaughter was a gift so precious to Jenni. The baby was an absolute love. She slept, woke, drank her bottle, burped, and went back to sleep. Compared to Jenni's memories of the boys as babies, Lily was no trouble at all. When she was awake, her eyes followed the adults around, especially Jenni. She watched and observed with a curiosity unusual in one so young.

Charlie seemed to have settled down over the last couple of days. Perhaps the shock of becoming a mother had passed. When Jenni came home from work yesterday, she found Charlie sitting cross-legged on the sofa whispering sweet nothings to her daughter. Jenni stood unobserved for some time, enjoying the precious sight. She was delighted to see the young woman finally bonding with her daughter.

Jenni had silently walked away with a smile on her face. Progress at last.

"Mum." Jimmy's voice interrupted her relaxation. He was banging on the bathroom door as he shouted.

"Oh for God's sake, Jimmy. Can I not have five minutes of peace. It is Sunday," Jenni shouted in frustration.

"I'm really sorry, Mum, but we have a problem." Jimmy's voice carried a tremor of concern. "Charlie's gone."

"What?"

"Charlie has gone. She left a note. I only just found it when I went to pick up Lily from her cot."

Jenni groaned as she realised her lazy Sunday was about to go horribly wrong.

Pulling the plug out with her toes, she eased herself out of the water. Grabbing a big, fluffy, pink towel, she dried the bulk of the bubbles from her torso and wound the towel around her, tucking the ends in above her cleavage. Sliding the bolt across, she eased the bathroom door open to reveal her son.

Jimmy held Lily in his arms. He was clutching a tatty piece of paper which he wafted towards Jenni. She flattened it out in her hands and read. The writing was rushed and messy, taking up valuable minutes for Jenni to decipher the words and take in their meaning.

Jimmy & Jenni

I'm really sorry but I can't do this. Lily will have a much better life with you two so I have to go. Please don't try to find me. I'm going away. I have taken the car. You will find it at Southampton airport. I will leave the keys under the wheel arch. Look after Lily and don't let her forget me.

I'm so sorry.

Charlie xx

"Oh, bloody hell," sighed Jenni.

She rushed to the bedroom window, her eyes confirming her fears. Her BMW was gone. This just didn't feel real. Who drives off in the middle of the night, leaving a note? Charlie must be in a right state to do something like that. After seeing her with Lily the other day, Jenni had been convinced Charlie was turning the corner. Obviously not.

Jimmy looked lost and bewildered as he held his daughter, following his mother with his eyes as she moved from window to bed. Panic filled his heart as he tried to figure out what was happening. He had slept in this morning after feeding Lily at 3am. Lily had been lying in her cot, her eyes following the elephant mobile which hung above her head. She had been calm and contented, hence the lie in for the family.

Racking his brains, he was certain Charlie had been in bed when he got up at 3am. Most nights he had been the one to see to his daughter's needs. Charlie would just roll over and feign sleep, even if she was awake. Jimmy hadn't minded. He had loved the quiet of the night, sitting with his beloved baby and telling her all about her father's plans for the future. Because he had plans, big plans.

"Look, son. Will you give me a minute to get dressed. Go and put the kettle on. Make yourself useful."

Not wanting to be rude, but Jenni shut the bedroom door in his face. There were times when you have to be forceful with your offspring. This was one of those times. A wave of sadness engulfed Jenni. How bad must things be for Charlie if she was willing to walk away from her precious baby? And what they hell did they do now? A new-born and both of them working.

The shit was definitely hitting the proverbial fan right now.

It didn't take long for Jenni to dress and join Jimmy in the kitchen. He had a bottle ready and Jenni naturally took control, taking Lily and settling down on the window seat to feed her. Jimmy made tea and laid a cup next to his mother.

"Right, first things first. Will you ring Alaistair and see if he will give you a lift to Southampton to find the car? I would ask Jeremy, but its Sunday so he will be busy. Once I have fed little one, I will ring Charlie's parents. They will have to be interested now."

Jenni was mentally ticking off activity. Charlie's parents had been silent since Lily had been born. Jenni had struggled to understand why they hadn't been to see their new granddaughter or even make a call to their daughter to find out how she was. Their behaviour was strange in the extreme.

"I don't want her parents taking Lily." Jimmy actually raised his voice in distress to her. "If they are that disinterested in their own daughter, I am not having them anywhere near Lily."

Jenni's heart was filled with pride for her son.

It wasn't the reaction she had expected, but his perception and his obviously protective nature for Lily was beautiful to behold. Things were going to be extremely difficult in the weeks ahead, but there was no way either of them would put Lily at risk. They would find a way to manage the situation which had been thrust upon them. Lily was the most important person to consider and her future must be protected, at whatever cost.

Jimmy returned from the study, where he had been ringing Alaistair. "Al will pick me up in thirty minutes, Mum. He's got a mate who works at the airport and they will check the CCTV to find out where the car is. He might even be able to find out which flight Charlie got on. If she got on a flight?"

"Good. She must have been planning this. I cannot imagine she just upped and left in the night without a plan," added Jenni.

"I thought she was a bit keen to get the birth registered. She insisted on doing it last week even though we had weeks to do it. We actually went on Friday."

"Oh no, I didn't realise. That sort of makes sense. Things could have been even more difficult if your name wasn't registered as the father. The other thing that worries me, Jimmy, is Charlie. Her physical state alongside her mental state. She only gave birth just over a week ago. Her body is still healing. She really shouldn't be doing too much so soon after giving birth."

Jenni decided she would ring the midwife, who had been checking in on Charlie and Lily this last week. She might have a view on how far Jenni should take things with the authorities. A mother is fully entitled to walk away and leave father in charge, but it is certainly not usual. It wouldn't hurt to be as open as possible with the health officials. Who knew what type of logistical challenges lay ahead. But that was for later. Right now the important thing was to find Charlie.

"Jimmy, pass me the phone. I am going to put a call out to Charlie's parents now."

Jenni knew she had to do this straight away, before her courage departed. She had never spoken to Mr or Mrs Wright before, let alone met them. It was the strangest family set up imaginable. Jenni had always been there for her own children, through good times and bad, so found it hard to imagine parents who had so little concern for their offspring.

The phone rang a number of times before a voice answered. "Mr Wright?

It's Jenni Sullivan here, Jimmy's Mum. I'm glad we are finally able to speak."

"Hello, what do you want Mrs Sullivan?" His tone was abrupt and certainly not welcoming.

Jenni was not put off, even if she was surprised at the rudeness of his manner. "It's about Charlie. Is Mrs Wright there? Perhaps it would be best if I spoke with your wife."

"Whatever you have to say about Charlotte can be said to me. We don't need to concern my wife with your trivia." Again abrupt and even rude.

"Alright." Jenni tempered her response, despite feeling angry with this arrogant, ill-mannered man. "Charlie has walked out overnight. She left a note and left her baby behind. We are worried about her. Has she come home to you?"

Jenni was pretty sure Charlie would not entertain the thought of going home.

"Perhaps she has come to her senses at last," Mr Wright responded. "Why saddle herself with a bastard baby when she has her life ahead of her. As far as I am concerned, she is better off as far away from your son as possible. Now goodbye Mrs Sullivan and please don't ring here again."

With that, he put the phone down on Jenni. She was totally discombobulated.

"I don't believe that," she stared at Jimmy with confusion written all over her face. "What a bastard. He didn't seem to care one fig about Charlie. Poor kid."

Jimmy reached across and took Lily from his mother. He lay the baby on his chest as he gently rubbed her back, bringing up her wind. Lily made little snuffling noises as she settled back to sleep.

"All the more reason to keep Charlie's parents away from Lily. They cannot be trusted anywhere near her. And fancy calling her a bastard. How awful are they? How can you say that about an innocent baby?" Jimmy was whispering, but you could hear the venom in his voice. "No wonder Charlie didn't want to go home when she found out she was pregnant."

Jenni shuffled across the window seat to sit next to her son. She draped her arm across his shoulders, rubbing his neck where his hair curled in tiny ringlets. He shivered as his mother's comforting touch tickled. Laying his head on her shoulder, he wondered to himself how anyone could survive with parents like Charlie. He was so lucky to have had loving parents, who had supported him throughout. He felt the loss of his father at this time. Reggie would have adored Lily and it was devastating to know he had missed out on such a precious time.

A car pulling up on the drive disturbed the peaceful moment between mother and son. The practicalities of finding Charlie kicked into action.

CHAPTER TWELVE
SOUTHAMPTON AIRPORT

Jenni's car was located in the long-stay parking facility.

Alaistair's mate had come up trumps, finding the car on CCTV as it entered the parking lot at 5am that morning. Everything seemed to indicate that Charlie had waited until after Jimmy had finished the night feed before she had sneaked out. She knew that Jimmy would be asleep again as soon as his head hit the pillow.

When the two men arrived at the site, Al's friend was waiting and invited them into the control room to view the pictures. A grainy image of the car showed the shadow of a person driving, which had to be Charlie. They followed the BMW to its final destination and watched Charlie park and leave the keys under the wheel arch. Once she was out of the car it was easy to confirm the shadow had been Charlie. Jimmy recognised her rucksack, their staple travelling companion, slung over her shoulder. CCTV then picked her up as she waited for the bus to take her to the terminal building.

"Look chaps, I know this is probably outside of my job remit, but why don't we head down to the main terminal and I will see what I can do. Hell, I might as well be hung for more than one crime," he sniggered. "Hopefully, my boss won't be in today so no-one will be checking up on my investigations. There must be a record of the young lady if she got on a flight." Al's mate, Tony, seemed to have contacts in all the right places. "Leave your car here, Al, and I will drive you down."

Tony had a security branded Range Rover, which could no doubt access parts of the airport to which they couldn't. Both men were concerned they might be getting him into trouble, but at the same time, were happy to take the help on offer. Unknown to them, Tony was a bit of a loose cannon. He had a reputation at the airport for flagrantly ignoring protocols. His job was only secure because he was the first to put his hand up to do the most unsociable shifts and grab any overtime that was going. Tony loved to show off to his friends and today was another example of that behaviour.

Al would not feel responsible for his contact's decision making, especially if it helped them to find out what happened to poor Charlie. He hadn't asked Tony to take any additional risks to find Charlie. Their only request of him had been to find the car. Anything else was a bonus. And was on Tony's head.

Jimmy took Tony's hand and shook it. "I really appreciate your help, mate. It is very good of you. I'm sure my mother would want to know where Charlie is. Anything you can do would be amazing."

On the trip down to Southampton, Alaistair had managed to get a better understanding of the events of the early hours of Sunday morning. He was horrified to think of Charlie, alone and scared as she fled from her child. He had witnessed for himself the care Jenni had given the mother of her grandchild, even if it wasn't necessarily reciprocated. The girl must have some deep-seated issues to be able to abandon her baby. However, after recent events with Peter, Al, for one, would not judge the girl.

No-one can ever understand what it must take to leave your baby, willingly.

Half hour later, Jimmy and Al were sitting in an interview room at the main terminal building. Tony had been as good as his word and had managed to trace Charlie's booking. However his investigations had been picked up by the ground crew manager who had insisted that Jimmy speak to the airport police before he left. Now it was becoming official, something Jimmy really hadn't wanted to do. The last thing he needed was to get Charlie into any type of bother with the police, especially if she wanted to come back into their daughter's life. As much as his relationship with Charlie was broken, he would never keep her from their precious bundle of joy.

Jimmy had insisted that Al join him for the meeting.

He respected his boss and also knew his mother would subject him to a thorough questioning when he got home so, having two heads involved, was certainly better than the one. They had been supplied with coffee, whilst they waited, and had sat in companionable silence for the last half hour. Jimmy was starting to get a bit nervous. Could he be in any sort of trouble? Would this impact on him keeping Lily? He really didn't know what to think.

One thing was certain, he would do nothing to jeopardise his care for Lily. Until she had been born, he could never imagine how deep love could be. His world now revolved around Lily Rose. Charlie's flight was confusing to Jimmy. He could not imagine ever wanting to be parted from his daughter. Not for a moment.

The door opened and a woman police office entered. "Good morning. My name is Detective Inspector Janice James. I understand we have a missing persons case to discuss."

Jimmy looked at Alaistair, his nerves kicking in. He might be nearly 23 years of age, but brushes with the constabulary were not something he was used to dealing with. Alaistair could see his reticence and stepped in.

"Good morning, Detective Inspector. My name is Alaistair Middleton. I'm a friend of the family. I'm not sure whether we can class this as a missing person. Jimmy's girlfriend left in the middle of the night and it seems she has boarded a flight to Mallorca this morning."

Janice closed her notepad with a look of frustration on her face. "Right, so why all the panic? A young lady decides to go away on holiday without telling her boyfriend. I'm really not sure that is a police matter."

"No, I guess it's not," said Alaistair. "But Charlie gave birth to a baby just over a week ago. She left in the middle of the night without the baby. I think we are all concerned about her mental well-being. It's not normal, is it?"

Janice reopened her notepad, her attention caught. "Now, that is unusual behaviour. Have you been in touch with any of her friends and family, James. It is James Sullivan, isn't it?" she said, referring to her notes.

Jimmy coughed as he cleared his throat. "Yes, Jimmy Sullivan. Charlie, my girlfriend, well its Charlotte Wright, she has been living with me and my Mum since we came back from travelling together. Our daughter, Lily, was born a week last Saturday." He paused collecting his thoughts. "My mum spoke to her parents this morning, but they hadn't heard from her. They weren't very supportive of Charlie and the baby. So she really only has me and mum."

"And how has Charlotte been since the birth? Did she have a natural birth?"

"She had the baby in Salisbury hospital and I think it was natural." Jimmy hadn't got a clue what she meant by that expression. Perhaps she meant one of those new-fangled water-births. Thank goodness Charlie hadn't wanted one of those. He could not imagine them sitting in a pool while she had her bits on display. "She's been a bit funny since Lily was born. She didn't want to hold her. I have done most of the work with Lily since we came home. That's why we are worried. It just doesn't seem normal. How could anyone not love Lily. She is gorgeous."

Jimmy pulled his mobile out of his pocket and was showing Janice photos of his daughter. The policewoman smiled thinking how sweet the lad's obsession with his child was. She made all the right noises, even though she had no interest in babies whatsoever.

"OK, Jimmy. Firstly, let me say that there really is nothing the police can do to prevent Charlotte from leaving her child. However, I do agree that, as it is so soon after the birth, we should just check on her well-being. I'm going to get in touch with my counterparts in Spain and see if we can track Charlotte down." She nodded as she captured notes on her pad. "I can't promise you that we can persuade Charlotte to come home. But we can check on her welfare. Make sure she is okay."

"Thank you, Detective Inspector," interrupted Alaistair. "I know Jimmy's mother is very concerned, especially as it is so soon after the birth. We would hate it if something should happen to Charlie while she is quite vulnerable."

"I understand. Leave me to make some investigations and I will give you a call when we find out more."

Janice was on her feet, dismissing them with her actions. There was nothing more for them to do except to make a trip back to the carpark to retrieve Jenni's car and start the long drive back to Sixpenny Bissett.

As he drove, Alaistair had a lot on his mind. With Charlie missing in action what would Jimmy do? Would he be able to work or would his labouring days be over far too soon? Al had enjoyed having Jimmy as part of his crew. The lad was a grafter who was not afraid to put his back into it. Al understood, but he felt sorry for Jimmy who had an uphill struggle ahead.

In Jenni's car, Jimmy was having similar thoughts. There was little love lost between him and Charlie, but she was useful. She would have looked after his precious daughter while he went out to work to provide for them. He didn't want to spend the rest of his life living with mum, even if it was the best 5 star hotel he had lived in for some years. Without Charlie, what was he to do? He couldn't contemplate the thought of another person bringing his Lily up. He couldn't expect his mum to give up her dreams for her grandchild.

It was a right muddle. And one they would have to discuss in the days ahead.

CHAPTER THIRTEEN
ROSE COTTAGE

"Shush." Jenni held a finger to her lips as she opened the front door. "Lily has just dropped off."

She waved towards the lounge, where the baby slept. It had taken far too long to settle Lily this evening. The last thing she needed was to wake her now. Jenni believed the chaos of Charlie leaving must have unsettled the new-born. The routine of her early days had given way to distress and colicky crying.

Richard kicked off his shoes as he followed Jenni into her kitchen. A bottle of wine was open on the island, with two glasses ready to receive its precious liquid. A welcoming sight after a busy day at work.

The friendship between Jenni and Richard had flourished over recent months.

They had put the kiss behind them, never to be discussed again or to be examined in any detail. Jenni had been mortified at the time and it had taken a few weeks before she could reach out to Richard. The arrival of Jimmy, back from Australia, with the news about Charlie and her pregnancy had distracted her. The only positive to come out of the kerfuffle was that Jenni had been given the time and space to put her embarrassment to one side.

She still fancied the pants off Richard, but had built a high, security wall around her lust, knowing that nothing could ever happen. How she wished she had listened to Kate and Paula and their words of wisdom. They had dropped enough hints that Richard was not on the market for a new woman. Jenni had ignored their warnings and rushed headlong into disaster. Unfortunately, she had run far too fast for her own good. Crashed and burned. She had pushed him too soon and nearly spoilt everything.

She had to make do with her informal arrangement with the beautifully formed Henrique to satisfy her lustful desires. If the Spaniard knew he was her booby prize, he never let on. Ever the gentleman, he was always ready for her, whether it was a regular visit or an impromptu one. Jenni did not think about the impact her comings and goings had on Henrique. As far as she knew, he felt the same way as she did. If she sounded selfish, she probably was.

But back to Richard.

Once she had finally got over her ego being dented, Jenni realised she liked Richard and wanted him as a friend. Being of a similar age and both being single, they were often thrust together at dinner parties and village events. Their friendship grew. Jenni would not make the same mistake again and she tempered her normal tactile nature when Richard was around. She never even gave him a kiss on the cheek. It was safer that way. Don't put temptation in her path, became a mantra she would live by, when it came to Richard Samuels.

Recently, they had got into a habit of sharing a bottle of wine of an evening. Richard had been a brilliant support to Jenni as she prepared to open the café. His knowledge of running a business was invaluable and he allowed Jenni to pick his brains on a regular basis. In return, Jenni would cook dinner and provide wine.

A mutually useful arrangement.

As it happens, Richard felt differently to Jenni's perception of their situation. He regretted his behaviour that fateful night of the failed kiss. He wished he could go back to that particular evening and do things differently. In his imagination, he would kiss Jenni back. He would have touched that seductive sliver of cleavage enticing him in. He would have taken her, right there on the cream sofa. It was those images which he took out and examined when alone at night, when he needed some relief.

But those were just imaginings.

He had ballsed it up. He had spurned her advances and even ran off like a prissy virgin rather than a red-blooded male. He regretted it the minute he closed her front door, but it was too late. Jenni had avoided him for weeks after that performance. Slowly she had allowed him back in, but made it very clear by her body language and behaviours that she was over him.

Or so he thought.

He would settle for her friendship, if that was all that was on offer. He deserved this outcome. If he hadn't behaved the way he had that night, how different things might have been. Maybe one day she would trust him enough to let him in. Until then he would prove himself invaluable to her as a friend and business confidant.

"Any news of Charlie?" asked Richard.

News had spread around the village fairly quickly, fanned by the mouth of Anna Fletcher, ex-schoolmistress and number one gossip resident of Sixpenny Bissett. Oh, she had delighted in witnessing more trouble for that woman, Jenni Sullivan. Anna Fletcher could not stand Jenni. Thankfully, the feeling was mutual.

"We had word from the Spanish authorities today. She's safe and well and refuses to come back. I think she plans to complete her world-wide travels now the little problem of a baby is sorted. Pick up where she left off." Jenni sighed. She really could not get her head around Charlie's mindset.

"Well, that's great for her, but what about Lily? Not being funny, but what are you going to do with a new-born to care for?"

Richard was not sexist, but he had instantly jumped to an assumption which irritated the hell out of Jenni. Why do people automatically think that the woman should look after a baby? Jimmy had been fanatical in his drive to care for his daughter given the emotional absence of her mother, especially in the days after she was born. He was far more capable of looking after Lily Rose than anyone else. She didn't blame Richard for expressing those thoughts out loud. He wouldn't be alone in thinking them.

"Jimmy has already spoken to Alaistair. He's going to have to give up work for now to look after Lily. He is an excellent father so I have no doubt he will do a fantastic job. Honestly, the timing of all of this is total pants."

Richard watched the sadness take the glimmer out of Jenni's eyes. Everything had been going so well for Jenni with the opening of the café and he could see how excited she was to set up her own business. She was thriving. It was such a shame that the birth of Lily could send this family into disarray.

Not the baby's fault of course. She didn't ask to be born. It wasn't her fault that her mother was just not the mothering type.

"I'm loving running the café, but perhaps I should have put things on hold when I first found out about Charlie and the pregnancy," she sighed.

"Of course you shouldn't," interjected Richard. "The last thing Jimmy would have wanted was for you to put your own ambitions on hold. It certainly wasn't your fault Charlie got pregnant."

He smiled reassuringly as he refilled both their glasses. They weren't sharing supper tonight. Richard had invited Jenni to have dinner at his, but she had declined. Being the loving mother she was, Jenni had insisted that Jimmy go for a pint at the pub. She had decided to babysit and give her son a well-earned rest. Jimmy had not left his daughter's side since the weekend and looked exhausted.

Jenni also had an ulterior motive.

"I know, Richard. Jimmy would never ask me to do that. I just can't help feeling frustrated that things have turned out the way they have. The reason I pushed Jimmy out to the pub tonight was to have a few moments alone with Lily. What with work and this debacle with Charlie, I haven't really had any time alone with her. My life is too hectic. That's what is really bothering me."

Richard just wanted to take her in his arms and cuddle her. He hated to see her sad at such a happy time. He dare not. If he invaded her personal space, it could ruin their friendship completely. He had noticed how Jenni held back when they were together. When she was with Kate and Paula or even The General, she was always the first to grab them in for a hug. When with him, she was much more reserved even though their friendship was blossoming. It did not occur to him that Jenni was protecting herself from another rejection.

"Can I have a sneaky look at the little love," asked Richard, thinking a reminder of the joy of Lily's arrival may blow away some of her worries.

It had the desired effect. Lily was sleeping in a wicker carry-basket in the lounge. Richard tiptoed across the carpeted floor to gaze at the baby. He was struck by how contented she looked, her rose-bud lips pouting, looking for sustenance, even while she was in repose.

"Oh, Jenni, she is gorgeous. What an angel. You must be over the moon."

Jenni was quite surprised by Richard's reaction. She was aware that he didn't have children of his own, but wasn't aware whether that was from choice or unfortunate circumstances. Watching his face light up with joy at the sight of the cute baby, warmed her heart. She could not fancy this man any more than she did right at this moment. Damn it that he was out of reach. What a shame it could never come good for them.

"She is so beautiful," Jenni sighed. "I know I'm biased. Every grandma must think their grandchild is the cutest. But mine is." Jenni sniggered, trying her hardest not to wake Lily. "Come on, let's go back to the kitchen. Fancy trying this new cupcake recipe out for me? You can be my guineapig."

The cupcake was salted caramel and apple in flavour and Richard showed his delight in it by consuming two. No wonder the café was doing so great with cakes like that. As he ate, an idea started to form.

"Jenni, why don't you and Jimmy run the café together?"

Jenni looked puzzled. "Run it together? How?"

"Sorry, that came out all wrong. I meant, why not train up Jimmy so that he can run the café a few days a week and you do the other days. It will give you precious time with Lily and give Jimmy a sense of purpose, outside of his daughter."

Richard watched Jenni as her mind cogitated on his suggestion. He sensed the moment when she recognised the merit in his idea.

"Bloody hell, Richard. Why didn't I think of that? You may be on to something. Jimmy is great with people and actually serving out the hot drinks and cakes isn't too technical. He would pick it up so quickly."

"It's worth considering. Jimmy is a lovely man and he strikes me as a kindred spirit. He loves his independence. If he was working it will surely help his self-esteem. His life has changed so much in the last six months." Richard had a soft spot for Jimmy, seeing many of his youthful characteristics from his own past. "After all that time travelling the world, independent of his mother, he now finds himself dependent on you for board and lodgings, along with the support of his daughter. His mind must be all over the place. Work will do him good."

Jenni knew that Richard was talking sense. She had spent so much time recently considering the impact on herself. The unwanted changes that Jimmy and Charlie had brought into her life. The way her idyll in the countryside had been hijacked. She had felt angry that her plans were being changed for her. The one consistency had been her drive to open the café. It had been something for her and her alone.

Richard had reminded her that she wasn't the only person affected. Jimmy was paying a high price for unprotected sex. Whilst he would never moan about his new responsibilities, his hopes and dreams had been shattered on the rock of fatherhood. He could never have imagined his life would be built around feeds and nappies for the next few years. Jimmy needed a purpose and Jenni had it in her gift to do something about it.

"You are right, Richard. This could kill two birds with one stone," she laughed. "I will talk to him."

"And if you don't mind a bit of extra advice?" he smiled.

"Go on."

"Focus on selling it to him that he is helping you. Male pride and all that. If he thinks he is doing you a favour then he might find it easier to square it in his mind. Especially the parental guilt of leaving his child with someone else so he can go out and work."

"Oh you are so wise, Mr Samuels," Jenni joked. "I think it's a brilliant idea and I really hope he goes for it."

As their conversation moved on to other things, Jenni could not help thinking about Jimmy. He was embracing fatherhood with a stoical air and was clearly enjoying spending time with Lily. The idea of giving him some shifts at the café had merit. Jenni was frustrated that she couldn't spend the time she wanted with Lily.

By the time she got home from work each night, she was usually shattered. Jimmy had slipped into the role of chef, having a meal ready for her return. Usually Lily was asleep when she returned and would go through until around midnight by which time Jenni would be asleep. If she was lucky, she would see the baby in the morning, for a quick cuddle, before she headed out to the café. Sunday was her only day when she could lie in bed with her granddaughter, giving Jimmy a much needed rest.

Jimmy never complained about his new responsibilities, but for how long would this last? Once the first flush of excitement wore off, would he resent the changes to his life plan? Working in a café was certainly not on his career path but being a family business may soften the blow.

Jenni had decided. She would talk to Jimmy and sound him out.

CHAPTER FOURTEEN
NUMBER 2, GREEN FARM COTTAGES

Paula's gaze was fixed on him. It was unnerving. He couldn't work out what she was thinking. Was she angry? Sad? Ashamed of him? Peter suddenly realised that this was the first time in his life that he was worried about what someone else thought of him.

Progress.

Making a mental note he decided he must talk to his counsellor about those feelings.

"Cup of tea, Paula?" he broke the silence, feeling increasingly uncomfortable under her scrutiny.

Before he could get up from the sofa, his ex was off into the kitchen, making herself at home. When Paula was in this sort of mood, it was best to give her the space to do her stuff. Peter might no longer be her life partner, but he knew Paula far too well. She would not be grateful if he interfered with her mission. She was determined to look after him and he best let her.

They had just arrived home from the hospital. It seemed like he had been away for ages and, as he looked around the living room, any signs of his desperate attempt to end it all had vanished. He was sure that either Paula or Al had been responsible for the clean-up. He really was the luckiest chap to have such good people in his life.

Why had he not seen how fortunate he had been? He had good people in his life who cared about him. If he had realised how blessed he was, would he have allowed himself to get so low? Ifs and buts were never worth contemplating. His mind was seeking out the future now. Not the past and his stupid mistakes.

Paula had insisted on picking him up from the ward, even though he had been planning on catching the bus. He really didn't want to impose on Paula. She had been an absolute brick and he didn't want to ask for even more help. Peter already owed her his life. How much more could he expect from her?

Before long Paula was back with a steaming cup of tea and a slice of cake. How he missed being looked after. He really didn't deserve it. Taking a nibble of the coffee and walnut slice, the reality of hospital food kicked in. He was starving. The cake hardly touched the sides as he gobbled it down. Paula smiled, enjoying watching his enthusiasm for one of Jenni's specials.

"Well, there is nothing wrong with your appetite," Paula grinned. She had been avoiding asking the question which had been bothering her for days now. But she knew she needed to broach the subject, otherwise the elephant in the room would grow and grow. "How are you feeling now Peter? Do you still want to die?"

Oh shit, she thought. That came out wrong. The question had been tormenting her for days. OK, Peter had rung her that night so perhaps it was just a cry for help rather than a real attempt to kill himself. But he had planned it out. No-one has that number of pills for the odd headache. He must have known what that amount of painkillers would have done to his body. And was it her fault that he was desperate enough to end it all? Was this her punishment for finally standing up for herself in the relationship stakes?

No wonder the question came out all wrong.

Peter was somewhat taken aback by the directness of Paula's tone, but he understood. It had only been ten days since that dreadful night, but in that time, he had made real progress in understanding his mental state and the triggers that had led him to try to end it all. His private medical cover had proved invaluable to get him the best psychiatric support money could buy. He was at the start of his journey of awareness. He wouldn't underestimate the amount of work he needed to do to accept how close he had come to ending his pain and to understand the triggers which had got him to that point. But the first step in that journey was recognising that he had a problem and that he wanted to get better.

One of the biggest steps he could take was to share his vulnerability with the woman who had shared the majority of his adult life with him. He drew in a huge breath and let it out slowly and surely. Looking at the floor, he decided eye contact was off the agenda. He didn't feel strong enough.

"I don't want to die, Paula," he paused. "I am so sorry that I put you through that awful night. You don't deserve that. Things got really dark and I didn't know where to turn." He raised his eyes gradually. Paula's gaze had softened as she listened. "I have been talking, I mean, really talking for the first time in my life. Dr Gibbs has been fantastic and I think I'm making progress."

"That's good," replied Paula. She could not imagine her husband talking about his problems. That was one hell of an achievement in itself.

"I owe you an explanation. I don't think I can put it into words just yet, but the main thing I need you to know is that none of this is your fault." He could see the tears forming in Paula's eyes. "I screwed up our marriage. I took you for granted, Paula, and I honestly don't blame you for kicking me out."

Paula had so much she wanted to say but was afraid to do so. She needed him to know that there was no way back for them, but how do you kick a man when he is down? The wife and woman, who had loved him for twenty years, naturally wanted to help him through his troubles. The last thing she wanted was to send any mixed messages. Her care and sympathy must not be mistaken for reconciliation. But how could she make that clear without pushing him towards that precipice again.

Peter wasn't afraid of her silence. He had gone to some dark places in his counselling sessions recently and he was still struggling to put into words how he was feeling. For Paula it must be so much worse. She had seen him at the bottom of his journey of destruction and hadn't been witness to the progress he had made so far. She looked scared and for once he understood that feeling.

"I know we cannot go back, Paula." His voice was slow and steady as he tried to express what he wanted, without hurting his dearest friend and supporter. "I will always love you, but I know it's over. You must move on and start a life without me. And I will do the same. I would love it if we can remain friends. I know that might be difficult, but we could try, can't we?"

If Paula was a blow-up doll, the plug had just been released. Perhaps not the best analogy, given the sexual behaviours of her husband in the past, but visually extremely apt for the circumstances. She sagged as if the air was sucked from her body. A virtual weight had floated away from her shoulders. She felt emancipated and alive for the first time since finding Peter's slumped body on the very floor before her.

"Thank you, Peter," she whispered. "There is no going back, but I was so worried that us parting had led to you to trying to kill yourself. I could not live with that knowledge."

Peter shuffled across the sofa to sit beside her. Taking her hand in his, he squeezed it just enough to indicate comfort. "I am so sorry for what I did, Paula. I know I can get better and I have great friends around me to help. Please don't feel guilty. It's my guilt to bear, not yours. I just want you to be happy and if that is with Al then I will give you both my blessing. Not that you need it, of course."

Peter could have laughed out loud at the look on Paula's face. He may have been the most arrogant bastard ever, but he was not stupid. He had seen the looks between Paula and Alaistair Middleton these last few months. Those looks had wounded him; slashes of a thousand knife cuts. Why did Paula have to fall for his best mate? He realised that he deserved the pain and humiliation of his wife falling for the village idiot. Not kind! But that's what jealousy can do to you. At the end of the day, Paula deserved happiness and if that was with Alaistair, then he would just have to suck it up.

Meanwhile Paula's current expression was one of horror and amazement in equal measures.

"What do you mean, me and Al? We are just friends," she whispered.

"Friends, my arse," he snorted, but in a friendly way.

It hurt, but he needed to accept that Alaistair was Paula's future, not himself. Perhaps they had been better suited all along. Even when they were all at school together Paula and Al had had a special bond. Perhaps if she hadn't got pregnant with Peter's baby they may have parted sooner, before they married. But that was all in the past.

He was learning to accept the past and use it to shape his future.

"Alaistair loves you and not just as a mate. Let yourself go, darling. And be happy." Peter squeezed her hand again as if to seal the deal. For the first time in his life Peter was thinking about what was best for another and not himself.

"I honestly don't know what to say, Peter."

Paula clung to his hand. For so long he had been the rock she had built her life on. He had been her friend and lover. Could they go forward only as friends? Paula knew that her husband needed her support over the weeks and months ahead. It was a duty which she did not feel burdened by. You cannot be married to someone that long without caring for their physical and mental well-being, no matter the hurt they had dished out to each other.

Paula was sure that between the three of them, including Alaistair, they might find a way to navigate the weeks ahead.

No matter how difficult it may be.

CHAPTER FIFTEEN
THE CAFÉ AT KATE'S

Sunlight beamed through the glass fronted shop window, filling the café with warmth and light. It was going to be another hot day. So far, July had been sweltering under unusually high temperatures, which was certainly not welcomed by all in the village.

It was Saturday morning and officially Jimmy's first day at work.

Richard's idea had been grasped with both hands by Jimmy, who immediately saw the benefits of him having some time away from father duties. He adored his daughter, but babies are not the most stimulating of companions. Once fed and changed, Lily could sleep for hours. Jimmy had missed the banter of work and had been jealous watching his mother enjoying time away from the house. Instantly he had felt guilty about those thoughts.

Welcome to the guilt triggers of parenthood!

He would not contemplate getting a nanny or using a childminder, especially as Lily was so young and she had already gone through more change than most children had, at such an early age. In the lonely, dark nights as he tended to Lily's needs, Jimmy's mind would focus on what lay ahead for him. His life plan had changed drastically and, whilst he would not change a thing as far as his wonderful daughter was concerned, something was missing in his world.

The previous weekend Jimmy had been given an impromptu lesson on the delights of the coffee machine. It was a sensitive machine which needed careful handling. Jimmy had passed with flying colours. Whilst on his gap year travelling, Jimmy had picked up a myriad of skills which he could turn his hand to. One of his most important skills, as far as the café was concerned, was his conversational capability. Jenni's ethos for The Café at Kate's was to create a space where customers could relax and enjoy a chat. Jimmy would be a welcome addition to the team.

The team being two of them, but a team all the same.

Jenni had agreed to spend an hour with Jimmy to help him settle in and to be on hand if there were any issues with the temperamental cash till. Lily was fast asleep in her pram, in the only bit of shade available. Jenni loved these new-fangled prams, so much better than the heavy-weight objects she had to manhandle around when the boys were little. Lily's was adaptable and doubled up as car seat. Ideal for moving her around when she was in the 'land of nod'.

Jenni sat back on the high stool behind the counter as she watched Jimmy work. He had a natural style and moved around the small serving area with considered actions. Cups and plates were placed, not bashed, into place and he cleaned up as he worked. Jenni nodded her head as she evaluated his performance. He would do well.

They had had a steady stream of customers during the last hour. There was rarely a queue, allowing time for Jimmy to talk to customers and ensure that relaxation, rather than rush, was the prevailing atmosphere. As Jimmy wiped down the counter for the umpteenth time that morning, The General arrived for his mid-morning piece of cake. Herbert Smythe-Jones was a regular. Living alone, he thrived on the company at Kate's. He would always find someone to sit and chat to, as the morning wore on.

"Well hello, young Jimmy. It is good to see you behind the counter. First day?" Herbert pulled his man-purse from his pocket and started to count out his coin. Herbert was old-school. He hated using plastic and much preferred 'the Queen's legal tender'.

"Morning, General." Jimmy flashed a big, beaming smile. He had a soft spot for Herbert. Most people did. He was a real gent. "Still got my 'L plates' on, but Mum hasn't sacked me just yet. What can I get you?"

Herbert took his time, viewing the various cakes and buns on display. "Americano and may I have a slice of the Red Velvet cake please. It looks wonderfully luxurious."

The two men chatted as Jimmy pulled his order together, spreading it out on a small tray, which he insisted on carrying over to a table by the window. Herbert's usual table, which was often seen by his parishioners as a drop in spot, allowing villagers to question their community leader. Herbert never turned anyone away. He was far too generous with his time.

"Jenni," The General had finally spotted his friend hiding in the background. "Have you got a moment?"

"Of course, Herbert. Let me just make myself a coffee and I will come and join you."

Herbert Smythe-Jones had been a good friend to Jenni since she moved into the village. His role on the council meant he had his finger on the pulse of the community. He had a soft spot for Jenni, who reminded him of his beloved, deceased wife, Bridget. She regarded Herbert as a surrogate father, having lost hers some years ago. Herbert had been keen to get Jenni onto the Parish Council, but so far, his pleas had fallen on deaf ears. She really hoped today was not another such attempt. She had enough on her plate right now.

The two friends sipped companionably on their coffees as Jenni awaited The General to make his opening salvo.

"Jenni, my dear. Now you aren't working every day I wondered if you could join me for luncheon at mine, one day next week. I have a business proposition you may be interested in."

Jenni was intrigued. "I would love to. I'm off on Wednesday if that works for you. I will have to bring Lily if you don't mind."

Herbert didn't mind one bit. He loved children.

He had five grandchildren of his own and actually preferred them to his own children. Poor Fraser and Eleanor had spent their childhood being moved from one army barracks to the next. Herbert had little time for them. Not through choice, but the demands of the job. Bringing up the children had fallen heavily on Bridget's shoulders. Once the grandchildren came along, Herbert had loved playing the fool and spoiling them, much to the disgust of his son and daughter. It was a different relationship completely, especially as he could hand them back once he had driven them into a state of extreme excitement.

"That will be lovely. How is little Lily settling down into a routine?" Herbert asked.

Jenni wheeled the pram over so Herbert could take a peek. "She is an angel. Doesn't seem to be bothered with her Daddy going back to work, although I'm not sure how Nanny will feel when it's her turn to do the night feed."

Herbert groaned as he imagined that. "She is a contented baby because she has a contented home. Lily is a lucky girl to have you and Jimmy as her carers."

"Too kind, Herbert. So will you tell me a bit more about this proposition?" Jenni hated surprises and didn't think she could wait until Wednesday.

"Not now, my dear. I will explain all when we have lunch. By the way, have you seen Peter since he came home? I do hope he is okay."

Jenni shook her head. "Haven't seen him, but I have spoken to Paula. She seemed to be quite positive. Looks like he is getting the right help. Something he probably should have had years ago. I do think it is so unfair for men. They find it incredibly hard to talk about their problems and it all piles up until they can't take any more." Being the mother of two grown up sons, she certainly understood the reluctance of some men to share their troubles.

"It was rife in the army," answered Herbert. "Culturally we were told to keep the 'old stiff upper lip', but I have seen too many young men take their own lives when a conversation with a superior could have sorted the problem out."

Their conversation was interrupted by Kate, who breezed into the café, announcing her presence with a wave, a drag of a chair from the neighbouring table and the plonk of her bottom on the afore-mentioned chair.

"Morning, Jenni. General. I need a favour, Jenni."

Jenni sighed. She really didn't have the capacity to provide anyone with a favour right now. This was her first Saturday off since the café opened and she believed she deserved some quality time with her granddaughter.

Kate sensed her mood change. "You will love this favour. Fancy coming to Southampton with me for a spot of shopping? Jeremy is minding the kids so how about a spot of retail therapy?"

Jenni's mood lightened immediately. Southampton had a massive John Lewis store, her favourite. The thought of exploring the baby department for clothes, and maybe even a christening gown, was too good to resist.

"Oh, yes please. That would be wonderful. Let me just check Jimmy is alright with that."

Looking over to her son, she spotted Florence Smith, daughter of the landlord of The King's Head, chatting with Jimmy. That's good, she thought. Another new customer. She hadn't seen Florence in the café before. Although looking at the animation on her face, coffee may not be the only attraction.

"Jimmy, love," she shouted. "Will you be okay if I head off with Kate for the rest of the day?" Jenni was already gathering her handbag and Lily's bag of essentials together.

"Of course, Mum. I will be fine. Enjoy yourself."

Jimmy was quite thankful to Kate for dragging his mum off. Having her watching him like a hawk was not helping. He was enjoying his day so far. Being out of the house and chatting to customers made him feel almost normal again. He was Jimmy again. Not just daddy or son.

And more importantly, the day had just got even better with the appearance of Florence.

CHAPTER SIXTEEN
WEST QUAY SHOPPING CENTRE
SOUTHAMPTON

Kate squealed with childish excitement as the two women stepped into the baby department of Jenni's favourite store.

"Look at this," she cried holding up the most beautiful christening gown. "It's gorgeous."

It certainly was.

Ivory silk laden with delicate, vintage lace which cascaded down the skirt of the dress. The bodice was shaped with a lace collar and sleeves and a beautiful wide ribbon sash. Jenni could imagine holding Lily for the christening photos, the lace falling over her arms. The baby would look absolutely beautiful. Jenni ran her fingers over the dress, feeling the quality. She noticed the price tag and was surprised that it wasn't too extravagant. Taking a quick picture on her phone, she sent a message to Jimmy, hoping he would agree with her.

Kate and Jenni made their way around the department, adding further goodies to a fairly laden shopping basket. Babies grow in size incredibly quickly. Lily was only four weeks old and was already growing out of some of her new-born Babygro's. Admiring the beautiful garments, Jenni decided she was in heaven. Having had two boys, she had missed out on the delights of dresses, frilly knickers and cute pastel dungaree sets. All too soon, the basket was overflowing with gorgeous outfits.

For once, Jenni was avoiding her favourite department, womenswear, in favour of spending her cash on her grandchild's needs.

Jenni's phone pinged. Grabbing it from her bag, she noticed a message from Jimmy.

Mum, that dress is beautiful. Go for it. Lily will look like a princess.

All good here. Have fun. Jx

She smiled as she read his words.

Thank goodness he was supportive of her choice, as Jenni had fallen in love with the gown. Her granddaughter would be the best dressed baby for her big day. The date was already booked with Jeremy for August and would form part of the normal Sunday morning service. Jenni was keen to introduce her lovely Lily to the church community, with all their new friends supporting them. George would be coming down for the weekend. Jimmy had already asked him to stand as godfather, an honour his brother was suitably excited about.

With an unspoken nod, the women made their way to the counter to pay. As she picked out each item from the basket and placed them on the counter for the assistant, Jenni turned to Kate.

"Fancy some lunch? The Place to Eat?"

"Ummm, yes please. All this shopping has made me hungry. And little lady here is now awake and probably ready for a bottle." Kate was pushing the pram forward and back, trying to delay the cries of a demanding baby.

The shop assistant was listening in. "Madam, would you like me to pack your items for collection once you have finished the rest of your trip?"

"Thank you, that's a wonderful idea. Where do we pick them up?" Jenni smiled at the helpful assistant.

"There is a pickup point on the ground floor, Madam, next to the carpark for ease. Now is that everything?"

"Thank you, yes. What's the damage?" Jenni gasped as she saw the bill. She hadn't expected that, but of course, a new baby is an expensive matter. Anyway who else was she going to spend her money on?

It didn't take them long to settle themselves in a booth on the fifth floor. Another helpful assistant had taken Lily's bottle for warming and, while they waited, Kate tucked into her fish and chips. Her choice of dinner looked delicious and Jenni was regretting her own choice. She had gone for a healthier option of Chicken Shawarma Grain Bowl, which did look tasty, and also less calorific. Unfortunately, there is something about fish covered in batter to get the mouth juices alert. And Kate's fish smelt amazing.

Never mind. Jenni would concentrate on the task in hand and ignore the rumbling of her tummy as it craved the succulent fish.

Jenni already looked a practised parent, balancing Lily in one arm, with the same hand holding the bottle to the baby's lips, whilst spooning the chickpeas into her own mouth. All done successfully, without dropping any food on Lily's head.

"Thank you for suggesting our shopping trip," said Jenni. "It's my first time bringing Lily out like this and it's great not to have to do it alone."

"No." Kate cut in. "Thank you. If you hadn't said yes, I would have ended up cleaning. Tragic, eh? On my day off too. Anyway it's good for Jeremy to experience the hectic dash from football practise to netball game. He won't volunteer again," laughed Kate. "I had to grab my chance while I could."

Kate's husband was the parish vicar. A quiet, lovely man who was ideally suited to his role. Kate was the absolute opposite. She was a whirlwind of enthusiasm, who could grab a room of people by the balls, colloquially speaking. She was confident and ebullient. Being the first person Jenni had met when she moved into Rose Cottage, Kate had taken the newcomer under her wing. It was just what Jenni needed to help navigate her way through the trials and tribulations of her first few months living in Sixpenny Bissett. It didn't take long for Kate to become her best friend and now her business partner.

"Kate, I wanted to ask you something." Jenni chewed on a piece of chicken. Her own mother would tell her off for speaking with her mouth full, but she didn't care. Jenni was learning to multitask with her new responsibilities. Sustenance needed to be taken whenever possible.

"Oh yes, what's that?" Kate was making good progress on her fish and enjoying it immensely. It was such a treat to savour her food, without the moans of her teenagers or the constant threat to her chips from Jeremy's fork.

"Jimmy and I have been talking and we would be absolutely honoured if you would be Lily's godmother."

Kate screeched making Lily jump in Jenni's arms and renew her suckling on the bottle. The baby had slipped into a milk-fuel stupor until her new godmother had frightened the life out of her. "Oh my God, serious?"

Jenni nodded. "We couldn't think of a better person to take on the role. You are my best friend and I honestly don't know what I would do without you in my life. Lily won't go far wrong with you as her guiding light."

"Oi, you soppy cow," laughed Kate. "That is so lovely of you, darling girl. I would be delighted to. And that means I get to hold her in that beautiful gown. Who else is joining me in the godparent stakes?"

"George is going to stand as godfather and one of Jimmy's best friends from university, Della, is the other godmother." Jenni loved the quirky friend who had always been at Jimmy's side throughout his university days. "I always thought Jimmy and Della would hook up as she was always coming to us during the holiday period. He seemed smitten with her at one time. Turns out she could only see Jimmy as a brother figure, certainly not boyfriend material. Seems she married a chap twenty years older than her. Actually her old university professor."

"Exciting. I cannot wait to meet her. Sounds a remarkably interesting young lady." Kate loved women with character, especially as she, herself, had the biggest personality ever. It didn't take Kate long to suss out a person and decide if she liked them. Fortunately for Jenni, theirs was a relationship which had hit it off instantly.

"Della is lovely and 'mad as a hatter' at the same time. I remember spending hours debating issues with her when she stayed with us. Reggie loved a good argument, especially over politics, and Della was the perfect contestant for him. She works at The House of Commons now; researcher for a minister, I believe."

"Oh, gosh. She will put me to shame," giggled Kate. "Not sure I will be able to compete with such an intellectual."

Despite her bombastic nature, Kate did have an annoying habit of undervaluing her own abilities. It was quite endearing.

Jenni was delighted, and somewhat relieved, that Kate was happy at being asked. It hadn't taken her long to convince Jimmy that she was the best choice out of all of Jenni's friends. She might not have known Kate as long as many of her Birmingham mates, but she loved her dearly and could not think of a better role model for her granddaughter. Sixpenny Bissett was the family's future. Birmingham its past. It made perfect sense to have her new best friend ready to guide Lily through the challenges of life.

"Anyway, once we have finished this, shall we head to M&S?" asked Jenni "I am in desperate need of some new sensible knickers."

Both women laughed. Jenni had two drawers for her underwear, a secret only Kate knew. One drawer had the sensible, comfortable pants for everyday use. The other held the more daring, sexy, lace ones which came out whenever her young lover, Henrique was around. There were standards to be maintained and Jenni would never be caught in the wrong set again.

Not since the embarrassment of their first encounter when he had been given full view of her Granny pants. An event which still made Jenni grin whenever she thought about it. Today was no different. She chuckled to herself as they prepared to move on to the next shop.

CHAPTER SEVENTEEN
THE MANOR HOUSE

The gravel drive was providing Jenni with one hell of a work-out. The wheels of the pram resisted the stones, spinning on occasions as she pushed Lily up the drive to the Manor House. Jenni was due for lunch at The General's house and was running late.

Lily had decided to projectile vomit all over the place as Jenni was about to tuck her into the pram. The milky vomit covered Jenni's skirt along with Lily's clean outfit. The sheer amount of liquid and its sickly smell left Jenni with no option. Lily had to be stripped down and bathed before they could consider leaving the house. Despite putting a new outfit on both her and the baby, Jenni could still catch the faint whiff of baby vomit.

It had thrown her timings up in the air. If there was one thing Jenni was passionate about above all else, it was timekeeping. Being late showed a distinct lack of respect. Hopefully, Herbert would forgive her, once he knew the reason.

It didn't take long for Herbert to answer the door and shepherd Jenni into the country kitchen. Being the gentleman that he was, he made absolutely no mention of his companion's tardiness. He cooed over Lily as he hurried around the stove, completing his preparations.

The General had made soup, home-made. It was one of his late wife's recipes, a potato and leek soup, enhanced with full fat cream. The smell wafting from the saucepan was delightful and Jenni could hear her stomach rumble at the thought of it. Without needing to be asked, Jenni placed spoons and bowls on the table and found side plates to hold the crusty rolls. She spotted a plate of her own ginger cookies for dessert. Last night her kitchen had smelt wonderfully with a ginger aroma. Her good friend had obviously been to the café as usual this morning.

The couple worked in harmony. It reminded Jenni of last year's New Year party when she had ridden to Herbert's aid. He had been let down by his caterers. That night they had been a formidable team, although Herbert would be the first to acknowledge that Jenni had been in charge. He was purely the sous chef.

Before Herbert served up the steaming vegetable soup, Jenni took one last look at Lily. She was fast asleep in her pram, parked the other side of the kitchen table, as far away from the hot Aga as possible. Despite bringing up a fair portion of her morning feed, Lily was exhausted and would hopefully sleep through their lunch. Fingers crossed, Jenni wished.

Jenni was still intrigued to find out what The General's big secret was. She was not great at being patient and was keen to know more.

As she blew on the hot liquid, Jenni fixed her gaze on Herbert. "Right, what's the proposition, Herbert? You have my interest piqued, so please, spill the beans."

The General finished his mouthful before speaking. He dabbed gently on both sides of his mouth with his pristine cotton napkin. "Right you are. I have a contact from my army days and he is in need of some help. He's hosting a regimental dinner for a group of retired officers. He is a widower like me, so does not have the help of a better half. He wanted the name of my caterers, but as you know I wasn't going to recommend them. Not after the debacle at New Year."

"Ummm, interesting. What sort of dinner party is he looking for?"

Jenni had been thinking recently about expanding her repertoire. Kate would, no doubt, urge caution, reminding her that not only was she running a café with her son, but she was producing all the cakes and biscuits they sold. Jenni needed to be sure that she had the capacity before expanding her business further.

Herbert's proposition sounded intriguing and she wanted to know more.

"I believe it is ten chaps, no ladies. Three course meal, focusing on high end rather than pub grub." Herbert smiled. There was no way that he imagined Jenni producing anything purporting to be pub grub. Her palette and expertise were further advanced. "He is open to suggestions, prior to confirming the job."

Jenni was genuinely interested. But she now had to face the difficult part. She hated discussing money, but that was a key part of business. She wasn't running a charity, was she? "Any idea of the price scale for the job, Herbert?"

"I think you are going to love this. £50 per head for the catering and he will cover the cost of the produce so you are looking at clearing £500 for your time and effort."

Jenni gulped. "Blimey. Are you serious? That sounds a huge amount especially as I'm new to this game."

"Darling girl, you are worth every penny. If you want to give it a go, I will pass on Terence's details so you can give him a call."

"You are too kind." That beautiful smile lit up her face, making it all worthwhile in Herbert's opinion. "Herbert, are you ok? You look a bit pale."

Jenni watched as the colour drained from The General's face. He was clearly in pain and his right hand came to his chest, clutching his sweater.

"Herbert." Jenni was out of her seat and around the table before he could utter a word. Clutching his free hand she gently rubbed it, providing reassurance and comfort. Slowly the pain appeared to disperse and blood rushed back to his face. "Herbert, what's up?"

The General let out a soft groan and continued to rub his chest with the palm of his hand. "Oh dear, that was a nasty one." He looked at Jenni with a fixed stare in his eyes. "I have had a few of these twinges recently, but that was definitely the worst to date."

Jenni was concerned. The General was very much trying to play things down, but it was clear that he was in pain, and considerable pain, if his expression was anything to go by.

"Herbert, have you spoken to the doctor about these twinges? It may be a good idea to just get things checked out." Perhaps it was just indigestion, but it was never right to ignore the warning signs.

The General eased himself up out of the chair and slowly walked around the room, breathing deeply and slowly. He felt quite embarrassed now, making such a fuss. The last thing he wanted to do was worry poor Jenni.

"I will do, my dear. I think I probably ate a bit too fast. That's normally the problem. But I will give the doctors a ring."

Jenni did not believe this was a simple case of indigestion, especially as The General was the slowest eater she had ever seen. He could make a plate of food last for ever as he expertly carved each piece into precision squares. It must have been his military background. She was also concerned that The General was a typical example of his generation when it came to health issues. He didn't like to make a fuss and felt that speaking to the doctor would be seen as an interruption to their busy day.

"Will you promise me you will ring the doctors? Please Herbert. For me?" It maybe emotional blackmail, but Jenni was not averse to applying a bit of friendly pressure to force the issue.

"Jenni, I will ring them this afternoon after I ring Terence and give him your number. Now let's get back to enjoying our lunch."

The conversation was clearly over despite Jenni's concerns remaining.

CHAPTER EIGHTEEN
LAUREL HOUSE

Sunday afternoon was proving to be a scorcher.

Paula lay back on the sun lounger after applying another layer of sun cream. Her skin was prone to burning so 50 was her 'go to' factor. Despite the challenges of protecting her skin, Paula loved the sun. She was never happier than on a holiday in the Med, on a sunbed from morning to dusk, glass of chilled wine and an excellent book. Today she had her kindle to hand and was absorbing a new novel by a fairly unknown self-published author. It was a gripping tale which she was finding hard to put down, even with company.

Paula was not alone.

Alastair seemed to be spending more and more time round at Laurel House these days. Not that she minded one bit. His presence gave her pleasure. In his company, Paula had learnt to laugh again. All too often he would have her in tears with some tall tale from the building site or the pub. He was the tonic she had needed in her life and, especially now, after what had happened to Peter.

Thinking of her ex-husband, Paula reflected on his progress. Peter St John was finally facing his demons. The cognitive behavioural therapy he was receiving was obviously helping. Paula could hardly imagine Peter thriving from talking to a stranger about his feelings. It was an eye-opener. He had never talked to her about what was going on in his head, but somehow a stranger had managed to tap into his worries and had given him the platform to examine them and learn from the past.

Only last week she had met Peter for a drink at The King's Head and she had to pinch herself. She was convinced it was all a dream. The man who came so close to ending it all, now seemed calm and reflective. He was the man she could have loved years before. If only they had talked more when they started their journey together. Perhaps he might have conquered his troubles before their marriage became roadkill. The new Peter was an interesting and attractive man.

But that was the past. And it should remain there.

Paula could not, and would not, fall in love with Peter all over again.

He had hurt her too much to risk that.

And you cannot go back, thought Paula. Life is not a dress rehearsal. It is not possible to return to the start and relearn your lines. What had happened must remain that way. Including their failed marriage. When she met up with Peter, and it was a fairly regular occurrence now, they tried not to pick apart their relationship. Both of them agreed that the past should be laid to rest.

The kitchen door slammed as the breeze caught it. "Sorry," shouted Al. He was washing up after the BBQ they had recently devoured.

Washing up!

Oh, how life has changed, thought Paula. She could not remember the last time Peter had washed up, without being nagged to do so. Alaistair Middleton was the perfect house husband. He had been dynamite with the BBQ, flipping burgers and spreading sauce across their sizzling tops. At the same time, he was tossing the salad and creating the most mouth-watering dressing. All she had to do was lie back and watch him take control of lunch. And now he was washing up.

Paula believed she had died and gone to heaven.

"Top up?" Al held out the bottle of Pinot.

"Please."

Paula sipped the chilled wine as she watched Al rearrange his towel on the neighbouring sunbed. He was sporting football shorts and nothing else. Under the cloak of her sunglasses, she ran an appreciate eye over his body.

Alaistair Middleton was proud to have kept his figure trim and, whilst it wasn't a six-pack, his chest was strong and powerful from hours spent lifting and carrying on the building site. He had a hairy chest but he could never be described as neanderthal; it looked well maintained and tidy.

He was an attractive man, both physically and emotionally.

Over recent months, Paula had got to know Al more deeply. They had shared many an evening together discussing their failed relationships, their hopes, and fears for the future. These honest discussions had helped them both deal with Peter's suicide attempt and the guilt they both felt about what had happened. They shared a bond, which was driving them closer together.

Paula wiggled over to lie on her front, discarding her kindle. "Al, darling, would you mind?" She wafted the sun cream in his direction. She had already undone the clasp o her bikini, her breasts squashed into the towel.

I thought she would never ask, thought Al. The chance to caress her beautiful body was not one to miss. Lucky towel, he sighed.

Al flipped the lid and squirted a generous helping on Paula's back. He shuffled his backside onto the edge of her sunbed as he gently worked the cream across her shoulders and down the centre of her back. As he spread the cooling liquid towards her sides, his fingers lightly touched the curve of her breast. Paula sighed. Taking that as a green light, Al caressed his fingers up and down her spine. He worked outwards towards her sides continuing to tease the curves of her breasts. He longed to take them in his hands and touch her nipples. Light touches, for now, to relax Paula and get her wanting him with a passion she could not ignore.

Gradually, his fingers caressed the top of her bikini bottoms, working out from the centre to her hip bones. He lingered over the dip between her buttocks, working his fingers in a circle, digging deeper into her flesh.

Paula wiggled with excitement as his fingers continued to caress her spine. Shivers ran up her body as a fire ignited between her legs. His touch was sensual and patient. There was no rush to his movement. It was all about her enjoyment. She was aroused like never before.

She wanted him.

Alaistair was breathing heavily now. The touch of her skin and the excitement of her whimpers was turning him on. God, he wanted her so much. Taking a calculated risk, he moved his fingers lower. Forgetting the sun cream, he ran his hands up her thighs, massaging the skin, whilst letting his finger tease between her legs. Paula groaned as his digit explored deeper. His lips caressed her shoulders, placing delicate kisses around her neck.

Unable to hold out any longer, Paula rolled over, reaching up to pull his head down. She kissed him, burying her tongue deep into his mouth. His hands were on her breasts now, releasing their wonderous mounds from the bikini top. He tweaked her nipples, sending shock waves of excitement through her body.

"I want you so much," he whispered in her ear. "God, you are so sexy, Paula. I don't think I can wait much longer."

She pushed her fingers into his shorts, feeling his excitement. He groaned at her touch.

"Let's take this upstairs," she whispered back. "I'm not sure the neighbours are ready for seeing what I'm about to do to you."

Al gasped.

Grabbing her hand, he pulled her to her feet. Playfully slapping her backside he laughed, "get up those stairs, wench. We have some ravishing to do."

CHAPTER NINETEEN
THE MANOR HOUSE

Jenni quietly shut her front door, stroking Lily's head nestled on her chest.

Recently, they had found a wonderful baby carrier which strapped their precious one to the chest. Jenni loved to use it, especially if she was not going far. Lily was getting heavy these days and the joy of having her close to Jenni's body, smelling the delightful baby fragrance, offset any concerns about the strain on Jenni's back. It was also so useful when Lily was sleepy, as the comfort of skin contact was guaranteed to let her doze contentedly.

Jenni was off round to see Herbert. It was an impromptu visit, but Herbert was a creature of habit and Jenni was confident he would be in. She wanted to tell him all about Terence's dinner party at the weekend.

The evening had been such a resounding success. Initially, Jenni had been quite nervous as she made her preparations, but once she got into the swing of the evening, her confidence grew and grew. Terence had agreed a menu with Jenni. They had met the week before the party to agree the format of the night and finalise the dishes he wanted his friends to savour. The similarity between her new client and her old friend, Herbert, was striking. He was tall and authoritative in stance, showing his military background. A kindly nature and gentlemanly behaviours confirmed his generation and heritage. Despite his formal nature, Terence made Jenni feel at ease instantly.

They finally agreed on a menu which started with fresh asparagus wrapped in prosciutto. Something simple, but fresh, to get the party started. The main was to be a luxurious rack of lamb in a redcurrant berry sauce, fondant potatoes and steamed vegetables. Jenni had been relieved that Terence had insisted on paying for the ingredients as she had contemplated the cost of rack of lamb for ten covers. That would have made a serious dent on her profit margin. Desert would be a berry meringue which Jenni could prepare in advance, allowing her more time to focus on the centre piece of the party. All in all, she had been confident she could deliver a splendid feast for her first catering job.

On Saturday evening, Jenni had driven over the valley to Terence's mansion. You really couldn't call it a home. It was huge, manorial, and very empty. It was so sad to see these old houses devoid of family, with an old gentleman rattling around on his own. The beauty of the building was crying out for a family to bring noise and chaos into the staid surroundings. Someone like Terence, and her own General, did not consider downsizing. A substantial home was part of the status symbol of their life's achievements and they could not part with it until death, no doubt.

Not that Jenni was complaining. This was her first paying job and she was determined to make it a tremendous success. And so it would be.

The kitchen had been old-fashioned, but practical, and it didn't take Jenni long to get settled in and have everything underway. She had dressed carefully for the evening, sporting a plain black skirt and white blouse with a sensible apron. She would be responsible for both cooking and serving, which allowed her to get a feel for how each dish was being received by the elderly gents. She hadn't felt embarrassed that she would be both chef and waitress. The military men made her evening a joy as they gorged on her food and settled back with their brandy and smiling faces.

It had been a busy evening and Jenni was relieved when she finished washing up and tidying the kitchen area. Terence had been delighted with her services and had embarrassed her with his profuse praise. There would no doubt be repeat business. Jenni realised that she had stumbled upon a further string to her business bow. And such an enjoyable string. The profit for one night's work was the same as a month's net profit for the café. Of course, not every job would pay as well, but with the prospective recommendations across Herbert and Terence's army friends, she could look forward to a prosperous future.

Not for the first time, Jenni congratulated herself on the changes she had made to her life. Before Reggie died, she had been content with her lot. She had never worked and didn't necessarily see a gap in her world. Losing

Reggie had been the catalyst to catapulting her into a new approach. She had discovered a need. A need for a new direction to her life. The café, and now her private catering business, was her future. A future she was so excited for. She couldn't wait to tell Herbert all about it.

There was a spring in her step as she neared the Manor House. She noticed Herbert's old bicycle leaning against the barn door. That's unusual, she thought. Herbert was such a creature of habit and would never leave his bike outside when it had been raining. A recent light shower had left its mark on the seat.

Running up the steps to the huge front door, she banged the door knocker with a satisfying boom. Silence. She tried again. Silence. She peered towards the kitchen window, which was at the front of the house, but couldn't see any evidence of movement.

"That's strange." Jenni spoke aloud to no-one in particular. "Where is Uncle Herbbie?" That was to Lily, whose interested eyes gazed at Jenni.

She gently stroked her grandchild's face as she made her way down the stairs. She found the side gate unlocked. The General's gardens were a thing of beauty. Jenni had often admired them when spending time with her friend. He was passionate about their maintenance and, whilst he found it too much to do the gardening himself, he was the conductor of the work. He orchestrated every action with his precision approach. Luckily, Henrique was as passionate about The General's garden as the man himself.

Jenni spotted Henrique as soon as she walked into the back garden, bent over a flower bed, pulling out weeds. She took a moment to appreciate the sight of his pert bottom. She had been remiss in seeing to her own needs recently. It had been too long since she and Henrique had shared some fun. She would put that right soon. The pressures of work and Lily had put sex to the back of her mind. She was not going to become a 'born again virgin' just because she was busy. That was for sure.

She could tell that the Spanish gardener had not heard her approach; she had spotted the earbud speakers. Not wanting to frighten him, she moved into his line of vision rather than tap him on the shoulder. Waving her arms around like some manic windmill she caught his attention. A wide grin broke across his face as he fiddled to remove the earplugs.

"Jenni, how lovely to see you." His response was genuine. Any thoughts that she had annoyed him with her lack of attention recently was dismissed. "It's been too long, mi amor."

He leant over and kissed her gently on the cheek. Out of habit, Jenni quickly looked around to see if anyone had spotted them. She was not ashamed of her relationship with Henrique, but she was fully aware that many on the village would see her as some sort of cradle snatcher. Henrique was only a few years older than her own Jimmy. Age didn't matter to Henrique, even though Jenni still struggled with doubts over why such a beautiful young man could want her, a middle aged woman.

"Henrique, it's so lovely to see you. I am really sorry. Just been frantic recently, but I will give you a call soon." She gave him one of her heart-warming smiles which always turned him on. If she didn't have more pressing matters in hand, she could quite easily make a trip to the potting shed with her lover. "Have you seen Herbert this morning? He's not answering the door."

Henrique shook his head "I guessed he was out. Have you tried calling his mobile phone?"

"Good idea." Jenni grabbed her mobile out of her bag as she and Henrique wandered over to the patio doors. As she dialled the number, she could hear the faint sound of a ring tone coming from within. They both peered through the windows looking for signs of life.

Nothing.

"I'm going to try the kitchen door," said Jenni. She remembered that Herbert kept a key under a flowerpot for emergencies. Not the most secure place to leave a spare key, but perhaps that was a generational thing too. Trust.

All of a sudden, she had a feeling of dread. She needed to get into the house. She wasn't sure why, but something was driving her forward with a worrying coldness in her stomach. Henrique followed as she rounded the house to the side door. As expected, the key was exactly where Herbert had told her. The lock was stiff and it took a fair bit of jiggling to get it to catch.

Once inside the house, Jenni made her way through the kitchen. There were no obvious signs of recent activity. A bottle of milk stood in splendid isolation on the vast kitchen table. She touched it. It was warm. Jenni could tell it had been out of the fridge for some time.

Jenni was really worried now. Herbert was fastidious and would never leave the milk out. Something was wrong. An icy chill travelled down her spine, making her shiver. Henrique picked up on her mood change. His fingers reached for hers and squeezed reassuringly.

"Herbert," she called. No answer. The house was silent, no radio or TV playing. The General always seemed to have some background noise playing. He hated silence as it reminded him of his solitude.

A quick check downstairs did not bear fruit so the couple made their way up the wide stairs. Lily kicked her feet against Jenni's chest, enjoying the bounce of her grandmother's step. The baby had not picked up on the heightened emotion of her grandmother. She was simply enjoying the ride.

Jenni called Herbert's name again and was greeted with silence. She had never been upstairs at the Manor House before and it felt strange nosing around without permission. There was the obvious worry that something was amiss, but also the awkwardness at prying into places she had never been invited, especially with her young lover in tow.

She opened the first door, at the top of the stairs, which appeared to be the main bathroom. A towel was draped across the bathmat, discarded in a hurry. Toothbrush and paste were left, haphazardly, on the side of the sink, unused. Jenni's worries were increasing exponentially. Deciding Herbert's bedroom could be the next door along the landing, she grabbed the handle and pushed it down slowly, worried as to what she might find within.

Herbert was lying on the floor next to the bed. He was wearing pyjamas, which considering it was nearly lunchtime, indicated he may have been there for some time. Herbert was face down on the carpet with one arm flung out, as if he was reaching for something. Jenni gasped. She quickly undid the straps on the baby carrier, handing Lily to Henrique.

The poor boy looked petrified as he stared at the small bundle in his arms. He hadn't held a baby for years. What if it cries, he thought?

Jenni crouched down beside Herbert and put her hand on his face. It was cold. She reached for his neck to check his pulse and couldn't find anything. She lay her face alongside his lips, trying to feel air breathing in and out. She knew she was wasting her time. There was nothing.

He was gone.

Jenni turned to face Henrique. The tears were already starting to seep from her eyes. "He's dead," she whispered.

Henrique made the sign of the cross as he took in those dreadful words. "Are you sure?" His voice had a tremble of emotion. Henrique was not just The General's employee. He loved the old gent. You could not ask for a kinder gentleman. He had never made Henrique feel like staff, but more a friend.

Jenni nodded. Her body started to shake with shock. She knew she shouldn't touch the body, in case of foul play, but she couldn't leave him alone on the floor. Holding Herbert's cold hand, she kissed his cheeks. The sobs increased as Jenni mourned the man who was like a father to her. Henrique sat on the floor next to her, cuddling Lily and holding Jenni's other hand.

They stayed like that for what seemed like hours, but was probably only minutes. Sentries guarding a fallen soldier, marking the minutes since his life had departed. Two people he had touched with his friendship and generosity who loved him and mourned his passing. They were alone in their own thoughts, but together in their grief.

Jenni came back to reality at the sound of Lily's wails.

The baby was not prepared to sit in companionable silence with the adults in the room. She wanted attention and knew the best way to get that was to make her presence felt. She also decided that now was a suitable time to fill her nappy. Jenni watched Henrique's face as the warm poo filled Lily's nappy, vibrating under his hand. It was a picture of shock and horror at the noise and the smell made by such a small human being.

Jenni burst into laughter.

It seemed so inappropriate in the circumstances, but gallows humour had kicked in. She took Lily into her arms, watching Henrique as he wiped his hands down his shorts. The disgust on his face made her giggle again. Feeling guilty she looked across at Herbert's body with an apologetic nod. The General would have been the first to join them in laughter.

There was nothing to feel guilty about.

Jenni pulled the emergency nappy and wipes from the baby carrier and set about cleaning up Lily. The baby wriggled in delight as the offending pile of poo was removed from her bottom. Her little legs kicked skyward as she gurgled in her own language. Jenni hoped Lily would not want another bottle any time soon. She didn't have a feed with her and then were formalities they had to manage. No doubt.

What to do next was troubling Jenni.

She had never been faced with such a position before. What should she do. Deciding that expert guidance was needed, Jenni put a call out to 111. A lovely lady dealt with their discovery with tact and kindness. She talked Jenni and Henrique through the actions they needed to take and held their hand, virtually, through the initial formalities.

As it was an unexplained death, the police had to be involved.

Jenni instinctively knew that those twinges Herbert had experienced the other week were a sign of some ailment of the heart. There were no obvious signs of violence, but a process had to be followed, however pointless it might seem to Jenni. She agreed to wait for the police to arrive and just hoped Lily would remain patient for her lunch.

Henrique remained by her side while they continued their silent vigil for their dearest friend. He would not be alone. They would be there with him until, much later, the funeral director arrived to carry his body away.

CHAPTER TWENTY
THE KING'S HEAD PUB

The bar area was packed with villagers milling around exchanging news.

Of course, there was only one topic of conversation, the sudden passing of Herbert Smythe-Jones. The village had resonated to the sound of grief. Neighbour had hugged neighbour as they thought of their own mortality, as well as the loss of one of the village elders.

Geoff Smith, the King's Head publican, rang the golden bar bell, stopping conversations in their tracks. "Can I have your attention everyone," he shouted as silence seeped across the room, reaching into all corners, where groups of friends sat sharing a drink. "I just wanted to say a few words."

Faccs turned towards the bar. A gamut of emotions could be seen across those faces. Some bore the weight of grief, others attempted to smile through sadness. The General had been a popular member of the community and his lack of presence was already being felt.

Geoff had their attention and pushed on. "Thank you all for coming at short notice tonight. I know we are all sadden by the loss of our dear friend, The General. He wasn't just the chair of our Parish Council. He was the person we would all go to for advice. Sixpenny Bissett just won't be the same without him." He paused as he steadied his trembling voice. "Can I ask that we all stand and raise our glasses to a loyal friend and gentleman. Herbert Smythe-Jones."

"Herbert Smythe-Jones." The bar rang out with his name.

"Thank you everyone. Jenni?" Geoff looked across at Jenni, who stood at the other end of the bar with Kate, Jeremy, and Jimmy. Kate's daughter, Mary, was listening into the baby monitor for the next hour, allowing Jimmy to join his mother at the pub. "Jenni, I know you spoke to The

General's son earlier and I wondered if you wanted to say anything."

The request caught Jenni off-guard. Jimmy noticed the panic on her face and squeezed her fingers. "You can do it, Mum. For Herbert."

She smiled at her son who seemed to have developed a new level of intuition. When had he suddenly grown up? Her son was a new man since the responsibility of caring for Lily had landed on his shoulders. It suited him.

"Thank you, Geoff. Yes, I spoke to Fraser this afternoon. He and his sister, Eleanor, are obviously very shocked at Herbert's unexpected passing. I passed on the condolences of the whole village, which they were very touched about." Jenni paused as she gathered her thoughts. It was disconcerting to see all the faces in the pub watching her intently. It did nothing to help calm her nerves at public speaking. She thought to herself that Herbert would be pretty proud of her right now. "Fraser said that once formalities for the funeral are in place, he will let me know the arrangements so we can all help out and be there for the family. I believe they will be asking Jeremy to conduct the service at the church here in Sixpenny Bissett. Herbert had told them he wanted to be buried with his beloved Bridget. That's all I know at the moment, but I will keep you updated. Thank you."

Jenni heaved a sigh of relief that her moment in the spotlight was over. She wasn't keen on public speaking, especially when her emotions were raw with the loss of her dear friend.

It had been a long, hard day.

Jenni had managed to slip out of The Manor House, after the police arrived. She needed to feed poor Lily, who was reluctant to wait any longer. She believed the police officer was quite pleased to see her go. Never easy dealing with a dead body when you have a screaming infant in tow. Kate had been a trooper. She had agreed to take Lily while Jenni returned to Herbert's house to deal with the doctor, who had been called to confirm the death.

Dealing with the doctor had been the hardest part of the formalities. Jenni hadn't warmed to him one bit. He seemed arrogant and dismissive of her concerns. She was an added inconvenience he wasn't prepared to put up with. No wonder Herbert hadn't got the support he needed, she decided.

Dr Patel admitted to the police that Herbert had been to see him a week or so ago about his twinges. He had run a number of tests but did not think Mr Smythe-Jones needed to see the cardiologist. A mistake the doctor would have to live with. All the evidence pointed to a huge heart attack which must have been building up for the last few weeks. Perhaps if Herbert had been a bit more forceful or if he had gone to A&E, he might have been saved. It was that knowledge which had felt like a kick in the gut to Jenni. He didn't have to die like that.

All alone on the bedroom floor.

"Well done, Jenni." Jeremy interrupted her thoughts. "Well said. And thank you for everything you and Henrique did for Herbert today. It must have been exceedingly difficult for you to find him like that. I know how close you guys were."

He reached across and pulled Jenni into a hug. Kate gently rubbed her back at the same time. She was so fortunate to have found such great friends. They were the rock for her to rest her troubles on, especially tonight.

"Mum," Jimmy tapped her on the shoulder. "We are going to shoot off now. Check up on Lily. I'm sure Mary has had enough of babysitting duties by now." He smiled at Kate and Jeremy. "I do appreciate Mary's help tonight."

Jenni noticed the use of 'we' rather than 'I'. She glanced over to catch Florence's eye. The publican's daughter definitely had a bit of a crush on Jimmy. She was a lovely girl and well suited to Jenni's son. Secretly Jenni was keen to encourage the relationship. Jimmy had matured since Lily was born and since Charlie had abandoned her family. He deserved a bit of happiness now. Although Jenni was concerned about what Geoff and Jacky Smith might think to their daughter hitching up with a man with a baby in tow. It was a lot for the young girl to take on. A readymade family.

"Okay, darling. See you later. Don't wait up for me, especially as it's your turn on the night feed." She grinned, secretly planning her own enjoyment for later.

Once Jimmy had left, Jenni joined Kate and Jeremy at one of the round tables which surrounded the fireplace. There wasn't the usual roaring fire tonight. It was far too warm for that. They had refreshed their drinks and settled down to talk about other things, rather than the loss of their dear friend. Jeremy was practised at moving the conversation onto safer ground, a skill honed through his ministry.

He and Kate launched into a conversation about their upcoming holiday to Greece. It was to be their first trip abroad with the children and the whole family was excited. Mary and Joseph, seriously the vicar named his kids after those famous biblical characters, had never been on an airplane and were both nervous and animated by the concept. Joseph had been picking Jimmy's brains about the experience; Jimmy being the seasoned traveller, of course. Joseph looked up to his worldly neighbour. He tended to follow Jimmy around, watching his moves and copying. The life of a pubescent teenage can be fraught with difficulties.

Jenni zoned out as her friends chatted, nodding, and smiling in all the right places. The emotions of the day had finally caught up with her. A deep sadness had nestled within her chest. A hard rock of emotion, which she would have to drag around for days, as she came to accept that Herbert was gone. She had loved that guy like a father. He had been generous with his time and had taken her under his wing. He had been her champion over the Peter St John affair, ensuring that the truth about the dreadful incident was known far and wide.

Life would be so very different without him.

She had got used to seeing him nearly every day as one of her most regular customers. Herbert would visit the café around 10.30 am every day for a cup of tea and a piece of cake. He had come for the company and to see Jenni. Often, he would just sit at the nearest table to the counter so he could chat to Jenni while she worked. He was an absolute darling and she would miss him desperately.

The only consolation was that Herbert was now reunited with his dear wife, Bridget. That was another thing Jenni and Herbert had shared in common. Both had lost the love of their lives and had found a way to keep putting one foot in front of the other. Herbert was the one person who understood her pain. She could speak to him about the loss of Reggie and the huge hole it had created in her life. And he got it. Despite Bridget having died many years before, Herbert continued to feel her loss.

Her sorrowful thoughts were interrupted by the ping of her phone. Noticing that her friends were chatting across the next table with Thomas Hadley, the local farmer, she pulled her phone from her handbag.

'Make your excuses and meet me outside'

Jenni grinned to herself. It was from Henrique and could mean only one thing.

Touching Kate's hand, which was resting on her wine glass, she whispered. "I'm off. Do you mind?"

Kate spotted the glow on her friend's face and knew it meant one thing. "Got a better offer?" she sighed.

"Something like that."

Kate was the only other person who knew about Jenni's secret assignations with the young Spaniard. She would never judge her best friend, despite wishing Jenni would find someone she could have a proper relationship with. It wasn't a view Kate could share with her friend, but she believed Jenni was avoiding a more stable, longer term connection with a man. Having Henrique, who would never be a future husband or even be declared as her boyfriend, was Jenni's way of avoiding commitment.

Kate decided Jenni was frightened of losing her heart again. She had tried to get close, romantically, with Richard Samuels, only to be rejected. Since then Jenni had closed herself off from the thought of another serious relationship. Henrique filled the gap and was happy to oblige.

Either way, good luck to her, Kate decided. I don't think I would turn down a young stud if I was in her place, she decided as she watched Jenni make her way through the crowded bar to the door.

CHAPTER TWENTY-ONE
THE CARAVAN IN THE WOODS

They waited until Henrique kicked the door of the van shut. Throughout their dash from the pub and into the woods, the anticipation was building, driving them to distraction. It took every effort to stop them touching each other before they were safe at the caravan. If hands had touched body they would have been done for and would probably end up making out on the leafy ground. Never a good idea when trying to keep their relationship quiet.

As the caravan door slammed with a satisfying crash the emotion of the day took over.

Henrique grabbed her t-shirt and pulled it one handed over her head as he wrapped his other arm around her waist, pulling her into his harden crutch. His actions were rough but controlled. His need obvious. His mouth sought out hers and his tongue explored her taste as he wrestled with her bra, one handed. It took a couple of attempts before it pinged open revealing her magnificent breasts. Cupping them, his mouth found her nipple.

Jenni groaned as her body thrust into Henrique. She ran her fingers down his spine, recognising the shudder of his body under her touch. He had the most sensitive back and she knew exactly where to stroke to drive him into a frenzy of passion. She wriggled her fingers under his shirt and caressed his back.

No prisoners would be taken.

Tugging at his shirt buttons, she quickly had them undone and pulled the garment down his arms, touching his side with teasing motions. She stroked his back yet again, feeling his passion rise. Appreciating the feel of his chest, she revelled in its firm muscular tone. Her touch reached his belt, yanking it apart with an urgency to find the secrets within. Her fingers worked their way into his boxers, releasing him from their confines.

Without breaking free from each other, they made their way into the bedroom. It was a strange dance of shuffles as their jeans flapped around their ankles. How they didn't fall as they careered into the kitchen cupboards like a pair of billiard balls bouncing against the pool table. Veering from one side to another, they made their way into the bedroom. Their mouths had not separated as they gorged on each other's lips with an urgency. Shaking their legs to free them from their jeans, they fell together onto the bed.

They made love.

This wasn't the frantic sex that they normally engaged in and that the build-up had predicted. They took time to worship each other's bodies. There was a heightened sense of affection. The loss they had just suffered was present with them, making them cling to the joys of life more than ever. As she came, Jenni wept. Not through sadness but with pent-up emotion.

Henrique held her in his arms as she cried. Stroking her hair, he kissed her head as she nestled into his chest. The comfort of his arms was just what she needed right now. Being single was hard, especially in times of trouble. She missed the comfort of a man's arms and Henrique had the most amazing ability to both drive her wild with passion and also make her feel comforted and supported.

They lay there, in comforting silence, for some time.

Henrique had news to share and he really didn't know how to start. His timing was going to be crap, but the longer he left it the worse the impact would be. He had been avoiding the conversation for weeks now and time had run away with him. His flight was next week. It just couldn't wait much longer.

"Jenni, my love. Can we talk?" Henrique squeezed her shoulders as she nestled against his chest.

"Umm," she sighed. Jenni was exhausted. Lying on his chest was relaxing her far too much and she could quite easily fall into a deep sleep. Her eyes fought the peace of slumber, conscious of the urgency in his voice.

Henrique nudged her gently and wriggled out from her side. Sitting cross legged on the bed, he looked far more serious that the current situation warranted. Jenni was alert now. Something was up. She pushed herself up against the headboard, pulling a sheet up to cover her nakedness.

"What's up? Why the serious face, darling?" Henrique was clearly wrestling with a problem. "Come on, spit it out."

The confusion on his face at her remark was endearing. The Spaniard struggled with some of the British colloquialisms which Jenni loved to employ. "Spit it out? I do not understand that."

"Sorry. I mean, just say what you want to say. It's just a silly expression. I don't mean anything by it."

Henrique rubbed his hands up and down his arms as he tried to find the right words to say. "Jenni, I'm going back to Spain next week." He rushed the words out and heaved a sigh of relief.

Jenni didn't pick up on his body language. "Oh, OK. Are you going for a holiday? That will be nice." Her first thought was that perhaps Henrique would be missing Herbert's funeral and was troubled by that.

He took Jenni's hands in his. "For ever," he whispered.

Jenni was confused. Where was this coming from? Henrique seemed very much at home in Sixpenny Bissett. He had plenty of work and loads of friends. He had always spoken of his desire to settle down in England one day so why the change of heart? She hadn't seen that coming.

"Why, Henrique? I thought you loved it here?"

He ran his fingers through his hair, the fringe flopping back into his eyes. The poor lad looked decidedly uncomfortable now. The passion and frenzy of their lovemaking was a thing of the past.

"It is my mother. She is not well and she wants me home. I'm getting married next month." He dropped a bombshell and then sat in silence; his head bowed.

Jenni was not planning on making a future with Henrique. She loved him, but not enough to face up to the scandal their relationship would attract. She had been absent from their relationship for weeks now because of Lily and the café, but in all the time they had been together Henrique had never mentioned the idea of marrying his Spanish girlfriend. If anything, he had suggested he was going to dump her this summer because he didn't think it was fair on her, waiting for him.

"Bloody hell, Henrique. This is all a bit fast. When did that happen?"

Henrique continued to look uncomfortable and embarrassed. He didn't look like the happy groom who had been hiding the depth of his relationship from his lover. "My mother, she arrange the marriage. To a girl from the village. I met her at Easter when I went home. Gabriela."

Jenni's mouth dropped open, with shock, as she listened. "What? So you meet this girl a few months ago and you are getting married. What happened to your other girlfriend?"

The whole story seemed unbelievable. He looked cowed, which was so unlike the man. Henrique had always come across as someone who knew what he wanted in life and wasn't afraid to go out and get it. Her, for example. And all of a sudden Mamma Gonzales clicks her fingers and he is running home to wed.

Unbelievable.

"My mother arrange it. She is a friend of my family, Gabriela. She's very nice. I think I will be happy."

The situation was becoming even more ridiculous. This didn't sound like the man she had known this last year. Suddenly bending to his family's will and marrying a girl he hardly knew. "But what about your work, your future? I thought you were happy here."

Jenni was trying not to sound needy. For once, she was not thinking of her own sexual gratification. She cared deeply for this man and he certainly didn't look like he was excited about his future with Gabriela. The whole situation seemed really weird.

"Sometimes you have to do what your family wants. Especially in my family, Jenni. I will really miss you and everyone in the village, but I have a duty to my parents." His voice fizzled out as if he was trying to convince himself and failing miserably.

Jenni slid across the bed and wrapped her arms around his body. His head fell to her shoulder as he planted small kisses across her neck. "I will miss you so much, Henrique. I have loved spending time with you. But if this is what you have to do then I wish you luck and happiness."

A tear spilled out of his eye and made a slow journey down his cheek. She reached up a finger to gently wipe it away.

"I love you, Jenni," he whispered into her hair as his lips kissed her head.

"I love you too, Henrique."

And she did. She wasn't lying. She loved him dearly, but not enough to fight for him. He would leave for Spain in a week or so and she would be sad, but she would survive.

What a day it was turning out to be. She lost the man who had filled a father-shaped hole in her life and now she was losing a lover.

They held each other and wept with regret for what was not to be.

CHAPTER TWENTY-TWO
ROSE COTTAGE

Jenni was lying on the rug in the lounge, admiring her granddaughter. She was biased, of course, but Lily was the most beautiful baby ever. And such a happy character, enjoying playing and content to entertain herself.

It was one of those days which was so very special for Jenni. Jimmy was manning the café and she had the entire day ahead of her to do whatever she wanted. And today Jenni wanted to spend quality time with Lily. Nothing else. Just the two girls together, having fun.

She had been up late the previous night, getting to grips with her baking. She had managed to get ahead of herself this week and the café was fully stocked until the weekend. The house was clean. Well, as tidy as it ever was with Jimmy and Lily. Jenni had certainly lowered her standards since she had opened her home to her extended family.

The joy of a baby definitely prevents a pristine home. Certainly, a bit of organised chaos was allowed, especially if it meant having time to play with little Lily. Babies grow so fast that it's worth putting some chores aside to share the momentous times before they pass.

Lily was lying on her playmat, next to Jenni. It was one of those interactive toys which designers make to irritate parents. Of course, it was great for babies who could learn about different noises, textures, and shapes. Just to get on the parents' nerves, the noises would always be spine-chillingly irritating, akin to chalk down a blackboard. The textures stuck to anything the mat came into contact with, including Babygro's. The shapes were the only redeeming feature in Jenni's opinion. But Lily loved it. And that's what counted.

Jimmy had acquired a plastic frame, with various dangling toys, to hang over Lily. Lily adored it. She would lie on her back, kicking her feet into the air and taking aim at the fluffy elephant, which was one of her favourites. A chewy ring hung before her, enticing the baby to pull herself up to a seated position. A little too early yet for Lily. She was only just at the stage where she could roll onto her front and hold her head up. It wouldn't take long before she would perfect the crawl. Once that happened, Jenni knew they would have to make some serious changes to their environment.

Lily was gurgling away to herself as she kicked her legs skyward. Her eyes focused on the fluffy elephant. At the same time, she kept moving her vision to check Nanny was still there. They shared a special bond, grandmother and child. Lily's eyes spoke of a wisdom beyond her age. They enticed Jenni to share her thoughts and hopes for the future as if she understood her Nanny had the need to offload.

Jenni was in reflective mood. It had been a tough few months, filled with ups and downs. When Jenni had first moved to Sixpenny Bissett she could not have imagined the changes she would have lived through. Who could have imagined that she would become a grandmother? She certainly would have scoffed at that thought when she was packing up her Birmingham home. Her mates back in Brum would be shocked if they knew. Jenni was ashamed to say that she hadn't kept in touch with many of her old friends. She blamed it on the pressures of time although if she was truthful, it was more about her desire for a fresh start.

The months had been packed with events, but Jenni wouldn't change a thing. She could not imagine her life without Jimmy and Lily in it. Okay, it would have been better if Charlie had found a way to live with her new family and share her love with her daughter. Because Jenni couldn't believe that Charlie didn't love Lily. She had panicked. Scared of her new responsibilities, she had done what many mothers wish they could do. Run a mile. Perhaps she was regretting her decision already and was afraid to admit her mistake. If only she had had the support of her own family. Things might have been different.

With Charlie gone, Jenni held a more important place in her granddaughter's heart. She was the mother figure. The main female influence over her development. Looking to the future, she would be the person Lily would come to as she grew up and discovered herself. But that was a long way off and so much could change before then.

"My little Lily." Jenni spoke softly, as the baby's eyes followed the movement of her mouth, watching Jenni shape her words. "You will never be short of love, even with your poor Mummy gone. Your Daddy is the best and he will walk over hot coals to keep you safe. I just wish your Grandpappy could have met you. He would have adored you, my darling."

Jenni smiled, reminiscing, as she imagined Reggie as a Grandad. He had left most of the baby activity to Jenni when the boys were little. They only really became interesting once they reached the age where football or cars were of interest. But deep down Reggie was a complete softie. She could see many of Jimmy's parental qualities came from his father. Reggie would have spoilt Lily rotten. Jenni would have had to temper his spoiling as the years went by. Poor Reggie.

"Melancholy thoughts indeed," sighed Jenni. "If there is one thing I would teach you, my darling girl, it is that life can be long or short. We never know what the future holds so grab life with both hands and hold on fast. It will be an exciting ride, no matter what happens."

The loss of Herbert sat heavily on Jenni's heart. A perfect example of how life can change on a sixpence. The ups and downs of recent months had been quite a roller-coaster. Losing Herbert, and Henrique leaving for Spain, could have dragged Jenni into a dark place. Her beautiful granddaughter made sure that Jenni's love of life would overcome any of the setbacks which were thrown her way to test her.

"Lily, we have so much to be thankful for." It felt strange talking to a baby in this way. Lily wasn't fazed or even bored by Jenni's chatter. She continued to watch her grandmother intently. "We have you, my sweet child. We love you so much. You have filled a big gap in the Sullivan family and you really have been the making of your Daddy."

Jenni reached across and let Lily grab her finger. Lily did what Lily always did. She stuck Jenni's finger in her mouth and chewed. No teeth had broken through yet, but Lily still had a good jaw action and squeezed tightly on Jenni's digit. She winced with the pain but smiled through it. That's one thing we will have to give up once her teeth come in, thought Jenni.

"And the café. Now that is something to think positively about," continued Jenni. "I didn't really know what to expect. Would early interest drop off? Would I manage to build a regular clientele? Would it save the shop? I think that's probably a yes to all those questions."

The café was doing extraordinarily well. Better than either Jenni or Kate had imagined. Jenni was loving working. It had given her a new sense of purpose. Some days she was exhausted after a shift, baking, and preparing for the next day. On those evenings when she dragged herself into bed, feeling tired to her bones, she would smile with delight. She felt more alive than she had for so long. She had a sense of purpose. She was making great friends with her customers and she had the pleasure of working with Jimmy. Together they were building a successful business.

Her Jimmy. God, she was proud of him. The caterpillar sleeping bag figure, who she had found sleeping on her doorstep months ago, was a changed character. He had grown up, of course. Responsibility does that to you. No, the main difference in Jimmy was that he had become the man she always thought he was capable of being. Kind, generous and a bloody nice person, if she said so herself.

Lily gurgled louder as if to catch Jenni's attention. A look of concentration flashed across the baby's face. She stared vacantly at Jenni then shuddered.

"Oh, Lily," cried Jenni. "I know what you have done. You little stinker." Jenni rolled over to stick her face towards Lily's nappy. "Yep, that is one big poop and in a nice clean nappy too."

Jenni laughed as she gently picked up the baby. "Come on sweetheart. Let's go and change that smelly nappy then. Make you all gorgeous again."

CHAPTER TWENTY-THREE
THE MANOR HOUSE

It had been the most beautiful service, reflected Jenni.

The General's funeral has taken place at St Peter's Church in Sixpenny Bissett. It seemed that everyone from the village had been in attendance, alongside Herbert's family and friends. Fraser Smythe-Jones gave the eulogy and there wasn't a dry eye in the church. Jenni had discovered more about her friend as she listened to Fraser's passionate speech. Herbert had lived a full and varied life and it was clear that he had touched many people's hearts with his warmth and kindness.

The number of people attending the service was testimony to that fact.

Jenni and Jimmy were providing the catering for the wake. It was the least she could do for such a wonderful man. Her last gift to him and his children. Young Lily was being her most accommodating. She slept deeply; her pram tucked away in the corner of the vast Manor House kitchen. Between them, mother and son had put the finishing touches to a finger buffet.

Jenni had watched Jimmy work with pride. Who would have thought her son, who had aspirations to travel the world, could settle down so well in their family business. She was incredibly proud of the man he was becoming, thoughtful, diligent, and passionate about doing an excellent job. They worked well together, which was another surprise for Jenni. Jimmy worked in a similar style to his mother, which made for an efficient operation.

Jenni enjoyed her son's company. When he had first arrived home, their relationship had been strained. Jenni resented the intrusion on her new life in the country. But since Lily was born and Charlie did a midnight flight, mother and son had reached a new level of contentment. They shared the responsibilities of caring for both Lily and their new business. And it worked.

Once Jenni was satisfied with the presentation of the buffet, large trays of goodies were carried through to the garden where everyone from the church had descended.

As Jenni rushed around, making sure everything was perfect, she spotted Florence pushing Lily's pram around the garden. Jenni smiled. It certainly looked like Jimmy's friendship with the local girl was blossoming and the fact that she seemed fond of his daughter must be an added bonus.

Jenni's reflections were interrupted by Fraser and his sister Eleanor.

"Jenni, we wanted to thank you so very much for the spread. It looks wonderful." Fraser reached his hand out to shake hers.

"It is the least I could do," smiled Jenni. "I am so sorry for your loss, Fraser. Eleanor. He was a wonderful man and I will miss him terribly."

Herbert's children bore uncanny resemblances to their father. Fraser certainly could be mistaken for his father at a younger age. Jenni noticed their partners and children mingling with the guests.

"Jenni, I wanted to let you know that Herbert left you a little something in his will." Fraser nodded across at his sister who produced a small jewellery box from her handbag. "It was one of our mother's favourite necklaces. Father wanted you to have it. He said it would be perfect for you."

Jenni gasped as Eleanor opened the case. Nestled inside, was the most adorable necklace. A fine, gold chain with a centre piece of two circular discs. The top disc held three small diamonds encased in a gold border. The lower disc was one solid ruby surrounded by a golden case. It was stunning.

"Oh, Fraser, Eleanor, it is beautiful. Are you sure? If it's your mother's don't you want it, Eleanor?" Jenni was quite embarrassed. The necklace was clearly expensive and a family heirloom looking at the work and size of the stones.

"Jenni, Mother would have wanted you to have it. You have been such a good friend to our father since you moved to the village. I know how much he loved your company and he even mentioned to me that you reminded him of our mother," smiled Eleanor. "I have plenty of Mother's jewellery to remind me of her. It's only right that you have this and think of father whenever you wear it."

"I will treasure it," agreed Jenni. "It is so beautiful and precious to me." Jenni did not want to keep Herbert's son and daughter from their guests for too long, but she was enjoying the chance to get to know them a bit better. "Have you decided what you will do with The Manor House?" she asked.

Fraser and Eleanor had been struggling with that decision since their father had died three weeks ago. Whilst they loved the house, it would be a millstone around their necks. "We are going to put it on the market," Fraser took the lead. "It's just too big for us to keep as a holiday home and too far from London for one of us to live in. It's a shame, but we have to think practically."

Jenni was surprised but understood their rationale. The Manor House must be stuffed full of memories of their parents. It was going to be a horrendous task sorting through the collectables of a lifetime. "Well, if there is anything I can do to help, you will ask me, please."

Both of them made affirming noises which Jenni realised were probably just platitudes. It was a tough ask and one that probably would never come to any sort of fruition. As she continued to make small talk with Fraser and Eleanor, Jenni spotted Anna Fletcher giving her the evil eye.

Anna hated Jenni.

It was a mystery to Jenni why Anna had formed such a strong view about someone she barely knew. Jenni had perhaps spoken to the woman a couple of times and never done anything to offend, in her opinion. Anna was the retired village school mistress and proud to be the number one busybody. She was the first to spread any rumour and was never happier than when she was passing judgement on another villager.

Anna had led the way in being beastly when Jenni was assaulted by Peter St John at the Christmas party. She had blamed Jenni for the incident which was totally crazy. How anyone could ever have believed Anna's twisted gossip, especially as the old woman hadn't even been at the party. But for some reason Anna Fletcher had taken a dislike to the newcomer and decided to make her life extremely difficult. To make matters worse, Jenni and her best friend, Kate, had stood up to the nasty woman. Anna Fletcher thrived on emotional bullying and, as with most bullies, could not take back what she dished out.

Anna had carried a secret aspiration to woo Herbert Smythe-Jones. Those plans were very secret. She hadn't even told the focus of her attention, The General. He would have spurned her if she had. Herbert was a kind gentleman. Anna Fletcher would never have been his type. Knowing this, Anna deflected this highly likely rejection on Jenni Sullivan, a middle aged floosy, who had captured the attention of The General, turning his mind against a much more suitable spinster.

Her mind was warped and poor Jenni was often on the receiving end of her bitterness.

Jenni shrugged off the evil eye from Anna and made her excuses to escape the grieving offspring of The General. A quick check of the buffet table revealed that the food was being received well. She saw Jimmy and Florence refilling a couple of platters and she waved across to them, in thanks.

Spotting Kate and Jeremy deep in conversation with Alaistair and Paula, Jenni made her way across the lawn. Despite Henrique's speedy departure from the village, the grass looked in perfect condition. The lawn was banked higher than the patio area and reached by an ornate staircase. Most of the rear garden of The Manor was on a gentle upward slope. If you walked right to the back of the garden, you had the most amazing view of the house and the surrounding village.

Jenni had shared a number of sunny evenings, sitting with Herbert, on a wooden bench which took advantage of these lovely views. It was his favourite spot. As she made her way towards her friends, Jenni noticed Peter St John sat on that particular bench, deep in thought. It was good to see him socialising again, thought Jenni, even if the social occasion was a funeral. Maybe not the easiest event, especially when you have had a brush with death yourself.

"Hi, Jenni, wonderful food." Jeremy had a mouthful of a prawn vol-au-vent in play. The thousand island dressing dribbling from the corner of his mouth. "You have done a great job." He tipped his sunhat in her direction. Kate pulled out her tissue and dabbed at his face. Never a good look, dribble on a vicar.

"Oh, thanks Jeremy," she replied. "I was chuffed when Fraser asked me to do the spread. It's a good advert for the business, if that doesn't sound too crass."

Her friends were quick to reassure her that in business you have to take any opportunities which come your way, even if it is the funeral of a friend. Jenni was picking up a fair number of catering jobs, built on personal recommendations. If things continued this well, she would soon consider employing staff, giving her and Jimmy greater balance to their working life. At the moment they were working at least a six day week between them. Neither complained as they were enjoying the thrust of building up a new business, but there would come a time soon when help would be needed.

"I saw you chatting to The General's children. How are they coping?" asked Paula.

Jenni decided it was best not to share the news of her new necklace, which was tucked safely in her handbag. Perhaps she would tell Kate when they were at work tomorrow. Kate would understand how precious the gift was. Others may question it especially as Jenni was the newest friendship The General had developed in the village. He had longer relationships which went way back over the years.

"They seem to be handling things," Jenni responded. "I was telling Fraser what a lovely eulogy it was. I learnt so much more about Herbert and his family. What a life he had."

Kate had known The General for over twenty years and had still found out something new earlier. "What a gent," she jumped in. "He has probably seen more in his 80 years than the rest of us put together. I will miss him, especially at the shop. At one stage he was the only thing keeping me going, financially." She smiled as the truth of that fact sunk in. The General was one of those people who avoided the big supermarkets if at all possible. He shopped locally and was a stalwart for supporting the village store, even before Kate took it on.

"Fraser mentioned that they will probably sell The Manor House," Jenni interjected. "Heaven knows how much they will get for it?"

"Bloody hell." Alaistair joined the conversation with his usual interesting use of words. "It will go for a packet and just think about the inheritance tax they will pay. Poor buggers."

Paula smiled at her new partner. She loved Al's straight talking. He was not one to put on a façade. You got what you were given with Al. Frank and to the point.

Paula and Al had made it fairly obvious to the rest of the village that they were now an item. They had arrived at the church earlier, hand in hand and, when Paula started to weep during the eulogy, Al had whipped a handkerchief from his pocket. Peter had actually sat with them both in church, as a subliminal gesture of support for the new relationship.

If anyone was surprised at that, they were unaware of the shift in dynamics between the three people. Peter was still struggling with the idea of Paula and Alaistair. He loved her still, but realised that particular boat had sailed. There was no going back. His relationship with Paula was dead and buried. The fact that she had chosen Al as the one to replace him, hurt deeply. However, all he wanted for Paula was to find happiness and if that joy was to be found with his old mate, Al, then so be it.

"Perhaps the house will be bought by some rich famous celebrity," said Paula. "And let's hope he's single." She laughed as she saw the horror on Al's face. "For Jenni, stupid. Not me."

Jenni pretended to act surprised. "For me. No thanks, Paula. I'm off men for now. Just me, Jimmy, and Lily. I don't have time for anything like that."

She sighed, considering she wasn't actually lying on that subject.

Henrique had departed last week with very little fuss at all. He hadn't wanted a big send off and hadn't told most of his clients until the week before. That certainly didn't go down well. Jenni had heard grumbling noises at the café from villagers who felt it was incredibly rude that their Spanish gardener had left them in the lurch, especially in the height of the summer whilst everything was sprouting up unbelievably fast.

Jenni was convinced Henrique was embarrassed at the speed of his departure. He didn't want to let people down, but at the same time he didn't know how to explain why he was going so suddenly. He never intended to return to Sixpenny Bissett so perhaps he could afford to annoy the locals. It was the least of his worries if he was honest.

Jenni and Henrique had one last evening at the caravan, before he left. It hadn't felt right though. Of course the sex was amazing, but they were both holding something back. Jenni felt she was saying goodbye to the man who had given her back confidence in her body. He had made her feel young and sexy, even when she knew she wasn't any such thing.

Henrique, on the other hand, was devastated. He had fallen in love with Jenni, even though he knew they had no future together. It was a dream he had treasured, or should we say, a fantasy. He didn't want to marry Gabriela, but he knew he had to. Family was far too important to allow him to rebel against his mother's wishes. He would make a go of the future placed in front of him, even if it wasn't what he wanted.

And now Henrique was gone. Jenni had decided to return to her celibate existence. She didn't need the inconvenience of a man in her life. Everything was busy with the café, catering business, Lily, and caring for her son.

If she needed any release then a battery operated one maybe her only option, for now. She smiled as she realised how different her world had become since she arrived in Sixpenny Bissett. She arrived a docile, nervous widow. Over the last year she had grown in confidence and self-belief. A successful business, a growing family, and a newfound awareness of her own needs.

Interrupting her mucky thoughts, Richard Samuels joined the group. Oh God, Jenni thought. He is still the sexiest man in the village. She fancied him. He would be the one she would certainly break her new celibacy promises for. The one guy who was out of her league, as he still carried a torch for his late wife. Let's face it you cannot compete with the dead. It's not a fair fight.

"Hey chaps, what are you laughing about?" Richard asked.

Kate grabbed hold of Richard's arm, bringing him into their circle of humour. "Jenni was just telling us she is off men for good," she grinned.

Kate was one of the few people who knew about that disastrous night, when Jenni had launched herself at the unsuspecting Richard, only to be spurned and embarrassed. Kate had tried to warn her friend that Richard Samuels was not the man for her, but unfortunately, she had not listened to Kate's advice.

"What a shame," Richard laughed, joining in with his friends.

He smiled across at Jenni, not for the first time, regretting his stupidity when she had tried to kiss him. If he could go back in time, he would do things differently. But he had his chance and he blew it. All he could do now was remain her friend. Like a moth to the flame, he was sentenced to constantly flutter around her golden star, never to get close enough to get burnt.

Perhaps one day Jenni would find her faith in men again. And when that day came Richard would be waiting. In the meantime, all he could do would be to admire her from afar and hope.

Yes, there is always hope.

CHAPTER TWENTY-FOUR
ROSE COTTAGE

Family and friends joined Jimmy to celebrate the christening of his adored daughter, Lily Rose.

The service had been lovely. Rather than a separate event it formed part of the normal Sunday morning worship, allowing both guests and the congregation to welcome the baby into the Christian family. Jeremy had performed the ceremony as Lily lay, like an angel, in Kate's arms. The christening gown looked exquisite on her and Lily had exceeded her Granny's expectations by declining to be sick or, even worse, soil the gown. What a result, thought Jenni. The idea of a quick change during the ceremony would have been mortifying.

For once, Jenni was not in the limelight. All too often, since her arrival in Sixpenny Bissett, Jenni had found herself the centre of attention. Even if she had no intention of being so. She sat towards the front of the church, with Richard, Al, and Paula, as she watched her son and his daughter's godparents promise to protect her from evil and propel her along a life of goodness. Lily didn't cry when the holy water touched her forehead. She blinked, looked around for her Daddy, and refused to wail in disgust.

A perfect performance all round.

Now, family and friends were gathered in the gardens of Rose Cottage for a BBQ. The weather had been kind. All week there had been showers, but this morning Jenni had woken to beautiful September sunshine. It was such a relief.

Jimmy and George were in charge of the BBQ. Displaying typically manly behaviour, they were determined to cook and had left Jenni to prepare a variety of salads. Everyone knows that being in charge of the BBQ was the easy part of any party. It was all the extras which took the effort and co-ordination, but at least the boys felt they were instrumental in feeding the hoards. Jenny was fortunate to have the helping hands of both Kate and Della, the two godmothers. They had already hit it off and the kitchen was full of laughter as the women worked together.

Della was such a character. Covered in piercings and tattoos, she had a mouth like a sewer. She had been on her best behaviour today, trying her hardest to look like a suitable godmother to the tiny Lily. Jenni had no doubt that Kate would provide the longer term emotional and religious support to Lily, whereas Della would probably be the first person to get Lily drunk and watch her vomit in her handbag.

It had been lovely to have her elder son, George, home for the weekend.

The previous evening, Jenni and her son had sat out in the garden with a glass of wine catching up on news. The car dealership was surpassing all expectations. George was a natural, probably even better than his father. He was finally seeing a young lady too, Francesca, Frankie for short. He hadn't brought her along for the weekend as the relationship was in its early days and George was worried Jimmy might scare her off.

By the sound of it, George was quite struck on his new girlfriend. That was unusual as George struggled to open his heart to another. Losing his father had affected George deeply. He had built a cold barrier around his heart to protect it from further emotional damage and it was great to hear that perhaps Frankie may be able to melt that blockade.

Jenni was dying to see him settle down with a good woman. He had devoted the years since Reggie's death to the business. He worked hard and forgot to play hard. Whilst it was great to see the profits rising and the family dividends providing security for the future, all Jenni wanted for her boy was to be happy.

What mother doesn't want that.

Jimmy and George seemed to be having fun over at the BBQ. A great deal of back slapping and jesting seemed to be going on. There had always been a good level of banter between the two brothers and today was no different. Interesting, George had actually mentioned to Jenni how surprised he was to see Jimmy all grown up at last. The shock of seeing Jimmy, the father, rather than Jimmy, the fool, who was always chasing some unreachable dream, had made George reflect that his brother had become a better man all together.

Finally managing to secure herself a plateful of food, Jenni found a free seat next to Richard. Balancing her wine glass on the edge of the chair, she tasted the beef kebab. She nodded her head approvingly. Cooked to perfection.

"You look happy, Jenni," said Richard. He chinked his beer bottle against her wine glass before taking a sip. "Lovely day isn't it. You must be so very proud."

Jenni certainly was. The service had been beautiful and there hadn't been any hitches, which was highly unusual for her. Always seeking perfection, Jenni was often frustrated by minor hiccups. But not today. The world was smiling down on her and her family, filling it with joy.

"Thanks, Richard. It has been wonderful, don't you think. Lily is such a darling. I really can't imagine a life without her now."

"And Jimmy looks a natural dad." Richard nodded over towards Jimmy, who had been relieved of his cooking detail and was now bouncing Lily on his lap. Florence, his shadow, was beside him. "Those two seemed joined at the hip. Are they an item yet? If that's what the youngsters call it these days."

Jenni smiled as she noticed Florence gently tuck Jimmy's hair behind his ear as he crooned over his beautiful daughter. The gesture was unconsciously tender and spoke of something more than friendship.

"I don't think anything official yet, Richard. Jimmy seems to spend all his free time with Flo and she does look pretty besotted with him. But it's a lot to take on. Not many girls her age would want to saddle themselves with someone else's baby."

That particular thought had been troubling Jenni for some weeks.

She was incredibly proud of her son for taking on the sole responsibility for

Lily Rose. He had never wavered from the moment she had been placed in his arms. He may not have pushed that child into the world, but his love for her was as strong as any mother's. Lily was an extension of his very being.

But being a single parent brings challenges, especially when trying to date again. Flo was so much younger and Jenni feared that she might get bored with the lack of excitement in Jimmy's life. A girl Flo's age surely wanted to be out clubbing, enjoying holidays in the sun, and generally having the independence of doing what she wanted, when she wanted. Her early infatuation may well cool as the routine of a young child doused the flames of passion. And then there was university. Jenni didn't know if that was something Flo was interested in or whether her parents, Geoff and Jacky, would want to push her towards, but a long distance relationship might not work.

"She seems a sensible girl Florence. Funny thing about living in a village is that you watch the babies grow up into young people," reflected Richard. "I remember Florence as a young'un. She was always serious and quiet. Really cared about the other children, rather than wanting to be at the heart of the rough and tumble. Perhaps Jimmy and Lily are just what she needs too."

Jenni hadn't thought about it that way before. She had been focused on her son and his needs, wanting to protect him from further hurt. Despite the fact that he hadn't loved Charlie, her departure had been a huge blow to Jimmy. He had questioned himself, trying to work out what he had done wrong. Maybe Flo was that steadying anchor he needed.

"Perhaps." Jenni sighed. "Relationships are never easy."

The troubled look on her face prevented Richard from saying more. He had come to value their friendship and certainly wouldn't risk it to satisfy his now blossoming needs.

They were star-crossed lovers. Fated to travel on differing paths. Now that he wanted her more than ever, she was sworn off men.

Theirs's was a true relationship disaster.

The two friends slipped into a companiable silence, each concentrating on their private thoughts. Jenni was thinking about Richard and how she had blown her chance. The closer she got to him as a mate, the harder it was to hide her true feelings. She was attracted to him and could visualise them living together. Her soul mate to fill the gap left by her dear Reggie. She could see her and Richard making a go of things together, but one stupid mistake had put a stop to that.

Richard, meanwhile, was having similar thoughts. His desire for Jenni was growing every day. His heart was starting to heal. He would never forget his wife, Nicola, but he was finally starting to live again. Jenni could have been the new woman in his life, but for one stupid mistake which had put a stop to that.

Don't you just wish you could knock their stubborn heads together and let them see what was right there in front of their eyes!

CHAPTER TWENTY-FIVE
THE CAFÉ AT KATE'S

The shrill cry of the phone woke Lily from her post-lunch doze. Looking around frantically, she burst into a loud wail of disgust.

Jenni sighed as she grabbed the handset. It had taken her ages to get Lily down and now that was all for nothing. Before she could even say hello, Jimmy launched into a rant.

"Mum, get over here now. We have a fucking big problem." His voice carried a mix of panic as well as anger and frustration.

"What's the matter, Jimmy love?" Jenni tried to remain calm especially as she was rocking Lily against her chest, trying to quell her cries.

"I'll explain when you get here. Just hurry."

With that, he put down the phone leaving Jenni with no other option than to gather her things and rush over to the café. Using the term rush is probably inappropriate. With a small baby it was impossible to rush anywhere. There is always a ton of equipment to be taken, which meant that the simplest task always required thought and planning.

As she wrestled with pram and shop door, pushing one with her arm and one with her bum, Jenni noticed a commotion within the café. Anna Fletcher was loudly declaring her disgust to whomever would listen. And, unfortunately, the café was packed with the normal lunchtime rush. Poor Jimmy was gripping the counter, his face burning with humiliation and no doubt anger, if his voice on the phone was anything to go by.

Leaving Lily in clear sight of the counter, Jenni pushed her way through the massed tables. "What's happening?" Her voice silenced Anna, along with numerous conversations which had sprung up across the café. All eyes turned to stare at the owner.

"A rat," mumbled Jimmy.

Picking up a plastic bag, he wafted the offending dead creature in her face. Thankfully, Jimmy had decided to pick up the rat and seal it in a plastic bag, minimising any immediate cross contamination, although the reputational damage may already have been done. The expression on Anna Fletcher's face would have been amusing if it wasn't for the seriousness of the situation. She looked like she could self-combust at any time, with excitement.

Jenni secretly wished she would. She really couldn't stand that woman.

"I found a dead rat under my table," Anna shouted, keen to ensure everyone could hear her complaint. The satisfaction she was getting from the current situation was playing across her face with a nasty sneer. "A dead rat in an eating establishment. That is disgraceful. You should be shut down immediately." Anna snapped the clasp on her handbag with a satisfying crack as she plonked in on the counter. "I demand my money back right now and I will never be frequenting your establishment again."

She glared at Jenni with a look which could kill, although her current focus was on killing Jenni's business reputation.

Interestingly, Anna Fletcher had never been to the café before. She was the only person in the village who had never tried Jenni's hospitality out. She would not be seen dead in that woman's business, a fact she had been vociferous about with her friends from the WI. The term 'friends' again had to be taken with a pinch of salt. Her fellow members of the valley's WI tolerated Anna Fletcher and her constant moaning.

What an incredibly strange coincidence that the first time Anna decided to visit she found a dead rat under her table. Her dislike for Jenni Sullivan was infamous. Would she really stoop that low?

None of these conspiracy theories were going through Jenni's mind at the moment. That was for later. Right now, she was feeling sick to her stomach as she frantically gathered her thoughts. It was an absolute nightmare she was living through. How she handled the next few minutes could be the difference between saving her reputation, or her business, from being mortally wounded.

"Okay, Anna, I am so very sorry. Jimmy, give Anna her money back please." Jenni turned to face the watching eyes of her other customers. She drew in a deep breath as she summoned every ounce of courage left in her. "I am so terribly sorry everyone. Please see my colleague, Jimmy, for a full refund. I will investigate what has happened here. We have extraordinary levels of cleanliness in the café so I honestly don't know how this has happened. We have never had any pest issues before." She noticed a number of understanding smiles from her audience. "I would like to ask if everyone could leave once your refunds have been processed. I am going to shut the café for the remainder of the day so that we can do a full deep clean."

As she drew to the end of her speech Jenni noticed Anna trying to take hold of the plastic bag containing the offending rodent. "Thank you, Anna, but you will need to leave the rat with me." Jenni was firm in her convictions and took the bag from Anna, quite forcibly.

"But it is evidence," shrieked Anna.

"Exactly, I need to investigate where this rat has come from. I will need to keep the evidence for that purpose."

There was no way she was allowing that dreadful woman to leave with the rat. Jenni was already becoming suspicious and, even though it was an awful thought which was unsettling her brain, she could not be seen to give in to the nasty old woman.

Gradually the café emptied.

Once the last person had departed Jimmy put out the 'cleaning in progress' signs, blocking the entrance. Because of the nature of the building, people could walk directly from the shop into the café. This had been a huge advantage for both Kate and Jenni, ensuring that they could share customers.

Today, Jenni wished she could lock a door and turn her face from the world. She was stunned and mortified. Both her and Jimmy crumpled down onto the nearest table. Jenni's head fell into her hands and she groaned. Her world was falling apart in front of her eyes. She had worked so hard to get the café established and then this happens. Jimmy put his hand on his mum's shoulder to comfort her. Even Lily seemed to pick up on the enormity of what had happened. She remained silent even though she was desperate for attention. Having spotted her dad, she wanted him to pick her up and cuddle her. But something in the atmosphere warned the baby that dad was not in a cuddly mood.

"I'm so sorry, Mum." Jimmy sighed.

Jenni raised her head and looked at her son. She could see the distress on his face. "Jimmy, it's not your fault, darling. I just cannot believe this is happening."

They sat in silence for some moments. Their contemplations were interrupted by Kate striding purposely into the café. "What the hell," she cried. "Claire rang me. A rat? Where the hell did a rat come from?"

Kate was angry, but not at Jenni and her son. It was an anger born of fear. The opening of the café was the main reason she had managed to keep the General Store in business.

Jenni reached across the table and took her friend's hands in hers. "It's got to be some big bloody mistake, mate. This room is spotless. You know how diligent Jimmy and I are. You could seriously eat your cake off this floor every morning. I just don't believe it. That's why we have held onto the rat."

Kate was slowly shaking her head in disbelief. "What are we going to do with a dead rat in a plastic bag then? What does it prove? Other than the fact that it was found in the café."

Kate wasn't trying to be difficult, but she was scared. What were the implications for her business? Rats in a café were bad enough, but what if she had a nest in the main shop. That could be a disaster reputationally. At the very least she could be losing stock if they were gnawing away at her dry foods.

"I don't know, Kate. I'm fucking making it up as I go." Jenni sank back in her chair, glancing from Kate to Jimmy, hoping for help.

"Look, Mum. First things first. Let's do a deep clean of the premises. We can put a notice up on the window to say we are shutting tomorrow to do that clean. I know that means we will lose a day's trade, but it sends a message. We do not compromise on cleanliness."

Jenni looked at Jimmy as he took control of the situation. Thank goodness she didn't have to handle this alone. Her wonderful son would be at her side. Together they could handle everything that Anna Fletcher chose to throw at them.

"That sounds like a plan, Jimmy. I will take all the stock out of here and take it home. We cannot sell it anyway so I guess we will be gorging ourselves on cake and biscuits for the next few days. I will have to make fresh for Friday, if we can reopen then."

Kate had been sitting in silence watching the exchange. "That's settled it. I am going to shut the shop now until Friday too. We have got to be seen to be taking this seriously. I'm going to ring for a pest control officer to review the shop and storerooms and see if they can find the nest." Kate was already scrolling on her phone as she spoke. "I remember we had a guy out a few years back when we had a wasp nest in the house. Let me give him a ring and see if he can come first thing tomorrow."

Suddenly, everything didn't seem so bad. Action is usually the best way of cancelling out fears. By the end of the day they would have the pest controller booked in and between the three of them, the deep clean had started.

Jenni had a nagging doubt at the back of her mind though. She was becoming more and more certain that the source of her problem was not rodent related but a nasty old woman issue. She couldn't prove anything right now so she would have to go through the motions of repairing the damage to her business. But something was gnawing away at her brain. Jenni didn't believe in coincidence and this was the biggest one ever. Anna Fletcher had never set foot in the café until today. And suddenly, they have an infestation.

Not bloody likely, she thought.

'Rat-Gate' had arrived in Sixpenny Bissett.

Scandal or sabotage? Only time would tell.

CHAPTER TWENTY-SIX
THE CAFÉ AT KATE'S

Jenni was on her hands and knees, scrubbing the floor. Her hands ached. Her back was screaming for rest. Her hair was matted with sweat. She had pulled it into a topknot to prevent it flopping in her eyes. Not a pretty sight, but she was working too hard to worry about her appearance. Vanity could not get in the way of a good dose of elbow grease. The café would be cleaner than ever before by the time she finished. Seriously, you would be able to eat your cake off the floor. If that was your desire.

Tables and chairs had been stored outside so she could make sure every last corner was spotless. Jimmy was taking apart the coffee machine and cleaning each part. He had finished the counter area, which again was now spotless. They had been working since early morning and were keen to finish as soon as they could to help Kate and Claire out in the main shop. That was a much bigger task which involved taking everything off the shelves to clean.

Luckily, Florence had stepped in to save the day. She had agreed to mind Lily for the day. A lifesaver. Flo hadn't seen it as a favour. She adored Lily and couldn't wait to get her hands on the baby. She planned to take the pushchair out for a long walk, hoping to meet some villagers and show off her new responsibilities.

News had spread rapidly the previous evening. It's amazing how bad news travels. So much faster than good.

It hadn't taken long for the messages of support to flood in. Jenni should never have doubted the goodness of others. Her café Facebook page was swamped with messages from her customers confirming what she knew to be the case. Hers was a clean and friending business and, whatever had happened the previous afternoon, was not a reflection on her, Jimmy and their cleanliness. As she read the messages, Jenni had cried with joy at the wonderful friends she had made since moving to the countryside.

Added to the supportive messages, Jenni had a call from Richard offering his help. He was working from home that Thursday and had offered to sort out some lunch for the four of them. Like any army, the troops could not march on an empty stomach and he knew exactly what was needed. Richard had just taken their fish and chips order. The workers were excited at the thought of stuffing themselves on calorific chips, which would be so very well deserved after a morning of hard graft. Jenni was determined that they could afford a break in the sunshine to recharge.

Her scrubbing was interrupted by a loud banging on the front door. "I'll get it," shouted Kate. "It's Steve, the rat man," she laughed.

Jenni was relieved that Kate was in a much better mood today. Despite her nagging suspicions, Jenni felt responsible for all the worry she was now heaping at her best friend's door. Kate had tried her hardest to hide her anger yesterday, but she had been moody for the rest of the day, which was a sure signal to Jenni that she was not a happy bunny. And Jenni felt responsible for that.

Steve, the rat man, had a cheery face with a large, hooked nose. It might be cruel to say he bore a passing resemblance to the pest he was responsible for catching or killing. But the truth was, he did. He was the spitting image of the child catcher from Chitty Chitty Bang Bang, an even crueller description but probably fair. Except that he had the happiest face ever.

Steve burst into the shop like a whirlwind and swept Kate up into a big hug. She had only used his services once before, but he was obviously one of those tactile people who never worried about invading an individual's personal space. His hug was not welcomed, especially as he had a pungent smell of rodent poison lingering on his overalls.

Kate glanced over his shoulder to catch Jenni's eye. She grimaced as she tried to extradite herself from his embrace. Her gagging mime told Jenni all she needed to know. She suppressed a laugh as she watched her friend's obvious discomfort. The whole situation was so ridiculous that you had to laugh.

"Right, ladies." Steve let go of Kate as he rummaged around in his huge, black bag. He slipped plastic covers over his shoes and a mask over his face. Anyone would think he was about to examine atomic waste with his hazmat on. It was a little over the top. "Where did you find the dead rat?"

Jenni directed Steve into the café area. His wheezing breath through the mask just added to the post-apocalyptic image. Despite the seriousness of the nature of his visit, Jenni was trying her hardest not to laugh. It was just a dead rat, one that had been deceased for some days, not a dangerous chemical spill.

"Jimmy, pass me the rat," she called over to her son. The offending creature had been sealed in an old tin box overnight. Jenni was not normally squeamish, but the idea of having this dead animal in a house with a new-born really didn't appeal. The garage had been its deathly resting place.

Steve took the plastic bag, opened it, pulled his mask off and poked his long nose into the bag. Jenni grimaced again. Gosh it must stink by now, thought Jenni.

"Umm." Steve poked the rat with his fingers. Rigor mortis had set in. "Interesting," he added.

Jenni and Kate both stood watching him in anticipation. He clearly wasn't going to tell them more, just yet. Putting the plastic bag and rat in his bag, he set off towards the storeroom.

"It's a bit of a shame you ladies have been cleaning already. It is going to make things a bit more difficult. Did you find any droppings?"

That was one of the things both Jenni and Kate had focused on before they set about their cleaning mission. Every surface both floor, windows and shelves had been swept, hoping to find some evidence of where the nest might be. But nothing. They weren't sure if that was a good sign or the very worst. Perhaps the rats had nested in the roof or within the cavity wall which would cause them even more issues.

"Nothing at all," responded Kate.

"Leave this with me, Kate. I will do some digging out back and see what I can find. Something just doesn't feel quite right though." He sniffed loudly. "I have a nose for these things, you know."

Jenni finally cracked.

Heading back towards the café entrance, she stuffed her hand over her mouth as she silently screamed with pent-up laughter. Kate ran after her, giggling too. It might be gallows humour, but the two women could not contain themselves. Jimmy looked confused. The second-hand telling of this story could not translate and offer the same level of humour. All Jimmy could do was watch the two women giggle and wait for them to calm down.

He felt somewhat left out and decided to change the subject. "I hope Richard arrives with lunch soon. I'm starving."

Jimmy was always starving. He had a healthy appetite and no matter how many carbs he ate, he remained tall and skinny. Jenni was quite jealous of his metabolism. She only had to look at one of her cakes and the weight would settle around her tummy. Fish and chips were calorific but she hoped their hard labour this morning might compensate for a moment on the lips and maybe not let it settle on the hips.

Kate must have left the front door unlocked as they were interrupted by a man peering round the corner. He didn't look like their normal clientele. Dressed in a grey suit, carrying a briefcase and clipboard. Very officious. He frowned at the two middle-aged women sniggering behind the cake counter.

Not a great start, he thought. Doesn't exactly look like they are taking this matter very seriously.

Jenni was the first to wipe the smile off her face. "Can I help you?" she asked.

The man stared at her over the rims of his glasses. "Yes. I'm looking for Mrs Jenni Sullivan." He referred to his clipboard and alternated his gaze from his notes to the two women standing in front of him.

"You've found her," continued Jenni. "What can I do you for?"

The man looked around the café, sizing things up, before he answered. "Allan MacPherson, Environmental Health Inspector."

Jenni and Kate looked at each other, horrified. That was an unexpected turn of events. How the hell had the Environmental Health found out about yesterday? And so soon. There was no obligation for Jenni to report the incident until she had a better understanding of the problem so how come they were getting such a visit?

"We have had a report of vermin contaminating a food premises. I need to inspect your business area, including all food preparation surfaces and storage facilities."

Jenni was fuming. There could only be one person responsible. "Who has made this report?" she asked trying her hardest to control her voice.

She wanted to scream at the guy out of frustration, but was conscious that Mr MacPherson probably had the power to close her down for good. Politeness was necessary even if she didn't feel very welcoming. Whatever happened they had to create a good first impression.

"I'm not at liberty to tell you that, Mrs Sullivan." He coughed awkwardly as he referred to his clipboard once again. "I understand a dead rodent was found on the premises yesterday. Is that correct?"

Jenni nodded. "It was found by one of our customers, Anna Fletcher. I can only assume it was her that reported the find. We shut both the café and store as soon as the rat was found, refunding all customers in the café at the time. We started a deep clean last night and we currently have the pest controllers here investigating." Jenni paused to take a breath. She could feel herself gabbling, in a hurry to defend her business. "So far we have found no evidence of rat droppings or a nest."

Fortunately, Steve chose that particular moment to stroll back towards them. Perfect timing. "Kate, I hope you don't mind me interrupting." Steve pulled his mask off and removed the plastic covers from his feet.

Kate introduced the pest controller to their new visitor. "Steve, this gentleman is from the Environment Health. They had a report about our rat. He is here to investigate our rodent problem."

Steve cleared his throat as he shook the other man's hand. Not wanting to be left out and, wanting to support his mother, Jimmy wandered over to see what was happening. It obviously wasn't lunch arriving, but he could sense something important was going on. If it affected the business, it affected him and Lily too.

"Well, Kate, you don't have a rat problem. I had my suspicions when I looked at the dead creature, but wanting to be thorough, I have done a good recce of the premises. There is absolutely no evidence of rats or any other pests." Steve turned his attention to the Health Inspector. "In fact, there is evidence that the dead rat has a broken neck, consistent with being caught in a rodent trap. In my opinion the rat was placed in the premises rather than died here."

Jenni looked shocked. "What?" she cried.

"I think someone put a dead rat in your café," Steve continued. "No idea why but I think someone was trying to damage your business. Sabotage, if you ask me."

Jenni slumped against the wall. She was struggling to comprehend what she had done to deserve such nastiness. She and Jimmy had worked so hard to get the café off the ground and someone's devious nature could have put paid to it.

Allan MacPherson looked decidedly uncomfortable. He started to pack his clipboard into his briefcase, deciding his work was done. What a waste of time, he thought to himself. A neighbourly feud, nothing more. His suspicions were raised when the anonymous caller had rung last night. They were very insistent that he make an urgent personal visit despite him explaining their normal processes. The caller had threatened to take the story to the newspapers if he didn't agree to make the visit a priority.

Allan should have trusted his gut and realised this was a vendetta rather than a health problem. Especially as Mrs Sullivan's café looked spotless. He had been to many food establishments which had a real rodent problem and that was usually because the premises were in a poor state of repair with totally inadequate cleaning regimes. This café did not fit that bill and he could tell that as soon as he walked through the door.

"Mrs Sullivan, I am satisfied with the explanation and my prima facie review of your premises does confirm that, to all intents and purposes, the food preparation area looks clean to a high standard. I will report back accordingly and will confirm the matter closed." He pulled at the collar of his shirt as if he was embarrassed to still be there. "I suggest you sort out your differences with the person who must have planted the rat. There is clearly a problem which needs sorting."

Oh, Jenni was fully aware of who was responsible. That bloody cow. But for now Jenni must keep her professionalism on display.

"Thank you, Mr MacPherson. Sound advice. I really appreciate you taking the time to visit us today. I'm sure you are very busy and you really didn't need to be bothered by such a trivial matter. Is there anything else we can do for you today? Do you need me to sign anything?"

"No, that's me finished," the Inspector closed his briefcase and headed at speed towards the door.

Clearly, he was pleased to be gone. He had a ton of work back at the office and this morning's interruption was not welcomed at all. His first impression of the village was that it was a sleepy backwater where nothing ever happens. As he walked back to his car, he chuckled. Who would have thought it. He couldn't wait to tell his mates down the pub about the Rat-Gate scandal of Sixpenny Bissett.

Steve, the pest controller, wasn't far behind. It was an easy job for him today, but he had definitely earnt his money, as far as Kate and Jenni were concerned. He even left the offending dead rat with the two women as a memento of the day. Not that either of the women looked pleased to have it.

As he handed over the offending dead creature to Jenni, she had grimaced and uttered her intentions. "Steve, I think I may well stuff it and put it on display to remind herself how evil some people can be. Not sure it is the best type of advert for my business but one day we will laugh about Rat-Gate."

As the shop door closed, Jenni let her anger vent. With her fists clenched she raised her arms in the air as she shouted out her frustration. She was determined not to cry. She had done too much of that recently. She was a strong, independent woman who would not get side-swiped by a stupid old woman with a personal vendetta. But boy was Jenni annoyed. That crazy woman and her pathetic attempt to hurt Jenni.

Now it was getting personal. Trying to ruin Jenni's business and put a dent in her income. It just wasn't on. It wasn't just Jenni she was hurting. What about Kate and Claire in the shop? And of course, Jimmy who had only just started to work in the café and was loving his chance to spread his virtual wings.

While Jenni screamed out her frustration, her friend and shop owner, maintained her silence. Kate slumped against the café counter and rested her head in her hands. The fight was oozing out of her now that the thought of a rat infestation had been disproved. Disaster had been avoided, but Kate didn't think she could cope with many more days like yesterday. The whole situation with Anna Fletcher needed sorting and quickly.

It may be quite funny, how pathetic that woman was, especially when it came to Jenni Sullivan. This latest attempt to wind up her mate had grave consequences. It could have been the nail in the General Store's coffin. All her hopes for the future up in crematory flames. Kate was not laughing right now. In time she would probably wet herself with giggling, but she couldn't even raise the energy for that right now.

The only positive thing to come from all of this, thought Kate, was that all her shelves had had a long overdue clean. And she had found some tins of tuna that were on their way out. She would rustle up her tuna pasta bake tonight. A firm favourite with Joseph and Mary.

Whilst all this was going on, Jimmy simply watched both women and remained silent. He couldn't understand what that woman had against his mother. Of course he was biased. She was his mum and she was a kind person who never really tried to wind people up. So what had Anna got against Jenni? He was relieved that their troubles with officials were over, but sensed this was just the start of another battle.

Out of the corner of his eye, he spotted Richard's car pulling up outside the shop. Perhaps food was what they all needed right now. Jimmy hurried across to the door to prewarn Richard. It wouldn't be fair to let him walk into the aftermath. Quickly bringing him up to speed, the two men unpacked lunch and set out tables and chairs. It didn't take long for the smell of the greasy delights to tempt Kate and Jenni outside.

Once they were eating, Richard decided to be brave, or perhaps foolish, and ask the obvious question. "Who do you think did it?"

Jenni was not in the mood to play games. "Seriously?"

Jimmy was making frantic faces at Richard, trying to stop the conversation before it began. But Richard was not the type to avoid a difficult discussion. He understood how upset Jenni had been, especially when he had spoken to her the previous night. This was her baby and she was passionate about the café. Anyone insulting her business was making it personal. He loved that passion in her. Watching her now, he was even more attracted to her passion, her anger and pent-up emotion, which she was trying hard to control and failing abysmally. She was one hell of a woman, he decided.

Passion, intelligent and bloody sexy.

"That bitch, Anna Fletcher, that's who," Jenni spat out that woman's name. She could not taste her food because of the acid bubbling away in her throat.

Kate reached across the table and took her hand, rubbing a finger along her palm. "Calm down now, Jenni. I'm just as angry as you are, but we need to handle this carefully. She's an old bitter woman and she needs our sympathy rather than hate."

"Sympathy? Seriously?" sighed Jenni. "I have done nothing to warrant this behaviour. This woman nearly destroyed my business and you want to let her get away with it?"

Kate had no intention of letting Anna getting away with anything but there were more ways to deal with this than confrontation. Kate didn't like confrontation. She was much more subtle in her revenge.

"Look, for what it is worth, this is my suggestion. Firstly, we put something on your Facebook page to explain that the rat was planted and that we have a clean bill of health from the environment people. Let's leave it up to the public to make their own minds up about Ms Fletcher." Richard and Jimmy were both nodding in agreement. Jenni was yet to be convinced. "Then we go round to see Anna. Just so we ensure she knows that we know. Nothing more than that. No-one can then accuse us of intimidating an old lady."

Kate's idea had merit and once Jenni had calmed down, she would see the sense in it.

Richard was keen to help and take some of the pressure off Jenni and Kate. "Why don't I sit down with Jimmy and compose a message for your social media. We will keep it fairly generalised, but detailed enough, so that people will know that you have been targeted." Richard smiled at Jenni and was pleased to see her mood lifting. "If we confirm it will be business as usual tomorrow, does that work?"

Jenni nodded, reminding herself yet again that she had some amazing friends, who were always there for her in times of trouble.

Kate looked at her watch. "Meanwhile, you and me, Jenni, are going to pay Anna Fletcher a visit. Yes?"

Jenni shrugged. "Not yet. I'm going to eat my fish and chips first." Her mood had taken a 360 degree turn. "These are probably the best chips I have had in years so I'm going to savour every single one before I face that woman."

CHAPTER TWENTY-SEVEN
THE RECTORY

Kate eased back into the bubbles, letting out an audible sigh.

Jeremy had been correct. A bath was the best way for her to relax and reflect on a hell of a couple of days. Thankfully, the damage to her business was not going to be a problem. If Kate was honest with herself, she had been worried sick. Sleep had deluded her for the last couple of nights, adding to her exhaustion.

Kate allowed the fragrant bubbles to settle over her body, leaving only her head out of the water. She had run the bath a little hotter than she normally liked, but she really couldn't be bothered to reach for the cold tap. She would just steam nicely instead. She could feel the benefits of the heat already, soothing her troubles away. She closed her eyes and let her body relax fully.

As she lay there, her thoughts strayed back to the earlier visit to Anna Fletcher's. Not the most pleasant of trips, but a necessity. It had been a difficult conversation, especially as Anna was not in the mood to confess her sins. Anna had started off by acting dumb to their accusations. Obviously, if she had been innocent of their charges, she would have quite rightly got angry with them and defended her position fervently. But no. She had simply pursed her lips and refused to acknowledge any part in the whole debacle.

Kate was extremely proud of Jenni. She had managed the whole conversation well, much better than Kate had expected. She had been worried that Jenni would go in there with all guns blazing. Something she would have been reticent to blame Jenni for doing. Jenni had been so angry. Whilst their friendly pest man had got to the bottom of the dead rat incident, neither of them would forget the fear they had felt. The worry that the café would be shut down for good and, ultimately, the store. Kate had been worried that her friend would not be able to control her temper when faced with the guilty party.

But Jenni had been calmness personified.

She had been reasonable and polite with Anna, a quality the nasty woman didn't deserve. Jenni had explained the findings of both Steve and the Environmental Health Inspector to which Anna pretended to express surprise. At no point did Jenni accuse Anna of being responsible, but there were plenty of opportunities for the woman to admit fault.

She simply refused to do so.

Neither woman wanted to be accused of bullying a frail old lady so they had left the unspoken accusation hanging there. They had made it clear that they suspected Anna, but no allegation was levelled which could be used against the two businesswomen. They departed, leaving Anna fuming on the doorstep. Her nasty plan had failed abysmally and it was clear that Jenni and Kate knew who was responsible, even if nothing was said directly. What the outcome could be in terms of Anna's standing in the village was left ambivalent.

Richard had done wonders with the social media. The number of supportive comments replying to his post indicated that Jenni's regular customers would continue to back her. Many comments expressed shock that someone could go to such lengths to sabotage a fledgling business. Luckily, Anna was not on any social media sites and wouldn't see the anger directed towards the anonymous caller. However, she would no doubt feel that tension in the weeks ahead.

A gentle tap on the door interrupted her musings. Jeremy popped his head through the gap. "Can I come in, my love?"

"Umm," Kate sighed.

Never any peace in this house, was her first thought. She only wanted half hour on her own to soak in the luxurious bubbles.

As she opened her eyes, she noticed Jeremy was bearing gifts. A large glass of red wine in one hand and a fragrant candle burning brightly in the other. What an absolute darling, was her second thought. He gently shut the door behind him and came to sit on the side of the bath. The candle, he placed at the foot of the bath, and its scent was already filling the room with wonderful smells. Kate was enjoying the height of decadence. She very rarely had a moment to herself, what with the store, the children and her husband's parish commitments. This was a treat.

"Jeremy, you are the best husband," sighed Kate as she took a sip of wine. It was delicious and just what the doctor ordered.

"I aim to please, my love." Jeremy slipped his fingers into the water, gently wafting the bubbles over Kate's breasts. "Are you ok, Kate? I have been worried about you lately. You seem so stressed."

Jeremy had been on the receiving end of much of that stress over the last few days. She had been snappy with him and the children, which was so unlike her. Jeremy had also noticed her midnight wanderings when sleep eluded her. Loving the woman as he did, he wished he could take the worry off her shoulders. He also felt incredibly guilty that he had pushed Kate into taking on The General Store when it was at risk of closure. Perhaps it had all been too much for his wife to take on. There was enough pressure on her as the wife of a village vicar. He didn't have a '9 to 5' job and could be called out at any time of day to support a parishioner in need.

"It has been a shit week, darling. You just can't imagine something like this happening in sleepy Sixpenny Bissett." She smiled. "I was just so worried about the consequences. If Jenni had been shut down, the shop would be next. I worked so hard to keep it afloat and the thought of losing everything was tormenting me."

Jeremy continued to rotate his hand in the water, stroking Kate's leg. He was worried that their troubles were not yet over. If someone like Anna Fletcher could go to such lengths to hurt Jenni and, by default, his wife then would she just give up?

"Are you certain it was Anna?" he asked.

"Absolutely. You should have seen the look on her face when we went round earlier. If she was innocent she would have been mightily offended.

But no. She sat there with a face like a bulldog chewing a wasp."

Jeremy smiled as he envisioned the old lady's expression. It was probably a good analogy. "Do you think she will stop this vendetta now? I honestly don't know what she has got against Jenni. What has she ever done to deserve this treatment?" he asked.

Kate had been pondering on the subject for hours. Jenni was the nicest person. She didn't have a nasty bone in her body. What could make Anna dislike her so much? She was risking the contempt of the rest of the village. If people found out the truth about her latest activity, Anna Fletcher certainly wouldn't find much sympathy from the rest of the community.

"I honestly don't understand her motives, Jeremy. For some reason she has taken a dislike to Jenni and seems hell-bent on making her life difficult. Anna had never even been to the café before this week." A fact which had not been overlooked by Jenni as soon as she got the phone call from Jimmy about the dead rat. "She would come into the shop as normal to buy her groceries but would never cross the threshold into the café. Even if The General had been in there."

"God bless his soul." Jeremy missed the old gentleman for his wisdom and guiding principles, which the village was happy to follow. Anna would probably have not taken such a risk if Herbert was still alive.

"I honestly don't think she is behaving rationally, Jeremy. We have sent a warning, but what if that just makes things worse? She knows that we suspect her so what has she got to lose?"

"I think it might be time for me to get involved in a professional capacity." Jeremy could not let this one fester. The village was small in both size and community. Having such a dispute going on was never good. "I think I will pay a visit to Anna. Perhaps I can try to understand her complaints and pacify them."

Kate was surprised at Jeremy's offer to get involved. One of his guiding principles as vicar was to avoid getting embroiled in personal disputes. This was a risky policy. "Do you think it will help, darling? Or will Anna get even more angry if she thinks you are against her?"

Jeremy stroked higher as he thought through his plan. He could see Kate's smile widen as his hand moved higher. "I think I can be trusted to treat the lady with my usual tact and charm," he grinned.

"Well don't be too charming, my love," Kate sighed as his fingers reached the spot. "It would be wasted on that old hag."

Jeremy's hand moved up her body to cup her breast.

He felt so decadent touching his wife in a sexual way, while the children were watching TV downstairs. It had been ages since they had slept together properly. The stress of both their jobs had got in the way of their sex life recently. Usually, by the time they got to bed, one of them would be too tired. Jeremy would never complain. It just wasn't his way but he was conscious that he had been letting his wonderful wife down recently.

Tonight he would make it up to her.

CHAPTER TWENTY-EIGHT
THE CAFÉ AT KATE'S

The morning rush had died down. Jenni took the opportunity to wipe down the tables and restock the sugar pots.

It had been a week since the debacle of 'Rat-Gate' and, at last, Jenni could laugh about the stupidity of it all. It hadn't had the desired effect of damaging her business. The desired plan of nasty Anna Fletcher, that is. If anything it had the opposite effect. Business was booming. Word had reached either end of the valley, stirring up new custom.

Jimmy, being Jimmy, had decided to make some humorous profit from the whole event. On Sunday he had taken a number of photos of the dead rat and created a collage picture, which was now displayed upon the wall. Many a customer was seen, hanging around the frame, laughing at the different poses Jimmy had perfected with Roland the Rat. Yes, he had actually named it and printed his identity under the collage. Who knows whether Roland was male. Neither Jenni nor Jimmy had been keen to verify.

Poor Roland had been given the honour of a funeral. Well, he had been buried with due ceremony in the back garden. Again, Jimmy with Florence at his side, had led the service. His serious expression had Jenni in stitches as she tried to take it all seriously. He had insisted on a rendition of Rat Trap by the Boomtown Rats as the finale to the moving ceremony. Guests had included the Penrose family along with Richard Samuels.

Once the ceremony was over, Jenni laid out the salads as Jimmy fired up the BBQ. The whole group laughed and joked about the scandal of Rat-Gate. It was good to laugh about it but things could so easily have gone the wrong way. While Jenni was in the kitchen, placing the finishing touches to a fruit salad, Richard had wondered in. Without saying a word, he joined her at the island. They fell into a comfortable companionable silence as he worked alongside her. Their friendship was growing stronger each day. She wouldn't want to lose Richard from her life and was prepared to just be his friend, if that was all that was on offer.

Breaking away from her reflections, Jenni returned to the counter to make herself a coffee. The lunchtime rush would probably kick in soon and the chance to recharge, and maybe put her feet up with a magazine, would be wonderful.

Unfortunately, she was not about to get that break.

Through the main store door a troop of ten elderly ladies marched into the café. They were led by farmer's wife, Winifred Hadley. She strode up to the counter in a meaningful fashion, plopping her handbag onto the top in a decisive way.

"Good morning, Jenni."

Winifred gestured her fellow ladies to gather around her. Jenni smiled as she imagined Winifred as the mother hen, guiding her chicks into formation. The ladies did her bidding in silence, waiting for their leader to speak.

"The ladies of the WI and Knitting Group have joined forces to show our support for your lovely café. We were hoping that you could accommodate us all for a mid-morning coffee, cake, and a natter. I hope we are not too big a party for you to cope with." Winifred rested her arms across her mighty bosom as she finished her speech.

Jenni was overcome. She looked around the now clucking hens, seeing a sea of smiling faces. There truly are good people in the valley, she thought.

"Winifred, how lovely to see you. Thank you, ladies. I would be honoured to serve you this morning. It would be my pleasure. Why don't I move a few tables together so you can get yourselves settled."

Jenni busied herself, moving tables together and rearranging chairs. She was also using the activity to disguise the choaking sound coming from her voice. It had gone all wobbly with emotion. She was deeply touched by this very real show of support.

"Now let me take some orders from you. I have a lovely date and walnut cake, some fruit scones, and a lemon drizzle cake, if you fancy indulging."

Jenni's quiet time was gone, but she wasn't bothered at all. In fact, she was buzzing. She didn't even mind the indecision of her customers as they switched from one cake to another. This was the boost she had needed to confirm not everyone over seventy was against her. These were the most senior ladies in the valley, endorsing her business.

As she worked her way through the list, Winifred joined her at the counter, intending to hand out the beverages, although she had an ulterior motive.

"Jenni, my dear. We want you to know that we are disgusted that this has happened to you. Whoever is responsible must be feeling incredibly guilty right now." She looked at Jenni as if she was trying to transmit a secret message.

Jenni smiled. "I really appreciate your kind words. I honestly don't know what I have done to make that person hate me so much. But this was potentially so dangerous a vendetta. It's not just my business, but the store too. Kate was worried sick about it."

Jenni was aware that a number of the ladies sitting nearest the counter were listening in. That wasn't a problem for her. Perhaps word would get back to Anna and perhaps she might just feel a little bit guilty for what she put Kate through. If she hates me, that's fine, she decided. Yet to try and hurt Kate, who did nothing but good for the village, that was low.

"I don't think the person concerned hates you, Jenni," responded Winifred. "I think its jealousy. You are everything they are not, and never were. Please don't let this matter trouble you any longer." Winifred lowered her voice, conspiratorially. "I believe the person concerned realises the error of her ways. The humiliation of having the vicar pointing out her very unchristian behaviours has hit home. You won't be seeing any more stunts from her."

Jenni nodded as she turned to face the coffee machine. Again she was taking some time to compose her face. This time she had a grin the size of the Cheshire Cat. Let's hope this is the end of it, she thought.

Anna Fletcher will not win and, if anything she has done Jenni a favour.

Her reputation was not damaged and she had gained a load of new customers. Now it looks like the Knitting Club and WI were going to be regular customers.

Things were looking up.

'Rat-Gate' could be the start of a business boom.

CHAPTER TWENTY-NINE
THE GUNDOG PUB

Jimmy stood at the bar waiting to be served.

Looking across he could see Florence glancing around the pub, getting familiar with her surroundings. He had chosen The Gundog, in the nearby village of Lower Winterbourne, for two reasons. Firstly, he wanted to talk to Florence and he couldn't do that with her mum and dad hanging around. Secondly, he had heard that The Gundog sold the most amazing beer, brewed by a local celebrity film producer and he was keen to try it. Florence had insisted on driving, which was an added bonus as he felt like he needed some 'Dutch courage'.

"Yes sir, what can I get you?"

The bar man was small in stature and large in gut. His hair was shorn severely into a crew-cut, greying at the sides. His smile was welcoming, which certainly helped Jimmy relax and feel comfortable in this new establishment. Pub landlords around the area got to know their regulars and the barman had never seen this young couple before. Perhaps they were tourists, he decided.

"Can I have a pint of the Dog's Breath and a half of orange and lemonade," said Jimmy.

"Excellent choice."

Jimmy hoped the guy meant the beer rather than the soft drink.

As he waited for his pint to be pulled, Jimmy looked over at Florence again. She really was quite beautiful. How had he not noticed that before. She had the most amazing red, golden hair, a striking colour, which hung down her back in ringlets. Her skin tone was pale. She avoided the sun unless she was fully layered up with protective cream. It was her eyes which had initially drawn him into her world. They were a piercing blue colour, eyes which he could dive right into and be lost for ever.

Over recent months they had spent a great deal of time together. He loved the way she could make him laugh with the silly expressions she made, especially if he was trying to be serious. They had become good friends. But could they be more than that? He was older than Florence by at least five years. Florence had only just finished her A-Levels, whereas he had finished university a couple of years ago. He honestly didn't know whether she could see him as boyfriend material or whether she regarded him as just her friend.

He definitely didn't want to make an arse of himself and ruin what they had. Especially if he was judging the situation incorrectly. Despite that, he needed to understand how Florence felt about him. If she saw him as boyfriend worthy then he would love to take her up on that. Jimmy hadn't really had a serious relationship with a girl. Charlie didn't count. They had sex and made little Lily, but neither of them had strong feelings for the other.

Paying for the drinks, he made his way back to the table. The pub was quiet, not unusual for a Monday evening. Many of the pubs in the valley didn't even open on a Monday because of a lack of trade. The young couple pretty much had the place to themselves which would help Jimmy.

He would much rather face humiliation without an audience.

As he approached the table Florence turned to look at him. Those eyes caught him in their laser beam and he was temporarily stunned. Feeling like a gawky schoolkid, he stuttered his words, as he placed a drink in front of her. Florence seemed to pick up on his nervousness and smiled once more.

"It's lovely to be in a pub where I don't live," Florence grinned. "Never been here before. It looks a lovely place."

Florence might be younger than Jimmy, but she was mature for her age. She could see that Jimmy was struggling with something tonight. All she could hope was that he wasn't going to dash her hopes. She had a huge crush on Jimmy and was so scared that he saw her as some silly schoolkid.

Perhaps he was only hanging around with her because she was a useful babysitter. She didn't think he felt like that, but you never know with guys.

Florence hadn't dated a boy before and certainly not one as old as Jimmy. When Henrique had been working at the pub, she had flirted with him, but soon realised he was way out of her league. Henrique had been lovely to her. He was such a nice guy, but he just saw her as his boss's daughter or a younger sister. Nothing more. The boys at school didn't interest her at all. They were so immature. Most of them still thought it was cool to fart in class and blame it on each other. They were certainly not boyfriend material.

"Have you decided what you are going to do next?" Jimmy asked.

Florence had left school that summer and hadn't mentioned university to Jimmy at all. He was surprised that she hadn't headed off to freshers' week, at whichever college she had decided to go to. He hadn't pushed the subject before as he really didn't want her to leave. And influencing her decision would have been so very wrong. He did what all good guys did, ignore the elephant in the room and hoped it would shuffle off. If he was going to put their relationship on some sort of footing then he needed to find out whether theirs's would be a long distance romance.

"Sore point," replied Florence. "Mum and Dad have been nagging at me constantly. I honestly don't see the point in going to uni. It's not my bag."

Jimmy tried not to show his relief and excitement at that comment. He nodded. "Not everyone's cup of tea, Flo. And bloody expensive."

"Exactly. I couldn't really decide what subject I would do at uni. I love history, but I don't want to spend my life teaching or working in archives. The pub has been my life and I can't see me doing anything else. As long as Mum and Dad don't kick me out." She sighed. "Seeing as I am a failure."

Jimmy grabbed her hand across the table. "Never ever call yourself a failure."

"I'm joking," she giggled. "I think Mum understands I don't want to go to uni and secretly I think she is happy about that. Shifts have been tough to organise since Henrique left us in the lurch. I'm doing more work hours in the kitchen which has got me thinking."

"Oh, yes?"

"I'm considering signing up to catering college. Night school. It would be a couple of evenings a week. Perhaps I can then take over more of the work in the kitchen. Take some of the strain off Mum."

Jacky Smith ran the kitchen at The King's Head. Henrique used to work a couple of nights, giving Jacky a break, but his flit back to Spain had thrown the rosters up in the air. Florence was able to help but wasn't up to the standard of her mother or the Spaniard. She couldn't run service on her own which meant poor Jacky was working six days a week.

"What a great idea." Jimmy tried to hide the excitement from his voice. "At least then you are learning a skill without a huge student loan to pay off. Luckily, Mum doesn't pay me enough for me to start paying back my loan. I think it will be years before I have that to worry about."

"Look at us," Florence laughed. "Both going to be in the family business. Next year we could be millionaires."

"No chance of that for me," sighed Jimmy. "After that business with the dead rat we will be lucky to break even this year. Although business has been booming recently, who knows Rat-Gate might be the start of something special." He laughed out loud as he thought about the stupid funeral he and Flo had arranged. That's what he loved about Flo. She got his sense of humour. "Mum has more plans too. Missus Entrepreneur is her new name. She wants to increase her private catering business too. I know, perhaps you can earn some extra money helping out when she has a party?"

Florence couldn't believe her luck. She had been meaning to speak to Jenni about that. "That would be great, Jimmy. If you wouldn't mind putting a word in."

Jimmy was starting to feel a bit more confident. Flo wasn't going to be moving away from the village and seemed keen to link herself more with his family. Lily adored Flo. The baby would kick her legs out in delight whenever Flo was around, looking for a cuddle. He just had to be brave now and risk everything.

"Flo?" he started with trepidation.

Florence took a sip of her drink, rising her eyebrows slightly. "Umm," she answered.

"I'm just going to come out with it so hopefully, I don't make a complete arse of myself." Jimmy took a gulp of his ale for courage. "Flo, would you like to go on a date with me?"

He put his head in his hands. Oh My God, he thought, how crass did that sound. He raised his eyes slowly, trying to gauge a response from Florence.

"Thought you would never ask," she laughed. "Of course I will. Doesn't tonight count as a date?" She smiled encouragingly.

The grin on Jimmy's face got wider and wider. Their eyes locked across the table. Slowly he stretched across the table and kissed her gently on the lips. He laughed. "Shit, I was so nervous about asking you out. I thought you would tell me to bog off old man."

"What are we like?" replied Florence. "I was thinking that you would see me as too young. I fancy you, Jimmy Sullivan, if you haven't realised that already?"

"And you don't mind about Lily."

That could be the showstopper as far as Jimmy was concerned. Lily Rose would always be the first girl in his life. Anyone else would have to love Lily as much as he did. His was an unusual situation.

"I adore Lily. And can I just say that being a father makes you even more fanciable."

Jimmy blushed. "You think I'm fanciable?"

Florence lent across the table and kissed him back. "God, I have had a crush on you for ages. I just thought you could never see me. I was too scared to say anything in case you didn't even want to be my friend anymore. I would have taken friendship over losing you."

Jimmy gulped down the last of his beer as he whispered across the table. "Can we get out of here. I want to kiss you properly without an audience." He nodded over to the bar where the landlord was watching their every move.

Florence laughed as she grabbed his hand. "Come on then. Let's go."

CHAPTER THIRTY
ROSE COTTAGE

Jenni paused at the door to the dining room as she watched her family. Her heart was full of joy and pride to see them all gathered around her this weekend.

Especially this weekend. It was three years since they lost Reggie. The loss didn't get any easier. She had just learnt to live with the gap in her life.

George had agreed to come and stay, bringing his new girlfriend, Frankie, with him. Jenni was warming to Frankie already. She seemed a lovely girl and clearly cared for George. Tall, very tall, towering almost as high as Jenni's elder son. She was athletic in posture, which certainly fitted with her career. She managed a gym. That was where her and George had met. Strangely, Jenni struggled with the idea of George at a gym. He hadn't been into sport when he was a school and always seemed to scoff at the idea of a fitness regime.

Flo was joining the family for Sunday lunch. Jimmy didn't need to tell his mother that his relationship with Flo had stepped up a gear. They were 'loves young dream' personified. He could not keep his eyes off her, following every word which dripped from her lips. It was adorable to watch. Jenni was so happy for the young couple. After the stress of Charlie, Jimmy deserved to fall in love.

Lily was very much part of the family lunch as she bounced happily in her baby chair. She had already been fed and hopefully would allow her dad to enjoy his dinner in peace. Jimmy's hand naturally dropped to one side so he could gently rock the chair, keeping his daughter content.

"George, would you pour the wine," Jenni asked. "I'm about to serve up."

"Jenni, can I help?" Frankie was on her feet before being asked. She followed Jenni back into the kitchen. "You have the loveliest home, Jenni," she continued.

"Thank you, Frankie. That's very kind of you to say. You and George are welcome anytime, especially if you fancy a break away from the bustle of Birmingham."

The two women served the vegetables into dishes, which would be placed in the centre of the dining table. Jenni took the leg of lamb and positioned that on the carving dish. She followed family tradition and handed the tray to George, who made a flourish by sharpening the carving knife. As Jenni watched him concentrate on the task, the similarities with his father were striking.

Arms crossed arms as everyone helped themselves to potatoes and vegetables. Jenni, sat at the head of the table, hovering between the couples as she served herself. She always insisted on ensuring everyone else had enough food before she allowed herself to dig in, even though she always made ample and was never known to run out. A family with three hungry men in the household had seen to that.

George captured everyone's attention by chinking his wine glass. He cleared his throat before speaking. "Everyone, I just wanted to say a couple of words before we eat." He looked around the family before his eyes rested on Jenni. "Today is always a difficult day for us. I cannot believe it is three years since we lost Dad. Let's raise a glass in memory of the best dad and husband ever. To Dad."

"To Dad. To Reggie."

Jenni wiped a tear from her eye. Three years had flown by, but the pain of loss hadn't diminished. Jenni had learnt to live with it, a bit better every day. In the months after she lost the love of her life, she struggled to put one foot in front of the other. Now, she could live her life, enjoying her new home in Dorset and the company of men. But there was still an empty space where her husband had been. She would never replace Reggie in her heart, but there was space for another. Whoever that.maybe she did not know. She had thought it would be Richard, but that boat had firmly sailed.

"I would have liked to have met Reggie," said Flo. She had lent across the table to Jenni whilst the others chatted. "Jimmy talks about him all the time. Sounds like he was a great guy."

"Thanks Flo. He was special. Although I guess if Reggie was still here, we wouldn't be down in Sixpenny Bissett. He was a Brummie boy and I really don't think I could see him living anywhere else. Not sure country life would have been for him."

Reggie was a home boy. He had lived and died all within a few miles. Only once they had made some serious money from car dealing, would he consider moving into the suburbs of Birmingham. And even then, he felt a little bit of an outsider. Reggie indulged Jenni's passion for travelling. They would have a couple of holidays each year to exotic places, but Reggie always took his brown sauce and English mustard with him. They could stay in the most beautiful hotels, but without his mustard he would have been lost. At the end of a break he was desperate to be home, pull on his comfy slippers and have a cup of proper tea.

George broke across the various conversations. "Mum, has the dead rat saga died a death? Excuse the pun."

Jenni raised her hands in pretend frustration. "I really hope so, darling. Jeremy, Kate's husband, had a word. He's the vicar. You remember?" George nodded. He had met Jeremy at the christening, although they hadn't really had a chance to chat. "From what he told us, Anna has agreed to bury the hatchet. We have never really got underneath why she did it. For some reason I irritate her enough for her to take this revenge. Not sure she really wanted to tell Jeremy too much. Think she was embarrassed."

"Well, I think she has got away lightly," replied George. "It could have been devastating for your business, Mum. You could have taken it to the police if you wanted."

With the passage of time Jenni had decided to forgive the silly old woman. She was not a vengeful person and decided holding onto hate was damaging Jenni herself.

"No harm done, George. Footfall has been increasing rapidly since the whole incident. We had a party of seniors in a couple of weeks ago from the Knitting Club and WI. I think they are going to be regulars."

George laughed. "How your world has changed, Mum. The old biddies are now your best customers."

Jenni smiled. Life was vastly different to her way of doing things in Birmingham. She would not change back for all the money in the world. Her confidence in her decision to move to the countryside was undoubted.

"I think I have found my niche, George. In fact, Jimmy decided we should open early on weekdays to catch the commuter traffic. If things carry on the way it's going, then perhaps we will need more staff."

Jenni had a plan. It had been jangling around in her brain for weeks now.

She hadn't really spoken to either of her sons about it yet. It had come out of a few conversations with Richard Samuels. He had a soft spot for Jimmy. They were kindred spirits. The sons who don't like to conform to their family's ideas for their future. Richard had taken Jimmy out on his boat a few weeks back. Jimmy had come home that Sunday evening buzzing. He had loved the feel of the sail rope between his fingers, as Richard put him through his paces. Jimmy was a man who loved to feel the quality of workmanship and had spent all evening telling Jenni what a beautiful boat Richard had.

Richard had floated an idea with Jenni last week and she was seriously considering it. He was willing to take Jimmy on part-time as an apprentice boat builder. Give him the chance to learn a new skill and give him a completely different challenge to the café. Jimmy was only working there because he had to. Jenni knew that wasn't what Jimmy wanted for his life. Circumstances had led him down that route. One day he would fulfil a different dream; Lily permitting.

If Jenni could make the sums add up, perhaps she could bring in someone part-time to manage the café while Jimmy worked at the boatyard. It would take some juggling as they had to think about the café and looking after Lily, but if the money kept rolling in the way it was at the moment, it felt possible.

Jenni's catering business was progressing well too. Florence had started to work with Jenni at some of the events. Jimmy had been true to his word and spoken to Jenni about Flo's ambitions. Jenni was more than happy to help her son's girlfriend gain some experience. It was help that she sorely needed right now. Jenni seemed to have a party every Saturday evening at the moment, which was killing her own social life.

Who was she kidding? She didn't have any sort of social life at the moment. And since Henrique had left for Spain, she had no sex life either. Things had dried up in that department.

But she was happy. For the first time since Reggie died, she could honestly say she was happy. Not just satisfied with her new life in the country. No, she was happy.

Today was a perfect reminder of all the good things she had in her life. She was fortunate to have two wonderful sons who would have made their father incredibly proud. Both sons seemed to be happy with their lives. With Frankie and Flo by their sides, perhaps there were serious relationships on the horizon. Lily Rose was thriving and seemed to cope well with the different people caring for her. She was not a clingy child and, at five months old, was a pleasure to look after. She was already sleeping through the night which was a blessing for both Jimmy and Jenni.

The café was fulfilling a need in Jenni. She loved running the business, coming up with new ideas for bakes and getting to know her regular customers. The catering side of the business had the potential for further growth. The only factor getting in the way of that was time. Jenni really could do with a clone of herself. Sometimes she felt she was stretching herself too thinly, but she would never complain. She simply loved what she was doing.

The only gap in her life was the love of a good man.

But, hey, you can't have everything. Can you?

CHAPTER THIRTY-ONE
THE KING'S HEAD PUB

To the casual observer they might look like three friends just having a drink together. To those who know them, it may seem a little weird. An estranged couple having a drink with a new love interest, who also happens to be husband's best friend.

The casual observer was not to know that this strange situation was becoming fairly comfortable for all three concerned.

Paula and Al had been asked out for a drink with Peter St John. It certainly wasn't an awkward situation for them. And that was all that mattered. They had run the gauntlet of the village gossips and survived. Their unusual relationship was no-one's business but theirs.

Since Peter's brush with the pills, the three friends had reached a form of silent arrangement. They hadn't specifically talked about it. It had just become natural to them. Al lived next door to Peter and kept an eye on his old buddy, always available if Peter had a wobble. Paula and Peter had entered a new stage of their relationship. No longer spouses, their friendship was finding a way to work for both of them.

Peter realised what an amazing woman his wife was. Why he had never seen it before was beyond him. He was working through his demons with talking therapy. And it was helping. He was already a changed man. There was a long journey ahead of him, but it was a journey he was confident he could make on his own. He didn't need Paula as a mental crutch anymore. He had to do this on his own.

Peter had spent a great deal of time examining his relationship, or lack of, with his mother. Many of his issues, especially his lack of respect for women, had their roots in his childhood. He had grown up thinking women were some sort of threat to him. He now realised that he had used women most of his adult life.

He had been an absolute bastard to Paula, putting her down, squashing any self-confidence she had, and being unfaithful to her without a thought for whether his actions would hurt her. The women he had affairs with meant nothing to him and he was ashamed of how he had used these faceless girls. It was bad enough that he treated them with so little respect, but the treatment he had dished out to his loyal wife was unforgivable.

Peter St John was learning to forgive himself.

Last weekend he had taken a huge step in his recovery journey. He had been to see his mum. Despite her lack of empathy for her only son, he had persevered. She really didn't want to listen, but he needed to speak. He had spent too long suppressing his emotions and now was his time to talk. And once he started to talk, he couldn't stop. It didn't take long for his mother to bend to his will and actually listen. By the time he finished talking, they were both in tears. This was no loving reconciliation, but it was an acceptance of the past. His rationale wasn't to hurt his mother. Hate was not a feeling he wanted to keep in his life any longer. He wanted to find forgiveness and reconciliation. Peter needed to heal his own past, and if it brought him and his mother closer together, then so be it.

The three friends had sat in silence for too long as they sipped on their drinks. They were all waiting for someone to start the conversation. Peter had issued the invite so, naturally, Al and Paula decided he wanted to share something. They had no idea what.

Peter cleared his throat, placing his pint on the table before him. "Guys, I need to tell you something."

Al stared at his buddy, while Paula picked at the corner of a beer mat. The tone of Peter's voice was nervous. They had been getting along so well since Peter and Paula had separated, but this was the first time he seemed worried about talking to her. What was wrong? Was he going to raise concerns about her and Al? She didn't want to give up her chance of happiness. It may be her last.

Peter took silence as an unspoken confirmation to continue. "I have got a new job. In Dubai."

"Bloody hell, mate," cried Al. "Dubai? What the fuck?"

Paula didn't say a word. It was a complete shock to her. Peter had worked freelance as an architect for years and had built a formidable reputation across the South-West. Why would he throw that all away on a whim? And Dubai? He had never been keen on the sun. Where the hell had that plan come from?

"Seriously mate, it's amazing money and free accommodation for at least two years. I couldn't think of a reason to turn it down." Peter laughed as he watched Al's face absorbing the news. "And the houses I am designing are being built round a PGA golf course. I get free membership to the course as part of the package. I had to think long and hard over that decision." He smirked at his last remark, heavily weighted with sarcasm.

Peter and Paula had both been keen golfers. Since they had split, Paula had been avoiding the golf club. She just didn't want to face the questions, even though she knew her friends at the club would be understanding and supportive. Golf had been something they had done as a couple. Her enthusiasm for the sport had waned since they split. It was a shared passion, which now lived in the past for her. She even questioned her own love for the sport. Was it something she had done for Peter more than for herself? It certainly wasn't a sport Al was interested in or would share her interest in. His passion lay with football and his beloved Southampton.

"Wow, Peter. That's one hell of an achievement. Congratulations." Paula raised her glass of wine in salute. "When do you start?"

"Thanks, Paula. I'm really excited."

Peter had some reservations about moving abroad, especially with his fragile mental health. He had spoken to his therapist before making the final decision. She had agreed that they could continue his discussions via video calling whenever he needed the support. His therapist also agreed with him that this change of scene may help him more than anything else. Having a fresh challenge to focus his mind on.

"Two weeks' time. Flying out of Heathrow on 3rd December. They are giving me a couple of weeks to get settled in and then it will be full on next year."

"I'm so happy for you, Peter." Paula's words were genuine.

She could see the happiness plastered all over his face. Looking across at Al, she could see the same excitement, but for a different reason. With Peter out of the country, their budding relationship could blossom. Paula had been thinking of asking Al to move in. He spent most of his time at hers anyway so why pay rent on Green Farm Cottage? As her mind turned to their living arrangements, she was suddenly aware of the issue of Laurel House.

"What are we going to do about the house then, Peter?"

Peter's mind had been mulling over that thorny issue for some time now. In fact he had been to see his solicitor earlier that day to finalise his new work contract and to get some advice about his obligations for the matrimonial home.

"Paula, I am going to sign the house over to you as long as you are happy to take on the rest of the mortgage. What do you think?"

Paula gulped as she took in his words. The house must be worth around £700,000 and they only had about £100,000 left to pay on the mortgage. Why would Peter be willing to throw away his share of the equity?

"Peter, are you sure about this? That's a lot of equity to give up. I really don't want you making a rash decision you might regret later?"

Paula was worried that Peter was moving way too fast with the changes to his life. Only months ago he was trying to end everything and now he was packing up and moving abroad. The idea that he could give up everything he had worked so hard for over their years together was a worry. She was uncomfortable about influencing his decisions. Was it all too fast? Was it all too final? Paula was ready to move on, but was Peter's enthusiasm for change false? Was he simply putting a brave face on his troubles and running away?

Peter reached across the table and took Paula's hand between his palm, in a prayer like pose. "Sweetheart, it's what I want. You love that house. It's filled with all your designs as well. And, if I am totally honest with you, the money they are paying for this new job is crazy. I can afford it."

Paula was stunned. Peter had always been the one who was careful with money in the early days of their marriage. This all felt so extreme and different to his normal characteristics. Perhaps spending time examining his own mind and behaviours was having a more drastic impact than she ever imagined.

Al continued to sup on his pint, conscious that this was not a conversation he could really contribute to. But he had an opinion. One he would keep to himself for now. Peter must be earning a small fortune to afford to be this generous. If he was going to seriously sign over the house to Paula, this would be the complete opposite position he found himself in when his ex-wife ran off with her body-builder girlfriend. She had fleeced him for everything she could get.

Not that he was bitter.

Of course not.

Paula didn't really know what to say. Words didn't seem sufficient. She settled for a simple thank you and the offer of another round. Perhaps in the days ahead things would change. She would not get overly excited, just yet, as Peter might say one thing now, but when faced with the legalities of what he was suggesting, his mindset might change.

If he did go through with his promise, things would be quite different for Paula. She could easily afford the mortgage on her income and now she could ask Al to move in without fear of upsetting Peter. The last year had certainly been a time of change for the St John's.

Last Christmas their relationship had reached rock bottom when Peter had assaulted Jenni Sullivan at the village party. Before that they had both been coasting through their marriage on autopilot. They were stuck in an emotional rut. Neither of them could have admitted how unhappy they were. They had done what many middle aged couples do, rub along together and avoid examining the problems too deeply. If Peter hadn't behaved so badly over Jenni, perhaps they would have carried on living their half-lives for ever.

This Christmas, Paula was happier than she had ever imagined. Alaistair was her one true love and she was determined not to waste any more time. She wanted to spend the rest of her life with the man and Peter's determination to move abroad would make everything so much easier. She wasn't being nasty about it, but Peter was doing her the biggest favour. Making the future easy for her.

Paula didn't care a fig for the gossips. They had their fill of it after she threw Peter out and after his suicide attempt. Paula had developed a thick skin to avoid the steely barbs hurting. Anna Fletcher would no doubt find time to spread the rumours when Al moved in. But Paula didn't care. She was going to grab life with both hands and enjoy the next roller coaster ahead.

Tonight had been planned as a friendly drink in the pub with the two significant men in her world. She had never anticipated it ending like this.

But tonight was not about endings.

It was all about new beginnings.

CHAPTER THIRTY-TWO
THE VILLAGE HALL

Music blared from the DJ's speakers, welcoming villagers onto the dance floor. He didn't have to wait for long. The regular offenders were soon up there, strutting their stuff with various degrees of expertise, ranging from none to fairly suspect.

The annual Sixpenny Bissett Christmas party was in full swing. And so very different from last year. The two protagonists from last year's event were absent, a situation remarked on by many attending. It was hoped that this year would be marked only by the number of sore heads on Sunday morning

Peter had already left for Dubai. He had messaged Al earlier that evening, with pictures of his new apartment and, of course, the golf course. Full of boasts about his new life, Peter seemed to have settled in already. He'd even decided to give up drinking completely, something he felt would help in his new Middle Eastern environment and would be a great improvement for his own personal struggles. Prior to his suicide attempt, Peter had got into a downward spiral with his drinking. Far too much and far too often.

Alaistair was happy for his mate who was making big strides forward towards a healthy new life. And more importantly for himself. With Peter out of the way, his life with Paula could really start. That might sound extremely selfish, but Al had waited too long for happiness and was determined to grasp it with both hands.

Jenni had cried off tonight's party. She really didn't want to relive the events of last year. Whilst it was forgotten and forgiven, she didn't want to reopen any wounds. Richard had tried his hardest to encourage her to attend, but she certainly didn't want that particular temptation placed in her path. She was protecting her heart from Richard Samuels and his many attractions.

She had insisted that Jimmy go to the party, while she stayed at home and looked after Lily. A quiet night in with a glass of wine and the latest series on Netflix was all she wanted, for now. How things had changed in the last year, she had smiled to herself.

The DJ changed the beat. The silky tones of Lionel Ritchie and The Commodores enticed couples onto the floor for a slow dance. Three Times a Lady, a beautifully sexy tune had the desired effect. Within seconds the floor was heaving with couples serenading each other. The change in mood was much easier on the eye for DJ Mark. He had just about had enough of the tragic middle-aged thrusting he had been witnessing up until now. But a gig was a gig and Mark could never turn down the lucrative Sixpenny Bissett Christmas do. It was a good earner.

Jimmy grabbed Flo's hand and twirled her into his arms. The music may not be to his taste but spending time with Flo was. Under the critical watch of her parents, he led Flo onto the dance floor. Florence looked amazing tonight. She had chosen a trouser suit in bright red, which fitted her curves, leaving nothing to his imagination. And he was having to live off his imagination for the moment. Out of respect for her youthful age, Jimmy was taking it really slowly. He didn't want to put any pressure on Flo to sleep with him. Even though his body craved for her, just holding her in his arms was taking him places which challenged his abstinence.

When the time was right, it would be worth the wait. For both of them.

Jimmy gently moved his fingers down Flo's back, tracing the track of her zip. His wished he could touch her bare back. He tormented himself with desire. Flo shivered under his touch. Her smile widened. She kissed his neck, as she nuzzled into his shoulder, enjoying the emotion of their dance. The only fly in the ointment was Jacky Smith. Flo could see her mother watching them. Her frostiness would not spoil the couple's first evening together in the glare of the whole village. Flo hadn't mentioned to Jimmy about her mother's disapproval of their relationship.

Irrationally, Flo worried that her mother might scare him off.

Nothing could put Jimmy Sullivan off the beautiful, funny Florence Smith.

As it happened, Flo and Jacky had had a blazing row earlier that evening.

You couldn't tell from the smile on Flo's face. She was putting a brave face on the situation.

Jacky was struggling with her daughter's fascination with Jimmy Sullivan. He was a lovely lad. She liked him, but he was not what she wanted for her only daughter. Jacky certainly didn't approve of Jimmy's past. The fact that he had a daughter by a young woman, who fled the scene and had no interest in the infant, added fuel to her fire. He may well have stepped up and taken responsibility for the poor babe, but that characteristic carried no particular weight in Flo's mother's eyes.

In Jacky's opinion, Jimmy lacked ambition. He seemed to stroll through life living on the goodwill of his dead father. A substantial inheritance still didn't make him a catch for her precious daughter. Jimmy had the job in the café fall in his lap, courtesy of his mother, and he didn't seem in any hurry to better himself. Jacky had never taken the time to talk to Jimmy about his plans for the future. No, she had made her mind up and was determined that her daughter could do so much better.

Jacky's prejudices against Jimmy did nothing to change Florence's mind. She was not going to be swayed by her mother's beliefs. Florence was a strong, determined, young lady and would do exactly what she wanted, despite her mother.

Or was it to spite her mother?

Jimmy sang the words of the song in her ears, seductively. He actually had a reasonable singing voice, which was good. One never wants to be off key when smooching a young lady. This was another first for Jimmy. Flo obviously brought out the romantic in him.

Flo tightened her hold on Jimmy's waist as she buried her face in his neck. Butterfly kisses peppered his nape as Flo's passion rose. Jimmy was keen to keep things going at a slow pace, not realising that Flo was desperate to sleep with him. She had never felt like this before. Jimmy was her future, whatever her mum thought.

Jimmy gently tucked her hair behind her left ear as he whispered, "I love you, Florence."

There he had said it.

He had been trying to pluck up the courage to say that for days. He had been frightened that it was too soon and Flo would be put off with his eagerness. He had never said those words to a female before, unless you count Jenni or Lily. And that was different.

Florence pulled back and looked deeply into his eyes. "Serious?" she whispered back.

"Very."

"I love you too, Jimmy Sullivan." She smiled before kissing him resoundingly on the lips.

Jacky Smith watched on.

Damn that boy, she thought.

****

Last year's Christmas's do had been a truly horrible experience for Paula.

Tonight was completely different. Alaistair was by her side. In fact, he hadn't left her side all evening, except to buy their drinks. They had circulated around numerous villagers, laughing and joking. Most of their friends and acquaintances seemed to accept this new relationship. Both Paula and Alaistair had lived in the village since childhood and Paula had always been a popular member of the community.

Unfortunately, Al had been the butt of many jokes especially after his wife left him, but people are not unkind in principle. Some may say that Alaistair Middleton was punching above his weight with his new relationship, but they wouldn't say it to his face. Others would say, lucky bugger, he deserves some happiness.

"You dancing?" asked Al.

Paula was taken aback. Al was a typical guy who never danced. Even when he was married to Ruby, Paula had never seen him hit the dance floor. She remembered Al and Ruby's wedding. The first dance had been Ruby and her bridesmaids. Perhaps that was an early warning sign that Al really wasn't his wife's type.

"You asking?" Paula tried a cheeky quip.

"I'm asking," he responded.

"I'm dancing," Paula giggled.

Al let rip a deep belly laugh as he took her hand and led her out onto the floor, sliding in between couples. The romantic tunes continued as the sultry tones of George Michael and Careless Whisper started to play.

Al had a firm grip on her bottom as he thrust his crutch towards her. Paula was reminded of those old school disco days. A slow dance comes on and it's an excuse for prepubescent teenagers to grope each other. She wasn't annoyed at her partner's clumsy touch. It was quite endearing. That was Alaistair all over. He was still like a young schoolboy when it came to their relationship. He delighted in making her laugh with all his silly tales and crazy voices.

Paula had never laughed as much in her life as she had since she started seeing Alaistair. Any embarrassment she might have felt, when she got naked with him for the first time, was soon dismissed as he bent over to take off his socks, farted then roared with laughter. Her 'love handle' concerns seemed irrelevant after that. They had fallen into bed, chuckling at their silly inhibitions. The sex was amazing. Far better than they ever imagined.

Falling in love in middle age lowers expectations but heightens passion, in Paula's opinion.

Since then their love life had gone from strength to strength. Paula now knew what it felt like to be loved, deeply, madly, seriously. Alaistair was her soul mate and she was committed to repairing his heart, broken by Ruby. She would make him trust again.

"Al, are you going to move in with me?" she shouted in his ear, trying to compete with the music.

Alaistair hadn't seen that one coming. After Peter had dropped the bombshell about moving abroad, things had moved quickly. Solicitor and banker had taken Peter's offer and completed all the necessary paperwork. And now Paula was the sole owner of Laurel House.

Why would she want to give up her independence so soon?

Al stroked her cheek as he gazed into her eyes. "Are you serious, Paula love?"

"I have never been more serious about anything in my life," she smiled. "You mean everything to me, Alaistair. I have wasted far too much time already. My future is with you."

Al nodded. He understood exactly what she meant. They had both survived toxic relationships and now was their time. He had no hesitation about moving in with Paula, if she would have him.

And he didn't give a damn what the gossip had to say on the matter.

****

Kate was enjoying herself despite Jenni's absence.

She was always the life and soul of the annual Christmas party. Without Jenni by her side and with Paula otherwise engaged, it fell on Jeremy to keep his wife under control this evening. And Kate needed a firm hand tonight.

The last few months had been a roller-coaster for Kate. The Rat-Gate incident had been regarded as one of the funniest things to have happened in Sixpenny Bissett in many a year. But the impact on Kate had been unseen by most of the village. Jenni had a good idea and, of course, Jeremy had been on the receiving end of her temper.

Kate had spent far too many sleepless nights in recent months, worrying about their financial future. A vicar's salary was not great. It was a vocation. People don't join the church to make money. With two growing teenagers their outgoings were increasing rapidly. Kate and Jeremy did not indulge the children especially when it came to designer gear. But just keeping their growing bodies in clothes put a strain on their funds.

On top of the normal financial worries, had been the threat to the store's income. Once the café had opened, foot flow into the store had almost doubled. Kate was making enough money to pay Claire's salary and take a small monthly wage herself. She had started to relax and look towards a more prosperous future.

That nasty woman, Anna Fletcher, had nearly scuppered all her plans. People may now laugh about what happened, but Kate couldn't. It wasn't funny at all.

Tonight, Kate was determined to let her hair down and forget her worries. She didn't care about the size of the hangover tomorrow.

"Come on, Jeremy." She grabbed her husband's hand and started to pull him towards the dance floor. "Let's dance."

Jeremy could have quite happily sat at one of the tables, nursing a beer. But it was wonderful to see his wife so happy and carefree tonight.

He could not let her down.

CHAPTER THIRTY-THREE
ROSE COTTAGE

They had only just sat down to lunch when they were interrupted by the sound of the front door knocker. A loud boom breaking the silence.

"Bloody hell, who is that?" sighed Jimmy. His plate was loaded with succulent roast beef and all the trimmings. He was seriously salivating at the thought of diving right in.

It was a brave person who got between Jimmy and his Sunday lunch.

"Would you, darling?" Jenni was seated at the furthest end of the dining table so it made sense for her son to answer the door.

Jimmy pushed his chair back in frustration, his eyes still fixated on his food. He was burning the image into his brain, to keep him going whilst he got rid of the rude interruption. People just don't make house calls during Sunday lunchtime. It's just not cricket. Doing an impression of Harry Enfield's Kevin, Jimmy slumped his shoulders as he strode down the hallway.

Jenni suppressed a giggle as she watched him. Her son, a dad, who could still be a stroppy teenager at heart.

Jimmy put his shoulder to the front door, easing the lock. Another job that needed looking at. The solid wooden door always seemed to stick and required a push to get the key to turn. As he pulled the door open, his face dropped with surprise.

On the doorstep stood Charlie.

She looked amazing. Her hair, which had been long and straggly, had been shaved, leaving only the slightest hint of stubble. She had lost weight and was back to her pre-pregnancy slender frame. Wearing shorts, unusual for the weekend before Christmas, and a hoodie, she gave the appearance of someone who had literally just got off a transatlantic flight and had completely forgotten what the weather in the UK might be at this time of year.

Jimmy continued to stare in wonder at the vision in front of him. Could it really be Charlie? She looked full of life and happy. Gone was the frowning face and miserable countenance, which he remembered so well. She had a glow about her which he remembered from when they had first got together in South America. The sight of his ex hit him in the solar plexus making him gasp.

"Are you going to let me in?" Charlie didn't say it unkindly. There was a happy tone to her voice. She was simply being practical. She was freezing cold and couldn't wait to get into the house.

"Course," muttered Jimmy. Standing to one side, he ushered Charlie in, slamming the door behind her. "What the fuck, Charlie?"

Jenni had heard Lily's mum's voice and rushed through to the hallway. Like her son, she was struck dumbfounded by the change in Charlie's appearance. Her heart sank as she wondered why Charlie was here. Please do not break my son's heart by taking Lili away, was her first thought. Or my heart, came a fast second thought. She could not bear to live without Lily in her life. When Jenni had first been faced with the knowledge she was to become a grandmother, she was surprised and decided she wasn't ready for such a change in her life. But once the baby was placed in her arms, she knew a love which held no boundaries.

"Charlie, you must be freezing. Come in. We were just having dinner. Are you hungry?" Jenni motioned the girl towards the dining room.

"Thanks Jenni. I could eat a horse. Been flying for hours and you know how shit airline food is."

Charlie strolled into the dining room as if she hadn't a care in the world, totally oblivious to the shock of her audience. She pulled out her normal chair, opposite Jimmy and sat, waiting for Jenni to serve her. The confidence, bordering on arrogance, of the girl's behaviour was certainly confusing. She seemed to have forgotten that she walked out of his house, taking Jenni's car. This was the girl who left her baby in the middle of the night with no explanation. And now she strolled back as if nothing had happened. Both Jenni and Jimmy were thinking the same. The girl has some front, that was for sure.

Charlie looked around the room as she waited for her food, obviously looking for her daughter. Jimmy had no intention of making things easy for her. He had put Lily down in her cot before they sat down to eat. She would sleep for a couple of hours. The last thing he wanted was to encourage Charlie to see her daughter and allow any maternal feelings to fledge.

Jimmy's appetite had vanished.

He watched as Charlie enthusiastically gobbled down her food, without saying a word. Meanwhile both Jimmy and Jenni pushed the cooling beef and vegetables around their plates, watching Charlie. Neither of them had the courage to ask why she was here. Putting it into words may make things real, something they were frightened to hear. The silence in the room was palpable, other than the crunching of Charlie's teeth as she devoured a crispy roast potato.

"So where is Lily?" Charlie stretched back in her chair, clicking the bones in her fingers. Jimmy hated that habit and today of all days, it was enough to grind his gears.

Trying to stay calm, he responded, "asleep."

"I want to see her. Go get her."

Charlie's attitude over Lily was the final straw as far as Jenni was concerned. That girl had no idea about baby routine and the importance of an afternoon nap. She had been absent from her daughter's life for most of it and, as far as Jenni was concerned, she had no right to interfere in how they were caring for her.

"Now look here, Charlie. You can't just rock up into my house after months and demand anything. You left that baby without even saying goodbye. You took my car without even asking and then jetted off to Spain without a backward glance. Do you realise what Jimmy has had to give up to take on sole parenthood of Lily? Do you?"

Jenni was shouting as she finished her tirade. She was just so incredibly angry with the arrogance more than anything. If Charlie had arrived contrite and seeking forgiveness then the conversation might have started so very differently.

Charlie was taken aback.

She had never seen Mrs Sullivan look so pissed off. It was perhaps the shock she needed to get her back on track. All through the long flight back from India she had been playing various scenarios through her head. She didn't know what sort of reception she was likely to receive and this was definitely not how she had seen things playing out. She had decided that if she acted all confident and gave the impression she had finally got her life together then perhaps Jenni would respect her and forgive her night-time flight.

She had misread the room, that's for sure.

"Look, I'm sorry, Jenni. I'm being an arse. I was just so worried about how you and Jimmy might be with me. Guess I came across too cocky." Charlie smiled sheepishly at Jenni.

"We were so worried about you, love." Jenni looked directly at the mother of her grandchild as she spoke. Jimmy continued to stare at his plate of congealing gravy rather than direct his gaze at the woman who had left her daughter so soon after giving birth. "We didn't know what to do when you left. I know you must have been unhappy, but it was such a shock to me and Jimmy. We tried to talk to your parents, but they wanted nothing to do with us."

"My parents are bastards." Charlie's eyes had started to fill with tears. "They don't want to know me, with or without Lily. I rang Mum when I landed and she couldn't wait to get me off the phone. Basically told me I wasn't welcome at home." Charlie slumped in the chair as the tears fell silently down her cheek.

Jenni couldn't help it. She felt sorry for the girl. Nobody deserved parents like the Wrights. They didn't seem to have a sympathetic bone in their bodies. Pushing her chair back, Jenni walked over to Charlie and motioned for her to get up. She enveloped her in a hug, squeezing tightly. Jenni rubbed her hand in a circular motion across her back, similar to the comforting gesture she gave Lily, when the baby had wind.

"There, there." Jenni's soothing voice did the trick.

The pent up emotions Charlie must have been holding on to for months were let forth in a torrent of tears. The girl cried as if her heart was breaking. Jenni held her close and let the pain wash out of her, while Jimmy continued to sit awkwardly, wishing he was anywhere else than here right now. A year's worth of tears needed washing out of Charlie. She had tried to be strong, all the way to Dorset, but the kindness of Jenni was her undoing. She had hated Jenni for long periods of time, but she was more of a mother to her than her own biological one.

Once the crying slowed, Jenni released the girl from her embrace and took a tissue from her pocket. Gently wiping away her tears, she kissed Charlie on the cheek. "Come on, sweetheart. Nothing is ever as bad as you think. Shall we sit down and you can tell me and Jimmy all about it."

It took some time for Charlie to gather her thoughts. She knew that it was important to be honest with Jenni and Jimmy. They had been the only adults who had shown her respect and love in recent years. She owed them an explanation, whether they would understand it or not. She took a deep breath.

"I didn't want Lily. I'm sorry, that sounds awful, but I hated every minute of being pregnant and when she was born, I just couldn't love her." Charlie was ripping the tissue to shreds in her fingers, pieces dropping onto the carpet. "I tried to. You have to believe me. I used to sit there for hours looking at her and hoping I could change. Hoping love would suddenly flick on like a light switch and I would care about her. But it didn't."

Jenni waited for a pause in her dialogue. "You probably were suffering from postnatal depression, Charlie love. We could see something wasn't right and, perhaps we are at fault as we didn't get you the help you needed."

"Don't ever blame yourself, Jenni," Charlie broke in with passion. "I couldn't have asked for a kinder mother-in-law." She used her fingers to indicate quotation marks around that title. "I am just so deeply sorry I let you down. And you, Jimmy. I know we were never in love, but I did care for you. I just wish it could all have been so very different."

Jimmy was gripping the edge of his seat. He really didn't like the way this conversation was going. There was no way he wanted Charlie back in his life. Not now he was madly in love with Florence. But the thing that was worrying him most was Lily. More importantly, Lily's future. Would Charlie fight for custody of their child? Wouldn't the courts look more favourably on the natural mother rather than the father? He really could not bear the thought of losing his daughter.

He would never let that happen.

The conversation was interrupted by the baby monitor. The sound of Lily's cries filled the room. Jimmy was on his feet and across the room before anyone else could react. He needed a moment alone with his daughter before he faced her mother again. As he lifted Lily out of her cot, he cuddled her to his chest. Forgetting the monitor was on, he whispered, "No-one will take you away from me, Lily Rose. You are mine." He kissed his daughter's frown away as he made a slow walk back to the dining room.

Charlie's stunned face greeted him along with a slow shake of the head from his mother. "I'm not going to take Lily away from you, Jimmy," said Charlie. "I promise." She walked towards him. "Can I hold her though?"

Jimmy glanced at his mother with a worried look in his eye.

"You forgot the baby monitor, love," sighed Jenni.

"Sorry, Mum," groaned Jimmy. "But I'm not sorry, Charlie. I mean it. I am not losing my daughter."

Jenni was conscious that the atmosphere in the room was on a knife-edge. "Come and sit down in the lounge, Charlie," Jenni said. "Then you can hold Lily a bit more comfortably. She has grown since you held her last." Jenni smiled, trying to break the tension in the room.

They watched intently as Lily lay quietly in her mother's arms. The baby seemed to be examining this new person's face. Lily was never normally this quiet when she first woke from her nap. She had been stunned into silence. Charlie gazed in wonder at her daughter, examining the changes in her features. Lily was almost six months old and had started to develop her own character, especially her expressions. She was so hugely different from the week old baby Charlie had left behind.

Jenni reached across and took Jimmy's hand, giving it a supportive squeeze. Glancing from Charlie to Jimmy, Jenni could see the tension on her son's face as he watched this intimate moment between mother and daughter. The look of devastation on her son's face was heart-wrenching.

Charlie had every right to meet Lily, but that didn't stop Jimmy's heart from being in turmoil. He had become so used to being a sole parent with all the challenges that brought. One of the big advantages of that solo state was that he, and he alone, was responsible for his daughter's future. He could shape her life and protect her from anything or anyone who might hurt her.

He did not want to share her. There, he had admitted it. He did not want Charlie back in his daughter's life. Did that make him some sort of bastard?

He looked towards his Mum. She would know how to handle this better than him. He would speak far too frankly and perhaps make the whole situation worse. This needed the careful handling his mother was an expert at. She nodded, passing a silent message of reassurance to her son.

Jenni took a seat next to Charlie on the couch. Charlie raised her eyes to Lily's grandmother and smiled. Her face showed a newfound love for her baby. This was going to be harder than Jenni had ever expected. Whilst she was keen to reintroduce Lily to her mother, the last thing she wanted was further disruption to her granddaughter's short life. She needed stability and continuity.

"Charlie, sweetheart, I know this is incredibly hard for you, but we do need to talk about Lily and what's best for her. You do understand that, don't you?" Jenni was choosing her words carefully. "She is settled here."

Lily had taken one of Charlie's fingers in her hand. It was a beautiful sight even though it was killing Jenni inside. Seeing the joy on the young woman's face made this so much more difficult.

"I know, Jenni. I don't want to take Lily away from Jimmy. You have to believe me. But I want to be involved in my daughter's life. In some way."

Jenni relaxed slightly at Charlie's words. Perhaps there was a way to navigate through the emotions to get to some sort of practical solution.

Looking at her son, trying to get a feel for his views, Jenni continued to explore Charlie's mind on the matter. At least if they knew what she wanted, they could try and make some sort of compromise. "Where are you planning to live, Charlie? And what about work?" The practicalities were always a good place to start, Jenni decided.

Charlie stroked Lily's head, not even raising her eyes to meet Jenni's. "Look my parents are bastards, but they have money. Mum was so keen to get me off the phone that she has offered me ten grand to stay away. I was thinking of renting somewhere nearby, if I can find some place. Then I will find a job."

Jenni nodded slowly, her mind jumping around with thoughts pinging at her randomly. She considered Thomas Hadley's farm cottage which Peter had been living in. Perhaps that was too close for comfort. Before she could say a word Charlie continued.

"I was thinking of finding somewhere in Southampton. I know it's not on the doorstep, but there is more chance of finding a job there. I can travel back here when I want to see Lily by train. I've got a couple of viewings tomorrow and I have a car hire until Wednesday so I was wondering if I could kip down here tonight. Promise I will be out of your hair tomorrow."

Jenni heard the sigh of relief from her son as Jimmy slumped onto the other sofa, opposite Charlie. "We can talk about when you can see Lily once you are settled," mumbled Jimmy. "It will be here, though. I'm not having her moved to Southampton."

His phone pinged with a text and without a word to either woman, he started to scroll.

"Of course you can stay tonight, Charlie," Jenni answered. "I will make up the spare room. I'm sure we can find a way to make this work for all of us. The most important person is Lily. As long as we all focus on what's best for her, I'm sure we can work this out."

Charlie was glowering at Jimmy who refused to make eye contact. She felt she was making big concessions and wasn't feeling the love coming back. If it hadn't been for Jenni and her understanding, Charlie would have been even more angry.

Jimmy stood up. "I'm going out," he grunted.

"Jimmy, we haven't had pudding yet," sighed Jenni. Things weren't fully resolved yet and she could really do with her son being a bit more understanding. The last thing she wanted was Charlie getting difficult. They would have to navigate some troubled waters ahead and Jimmy going all caveman was not going to help.

"Don't want any. I'm going to see Flo."

Jenni stared at her son's back as he flounced down the hallway. I guess it will be up to me then to tell Charlie about Florence, she thought.

Bloody kids. It doesn't get any easier.

CHAPTER THIRTY-FOUR
THE KING'S HEAD PUB

The pub was closed after the lunchtime rush. Jimmy headed for the backdoor.

Florence was waiting for him and threw herself into his arms. She squeezed him tight to her body, moulding her shape to his. Since Jimmy had confessed his love for her, Florence wanted to be with him every waking hour. Practicalities got in the way of that, but as soon as she was free from her waitressing duties, she had texted Jimmy and he had come running.

She had an ulterior motive too. Richard Samuels had been in the pub for his usual Sunday roast. Florence had overheard him tell her father that Charlie had turned up at the Sullivan's. He had seen her pull up in a car outside Rose Cottage as he was strolling down to the pub. Florence's head was all over the place with that news. What the hell was she doing back in Sixpenny Bissett? She better not want Jimmy back.

Florence was not giving him up without a serious fight.

Before he could utter a word of explanation, she kissed him. A kiss full of promise. Her tongue probed into his mouth, exploring and tasting him. A mixture of roast beef and red wine sprung into her mind. She ran her fingers through his hair, stroking the back of his ears. She knew that would get him going. He shuddered as she hit the sweet spot.

"Oh Flo, it's so bloody good to see you," gasped Jimmy as he came up for air. "Your message arrived just at the right time too."

"Why? What's up, Jimmy?" Flo certainly wasn't going to let on she knew about Charlie. She convinced herself she wasn't being dishonest. Florence didn't want him thinking that he was being talked about in the pub. She knew how sensitive Jimmy was about such things.

"Bloody Charlie. That's what. Stupid cow is back."

Jimmy jumped up backwards on to the worksurface. They were in the pub's kitchen. Luckily, Mr and Mrs Smith were not to be seen. He would never have entertained the thought of sitting on the worktop if Jacky had been around.

Florence joined him, grabbing his hand. "What do you mean she is back?" Her voice trembled as she secretly dreaded his response. Would she have to fight for her happiness?

"Strolled back in, bold as brass, and says she wants to get to know Lily. Over my fucking dead body." The anger seeped from Jimmy as he swung his legs back and forth. "There is no way she is taking Lily off me."

Suddenly he slumped forward with his head in his hands. Florence initially just watched, shocked at his words. How could Charlie turn the motherly feelings on and off like a light switch. It just wasn't natural. Then she noticed Jimmy's shoulders slowly heaving. She realised he was crying. Florence reached out for him and Jimmy grabbed hold of her as if she were a lifejacket, saving him from a turbulent sea. His body shook with emotion as he clung to her.

Over his shoulder, Flo saw her dad come into the room. With silent signals she waved him away. Luckily, Geoff could read the situation and he retreated quietly, saving Jimmy's blushes. Geoff had a soft spot for Jimmy Sullivan. He understood that Jacky wanted better for their only daughter, but that was not a feeling he shared. He respected the lad for stepping up and taking responsibility for his little Lily. From what he had seen, Jimmy was a natural father and what guy doesn't want a kind and gentle man for their only daughter. Florence could not go far wrong with Jimmy, in Geoff's opinion. Let's hope the arrival of Charlie wasn't going to screw things up for his precious darling.

Gradually the sobs subsided. Jimmy wiped them away on his sleeve, looking embarrassed at his show of emotion. "Sorry Flo. What an arse." He tried to laugh as if to dismiss what had just happened.

Florence kissed his cheek, still wet from his tears. "Never apologise for showing how much you care about Lily. It's one of the reasons I love you so much." She squeezed his hand then entwined her fingers in his.

"I love you too, Florence Smith. I don't know what I would do without you."

She looked into his eyes with an intensity. They needed to talk about this seriously though. She would never want to play second fiddle to Charlie Wright and if Jimmy had any such feelings for the mother of his child, then she needed to know that now.

"So what does Charlie want? Does she want to get back with you?"

Jimmy laughed. "Fucking hell, Flo. Can you imagine." He doubled over as he belly laughed. "Well, she certainly didn't say she wanted me back, but if she had done, she would have been sorely disappointed. I do not love her, never have and never will. So please, don't worry about that."

Flo tried to keep things light and made the sign of wiping sweat from her brow. "Phew. I didn't fancy fighting her for you. She's a tough cookie. Think she could floor me in a fist fight." Florence was waif-like compared to Charlie, although she would give it a good go, especially if Jimmy was the prize.

"I left her with Mum to sort things out. She reckons she's going to get a place to stay in Southampton, get a job and then come and see Lily when she wants." Jimmy seemed to be gazing into space as he spoke.

"And how do you feel about that, babe?"

He shrugged. "Southampton is good. Far enough away. I guess I can't stop her from seeing Lily. She is her mother, even if she doesn't behave like it. But there is one thing I will insist on. If she wants to spend time with Lily then she does it with me in control. I'm not having her swanning off to Southampton with her. Not until I can trust her. And I don't trust. Not yet."

"That sounds sensible, Jimmy." Flo kissed his cheek again, reassuringly. "You have got to protect Lily. Who knows she may bond with her and then you guys can come to a sensible arrangement. But with her track record, she may just find it all too much and bugger off again."

That scenario was what Florence secretly wished for. Okay, it wasn't fair on Lily, but did she really need a mum like that when she had Jimmy, Jenni and, of course, herself? Florence loved Lily almost as much as if she were her own. In her mind she pictured her and Jimmy living happily ever after with baby Lily. That was her dream and she was damned if Charlie was going to ruin that. If Charlie was determined to be part of her daughter's life, she would have to accept Jimmy's new relationship. Like it or not.

"Anyway, when's she leaving for Southampton?" Florence could not wait to see the back of her rival.

"Think tomorrow morning. Mum is letting her stay over tonight."

Florence gasped. "She better not try to sneak into your room tonight." She giggled, trying to disguise her true thoughts.

"Don't you worry, Flo. I'm locking my door and sleeping with one eye open." Jimmy reached for his girlfriend, hugging her firmly. "And I'm sleeping with the baby monitor so if she tries anything with Lily, she will have me to contend with."

It might sound like Jimmy was joking, but there was a serious point behind his words. His mother might be the most trusting woman in the world, but Jimmy had a huge dose of scepticism bubbling under the surface. Charlie might be a changed woman. She might want to get to know her daughter, now the heavy lifting of the early months was over. Any changes to her relationship with Lily would have to be agreed with Jimmy.

He didn't think Lily needed her mother. Charlie might think she needs Lily, but her daughter didn't even know her. If she had never come back, Lily would have grown up with little or no knowledge of the woman who carried her for nine months. In Jimmy's mind, carrying the baby was the easy part. Picking up sole responsibility for the baby, and surrounding her world with love, was the important part of being a parent.

Jimmy would not forgive Charlie easily for abandoning his daughter and he certainly would take some convincing to trust her again.

CHAPTER THIRTY-FIVE
ROSE COTTAGE

Jenni eased herself back in her chair, lifting her tired feet onto the footstall. It had been a wonderful day, having her family around her to celebrate the festive season. So very different from her first Christmas in Sixpenny Bissett, when she only had George for company.

Slowly she surveyed the room, observing the damage of the post-Christmas festivities. Wrapping paper lay where it had landed. Half empty wine glasses and the remains of a tub of Quality Street sat on the coffee table. George and Frankie were curled up together on the opposite sofa, Frankie resting her head on her boyfriend's chest.

George was clearly asleep and catching flies, with his mouth flopped open. The odd snore escaped his mouth and with each snort, Frankie smiled. This was the traditional post-dinner position for George, a testament to the huge meal Jenni had prepared for the family. Frankie was watching TV, trying her hardest to keep her eyes open. The seemingly annual rerun of ET filled the screen, a bit of easy watching for the family. Although Jenni wasn't sure if any of them where really watching. It was purely background noise.

Jimmy and Florence had taken ownership of the other sofa. Florence had only just made her entrance, after having lunch with her parents. Their relationship wasn't yet at the stage that either of them could forgo the mandatory family duties. Florence had tiptoed into the lounge, kissing Jenni on route and wishing her a Happy Christmas. She was such a considerate young lady. Adamant that she didn't want to wake up George, she insisted that Jimmy hold off her presents until he woke. Jimmy was itching to do more present unwrapping.

The kid in him loved Christmas with a passion. Never mind that he was now a father. It purely meant double the excitement for him as he could open Lily's presents too.

The young couple sat together on the sofa holding hands, whilst Jimmy cradled Lily in his arms. Lily had joined her uncle in a snooze. Jenni watched the three of them together and could see the future with greater clarity. They were made for each other and Florence would be a perfect role model for Lily as she grew up. As long as they could navigate the turbulent seas ahead, theirs could be a strong relationship. It wasn't going to be easy for the young couple to make things work, but Jenni felt confident that they had a strong foundation to build on.

Jenni was reflecting back over the last week. Life was never dull in the Sullivan household. The last week was yet another example of that. Since she had moved to Sixpenny Bissett, there didn't seem to be a day when her world wasn't spinning in one direction or another. It was enough to give you motion sickness.

The last week had been no exception.

Charlie, arriving back, had been a seismic shock, the impact of which was not entirely certain yet. That Sunday evening had been particularly fraught. Jimmy had disappeared for most of the afternoon and, when he did show his face, had behaved in a fairly monosyllabic way, grunting responses to questions. He made it abundantly clear that Charlie was not welcome. Giving her due credit, Jenni was impressed with Charlie and the way she had tried to bridge the gap between her and Lily's father. There had been an awful lot of hurt between the two young people. It was a huge gap to bridge, but Charlie seemed determined to try.

Jenni had not slept a wink Sunday night.

She was worried about what the future held for her family. Lying in bed, tossing and turning, she tried to sort out the problems in her head. Unfortunately, she was a bit part player in the decisions about Lily's future. She could influence and have her say, but ultimately, it was down to Charlie and Jimmy to agree a way forward.

Jenni could sense the pain oozing from her son as he feared that Lily would be taken from him. She wished she could make things right for Jimmy. She didn't own a magic wand so would have to settle for being there for him.

She would catch him should he fall and she hoped, with all her heart, she wouldn't need to do that. That child was Jimmy's purpose in life now. He had thrown himself into being a father when he hadn't really wanted the trappings of parenthood. And he was doing a really decent job of it. Lily was happy and contented, which is really all anyone wanted for a baby's first year.

However, Jenni could see a need burning in Charlie which hadn't been there before. In the week after Lily's birth there appeared to be a lack of motherly feelings displayed by Charlie. She looked disinterested and completely at a loss to know how to interact with the poor little mite. Watching her holding Lily now was completely different. Her initial nerves were soon replaced with a newfound confidence. She had held Lily the rest of that afternoon, even having a go at changing a nappy, a whole new experience.

When it had come to bath time, Jimmy had grudgingly agreed to let Charlie help. Jenni had stepped away, seeing this as an opportunity for the two parents to find some common ground. And that common ground proved to be Lily Rose. Standing at the bottom of the stairs she had overheard the squeals of laughter from Charlie as Lily splashed the water. What surprised Jenni was hearing Jimmy's laughter too.

Jenni had smiled and left them to it, grabbing a glass of wine and settling down to watch TV. Perhaps there was light at the end of the tunnel and that could be compromise. Always the hardest action when the love of a child is at stake.

The following morning Charlie appeared distraught at the thought of leaving her daughter behind and travelling to Southampton. She had cried as they parted and only agreed to get in the car once Jenni promised to text her every day with an update on Lily's progress. Jimmy had been running the café that Monday morning so was excused from seeing Charlie off. Which was probably for the best. Despite the bath time fun the previous night, there remained a tension between the parents which needed careful handling.

As Charlie got into her car, Jenni had spotted Florence watching on. The girl looked troubled to see Lily's mum. Jimmy had purposedly kept the two women apart the previous night. He had told Charlie about Flo, but the last thing he wanted was for them to see each other. As the car drove slowly down the high street, Florence could not hide the feelings of relief, displayed across her face.

After Charlie had left there had been little time for Jenni to talk to her son about the future. The café was heaving with the build up to Christmas. Trade was brisk. Any hangover from 'Rat-Gate' had been well and truly forgotten. Jenni had never known business to be this good. Jimmy and Jenni had been working flat out right up until Christmas Eve. All thoughts about the difficult future ahead had to wait.

Charlie had been in touch with Jenni to tell her that she had found a flat. Well, to be precise, it was a room in a flat, but well within her budget and also fully furnished. She'd also managed to sign up to a temp agency and had a job lined up to start after Christmas. At least the girl was being true to her word. Sticking around for the sake of Lily may have given her some much wanted structure in her life. Jenni still could not believe how dreadful Mr and Mrs Wright must be. How can any parent turn away from their child? No matter what they had done.

Charlie was coming to Sixpenny Bissett for the day tomorrow so she could spend some time with Lily. Trying to be as supportive as possible, Jenni had planned a long walk across the valley with a stop at The Gundog pub for lunch, allowing Charlie to have the house and, more importantly, Lily to herself. That hadn't gone down well. Jenni and Jimmy had a huge row over that decision. He really wasn't ready to trust Charlie alone with their daughter, and he was pissed with his mum for agreeing to it. He actually called Jenni an interfering old cow, which had hurt. Eventually Jenni had managed to persuade him that by being reasonable now, they might prevent things becoming difficult in the future. It would be a long time before Charlie had the means to look after Lily alone, so Jimmy's position as principal carer was safe for now, at least.

The interfering old cow comment hung between them for the rest of that day like a miasma.

The coming weeks ahead were going to be difficult for Jenni and her family. Their world had been centred around Lily for the last six months. Just Jenni and Jimmy, wrapping the little girl up with love and attention to make up for a lack of her mother's presence. Now the three would have to find a way of accommodating a fourth person on the periphery.

And of course there was now Florence to be considered.

Jenni adored Flo. She was just right for her son. She might be young in years but was mature in heart. She brought out the best qualities in Jimmy, who had been a different man since he and Flo had become close. Due to the objections of Florence's mother, Jacky, the couple spent more and more time at Rose Cottage. Jenni was not a prude, hell her relationship with Henrique could testify to that, but she wasn't sure she could cope yet with Florence staying over. The last thing Jenni had wanted was to fall out with Jacky.

So a difficult conversation had been had with her son. Jimmy, being Jimmy, had not made it easy for her. Acting dumb, before playing the fool, had ended in Jenni slapping him around the head and telling him, no sex when your mother is in the house. What you get up to when I'm not around is up to you, she had said. At least then she didn't have to lie to Jacky Smith.

And wear a condom, had been her parting shot.

CHAPTER THIRTY-SIX
ROSE COTTAGE

They had finally left.

After the noisy chaos of Jenni, the boys and Frankie struggling into boots and coats, there was silence. Charlie lent against the door, sighing deeply. For the next few hours it was just her and her daughter.

She was frightened and excited in equal measures. Not being alone with Lily since her return, she was worried that she would fail. What if Lily screamed the house down when she found out she was being cared for by a stranger. Of course, she didn't let on her fears to Jenni or Jimmy. She pretended confidence, and they had believed her, so it seemed.

Lily was asleep in her Moses basket in the lounge. Luckily, Jimmy had only just finished giving her a bottle before Charlie had arrived so she decided she had a few moments to herself before she should wake Lily up. The last thing she wanted was for her daughter to be all grouchy.

Strolling into the kitchen with a confidence she really didn't possess, Charlie made herself a cup of tea. It seemed strange to be in Jenni's house alone and making herself at home. Quietly, she tiptoed into the lounge. Sitting on the sofa, she watched Lily breathing in and out as she slept. She looked so peaceful and content. In her heart she knew what a fantastic job Jimmy had done. He had really stepped up. Not that she could tell him that, just yet. It still felt too raw.

As she watched her daughter sleep, she reflected over the last six months.

Charlie wasn't proud of herself for leaving Lily when she did. The last year or so had been crazy for Charlie. She had been desperate to escape the UK after university, mainly because she couldn't bear the idea of going back home to live with her parents. She hated her mum and dad. The feeling seemed to be fairly mutual. Honestly, why they had even had her was beyond belief. They clearly didn't want children so she figured she was a mistake, which they resented interfering with their life. Her mum and dad were totally disinterested in her. The fact that she obtained a first class degree in computer science didn't even merit any sort of congratulations from her parents.

Charlie had nothing to anchor her to home. She had no idea what she wanted to do career-wise and travelling seemed an obvious choice. Her parents' typical behaviour was to throw money at a problem. She was a problem. Which was quite fortunate as they were generous in her travel fund. Charlie lacked close female friends and decided that travelling alone was her only option. It never entered her mind that, if her mother loved her, she might have been worried about her only daughter travelling the world on her own. No. Out of sight, out of mind. Her mum never tried to contact her whilst she was away. She could have been dead for all they cared.

It was in Argentina that Charlie had met Jimmy. He really wasn't her type. Not that she knew what her type was. She hadn't had a serious boyfriend before and only had sex a few times at university. She was far too busy studying to bother with boys. Jimmy was like a whirlwind crashing into her life. He was funny, clumsy, and incredibly adorable. She had fallen for him far too quickly.

A few drunken nights had led to them sleeping together. Charlie wasn't on the pill. She had never needed to bother with that and she had just assumed that Jimmy was using protection. That's what happens when you assume. 'It makes an ass out of you and me'.

When Jimmy had asked her to go to Australia with him, she didn't hesitate. He was fun and she was totally into him. They had only been in Australia a few weeks when she started to feel sick and realised that she hadn't had a period for a few months. Why she had kept things quiet from Jimmy, until it was almost too late to abort the baby, was something she still struggled with.

She didn't want a baby. It wasn't part of the plan. She wasn't even sure whether her and Jimmy were working any more. The early glow of the relationship had diminished into a small flicker. She didn't want a baby, but the thought of killing it tormented her. That was one decision she did not regret. Lily deserved to live, even if her mother was an absolute failure.

Once Charlie was back home, living with Jenni, the rot had really settled in. She felt an outsider in Sixpenny Bissett. Jimmy wasn't interested in her. Jenni put up with her. And the village was in the backend of beyond. She regretted her decision to come home, to have the baby. She wasn't ready to be a mum, but the thing growing inside her had to come out. Somehow.

When Lily was born, she felt nothing. She had waited for a rush of love. But nothing. She could see the love splashed across Jimmy's face. He had never looked at Charlie the way he looked at his new daughter. It was just another reminder of how alone in the world she was. The way Jenni looked at Lily was beautiful, full of love, pride, and joy, but Charlie felt nothing at all. That's why she ran. She couldn't bear to sit and watch those two adore the baby, while she felt nothing.

It made her feel even more of an outsider.

The change to her attitude happened in India. She joined a retreat out in the countryside near Kerala. It was all a bit hippy with a lot of contemplation of her navel, yoga, and meditation. Charlie unpacked her life and started to sort through it. She examined her mistakes. She examined her relationships, especially that with her parents. All of a sudden, she realised that Lily was not to blame for her awful bond with her mum and dad. Lily did not deserve an absent mother. Charlie needed to face up to her responsibilities

Coming back had been hard.

Jenni had been amazing. She welcomed her back into her home without any animosity, well except for an initial outburst, which had been Charlie's fault. She fully deserved the reaction to her cocky approach. But Jenni was quick to forgive. She really was a decent woman.

Jimmy didn't want her there, that was clear. She knew it was going to be difficult, but she wasn't prepared for his hatred. Especially as he looked amazing. She couldn't get over the changes in Jimmy. He had grown up. He had a new-found confidence which oozed from him. She actually quite fancied him again. But she was too late. Florence had muscled in on her territory.

She was jealous.

Seeing Florence had been a shock to her system. The girl was stunning and clearly mad about Jimmy. Charlie had seen her when she was leaving the house to drive down to Southampton. Glaring across the street, as if she was warning Charlie not to mess with her man. It was a reminder that there was no way back to Jimmy.

That boat had definitely sailed.

Her thoughts were interrupted by Lily's snuffles. Reaching into the basket, she lifted her daughter into her arms. Rocking her from side to side, she gazed at her daughter. Jimmy had done something right, she thought. Lily is one contented baby. And she really is so beautiful, angelic with light, wispy blond hair and the most amazingly piercing blue eyes.

Settled down on the sofa with Lily in her arms, Charlie kissed her gently on the forehead.

"Oh, my sweet girl. I'm so sorry I left you behind. I promise I am going to try and be a good mother now," she pledged. "Between me and your dad we are going to find a way to make this work. I promise."

Charlie was determined to find a way. It was going to hurt, watching Jimmy and Florence as a couple, especially if Lily favoured that girl over her. But if things are precious, it's worth fighting for them.

Charlie had made enough mistakes in her life and her reunion with Lily would not fail. She would find a way to balance work, living in Southampton and spending time with her daughter.

Her pride would just have to take a back seat for now.

CHAPTER THIRTY-SEVEN
POOLE HARBOUR

"Take my hand, Jenni." Richard stretched his arm across the watery gap, encouraging her forward.

Jenni was no sailor. The last time she had been on the water, she and Reggie had taken the boys on a cross-Channel ferry. Jenni had spent the whole journey throwing the contents of her stomach over the side of the boat. And that was a calm, summer day, not the middle of bloody winter. Why, oh why, had she agreed to this trip.

Of course, she had agreed to the trip because she wanted to spend some time with Richard and was far too embarrassed to tell him she was scared of the water. She could have suggested a walk in the countryside rather than jump at his idea of a jaunt on the sea. She would just have to pull her big girl knickers up and get on with it. She actually did have her sensible pants on today as it was freezing cold. Layered up, she resembled the 'Michelin Man Blimp' rather than the sexy woman she hoped to portray.

Jenni tentatively stepped into the boat. As she landed, the craft swayed from side to side. She shrieked, grabbing hold of Richard. Fortunately, he was used to first timers and was ready to steady the boat under their feet and land her safely on the seat. There were only two seats, next to each other and behind the central navigation console. He could see she was scared and that she didn't want to say anything to him, but hopefully once they got underway her nerves would settle, or so he hoped.

It had been Richard's idea to take Jenni out on his boat. Sailing was his passion and he thought it would be a fantastic way to give Jenni a break after the crazy few weeks she had been through. Because it was January and putting a sail up could have been a bit too challenging, he had decided to take his Captain's Launch, which was small, and robust, and had a decent inboard engine. Whilst they were in the harbour, they were fairly protected from the waves and, looking out over the Channel, the conditions seemed perfect for a bit of winter exploring.

Jenni started to relax as she watched Richard take control of the craft. He certainly knew what he was doing and looked confident as he started the engine. He patted her leg and smiled reassuringly. This could be fun. Forget your silly nerves and relax, she thought.

It didn't take them long to move away from the dock and head out into the harbour waters. There was little traffic around so Jenni didn't have to worry about some of the huge specimens which were tied up alongside the docks. There were some monstrosities anchored up. Definitely some money in evidence down here, she decided.

"Okay, Jenni?" Richard asked. She nodded, smiling. "I thought we would take just a short trip across to Arne. It's just across the channel from here and we can tie up on the beach. I even packed a picnic for us."

Jenni was overwhelmed. How thoughtful. She had honestly only expected a quick trip round the harbour then lunch in a pub. His idea was positively romantic, even if romance was the furthest thing from either of their minds.

"Richard, that sounds amazing. What a treat." She reached for his hand and squeezed it. "This is just what I needed. A blast of fresh air and a chance to forget about family for a few hours."

Richard had a good idea about what had been happening. He knew Charlie was back which was probably adding some tension. "How are things going with Charlie and Jimmy?" he asked.

"Remarkably well. Charlie is being very grown up about everything. It's quite refreshing to see. Not that Jimmy is coping with her being around. He is so scared that she will get her act together and take Lily from him." Jenni sighed as she worried about her younger son.

"Do you honestly think she would? Or even could? Surely the courts would look more favourably on you and Jimmy." Richard had a good point, but Jenni really didn't want things to get that far. They would have failed Lily if custody ended up being decided in court, she believed.

"I really hope not, Richard. She has got herself a job working for a small IT company. They do flexible working, which gives her one day off during the week. Her latest proposal is that she has Wednesday off each week and spends that in Sixpenny Bissett with Lily. I am trying to work on Jimmy to agree to that."

The conversation tailed off as Jenni became absorbed by the sights and sounds surrounding her. The lapping of the waves and the wind in her hair had made her completely forget about her nerves. Richard expertly controlled the vessel as he headed out into the main channel. Jenni laid back in the seat enjoying the weak rays of the wintry sun, warming her face. She was really enjoying herself. Now she understood why Jimmy had been so enthusiastic when Richard had taken him out on the boat. There was something about being out in the elements, close to nature.

It didn't take long for the boat to reach a small, deserted beach. Richard stopped the engine short of dry land and tied the boat up to a strategically placed buoy. Jenni looked around puzzled. There must be some means of getting from boat to shore without getting soaked. Okay, she had her old jeans on, but she certainly didn't feel like getting wet legs. Not in this cold.

Before she could ask, Richard was out of the boat and knee deep in water. He had put long waders on, she noticed. "Come on then?" He held out his arms towards Jenni. "You are going to have to let me give you a lift, unless you want a soaking." He laughed at the expression of shock on her face. "Trust me. I won't drop you."

Jenni made the undignified movement into Richard's arms as he waded to the beach. She was able to regain her self-control, while he returned to the boat to pick up the picnic basket. Jenni had enjoyed the feel of his arms around her body. It felt comforting and he smelt amazing. A mixture of aftershave and salty water. A heady mix. Her imagination could have run wild, but she gave it a quiet talking to and put it firmly back in its box.

They found a quiet spot where the beach met sand dunes, sheltered from the wind and with the sun beaming down on them. Richard had brought a blanket which he spread out on the ground. He produced a thermos flask with hot soup and fresh crusty rolls which had been vacuum-packed to keep them warm. As they dipped their rolls into the soup, Richard also opened a bottle of Prosecco. An impressive host who had obviously planned out their meal to perfection.

"Richard, you have thought of everything. Thank you." Jenni toasted him with a clink of glasses before she took a sip. "What a unique way to spend lunch. You are a darling."

She blushed, hoping she hadn't gone too far with the compliments. Whenever they were alone together, they spent their time dancing around a conversation, always worried about saying the wrong thing if their chat became too personal.

"I have even got some of your cake for after," he smiled. "If you don't mind making do with your own baking."

"Only the best," she grinned. "But seriously, I really appreciate you bringing me out today. I have had the most amazing time. Thank you. Jimmy was in one of those moods this morning. The idea of being stuck in the house with him all day was not the most appealing."

Richard had a soft spot for Jenni's younger son. He could see a likeness in the lad with his own youthful struggles. And it certainly can't be easy dealing with a new-born at his age.

"Thinking about Jimmy, I wanted to ask you something." Richard's face turned a bit more serious. "You mentioned Charlie was looking to spend a day in the village looking after Lily."

"Umm," Jenni nodded as she wiped the last of her roll around the remains of her soup.

"What if I take Jimmy to the boatyard on a Wednesday? I could give him a day's training each week with one of my guys. I think he has a real passion for boats and, if he has the talent to go with that passion, we may make a boat-builder out of him. What do you think?"

Jenni turned to look him in the face. "Would you really do that for him?" The smile on her face was payment enough for the favour in Richard's eyes.

"Of course. I would love to. Jimmy has shown such character dealing with the cards he has been dealt. I would like to give him a chance."

Richard believed that once Jimmy started learning the trade, he and Jenni would find a way for him to fulfil that as a career. Not just a hobby. He believed that Jimmy needed a fresh challenge and he had the means of making that happen.

"You are such a wonderful man, Richard Samuels." Jenni took his hand. "That's why I love you." The words were out of her mouth before she realised it. Oh My God, she thought. Why the hell did I say that? "Sorry," she whispered. "I didn't mean it like that. You are such a great friend. That's what I meant."

Richard grinned, clearly not offended. Jenni realised she had been holding her breath, hoping that she hadn't made the same mistake she made last time she overstepped the mark with Richard. Their relationship had grown into one of friendship and she valued that deeply. The last thing she wanted was to muck it up again.

"Can I tell you a secret, Jenni?" She noticed he hadn't withdrawn his hand and was actually stroking his finger across her palm. "I really fancy you."

Richard groaned internally. Bloody hell had he actually said that out loud. He sounded like a pubescent schoolboy. Jenni continued to stare at him in shock.

"Oh shit, that sounds a bit creepy." He grinned trying to make light of the situation. "What I am trying to say is, will you give me a second chance? I made a complete arse of myself last year and I regret it so much. I don't think I was ready. But I am now."

Jenni still didn't say a word. She looked deeply into his eyes as if she was examining his soul to find the truth.

"Jenni, if you would agree to go on a date with me, I will be the happiest man ever. Please say yes." His voice verged on pleading as he waited for her answer.

"Richard, are you sure?" Jenni was not prepared to put herself through another level of humiliation.

"Look, I was too scared to live again when you kissed me last year. The minute I walked out your door, I realised I had made the worst mistake of my life. I have spent the last year hoping that you would forgive me and give me another chance." Richard looked down, averting his eyes. He could not face seeing her rejection.

"What about Nicola? I'm not being nasty, but I really couldn't play second fiddle to a ghost." Jenni shuddered at her words. That sounded awful. "Sorry, Richard. That didn't sound right either. I do understand the depth of your grief so I need to be sure you are ready to move on before I agree to anything."

"You are right to be cautious, Jenni. I will always love Nicola and I will always miss her. Probably the same way you miss Reggie. But I am really attracted to you. I would like us to go on a few dates and just see where that takes us." His eyes found hers again. "We have become really good friends, but that's not enough for me. I want more."

Jenni smiled. "I want more too."

"So can we go on a date?" That serious voice crept in again.

"So today doesn't count as our first date then?" asked Jenni. She was playing along with him.

"Not officially," he grinned. "I want to take you somewhere really special and wine and dine you. Just like you deserve."

"That would be lovely," she whispered.

Jenni moved towards him, slowly, her eyes fixed on his. Her lips quivered as she found his. She kissed him. Richard's hand went behind her back, pulling her into his embrace. Their kiss became deeper, full of desire.

Jenni knew this was where she wanted to be.

In his arms.

CHAPTER THIRTY-EIGHT
ANTONIO'S RESTAURANT

Jenni gazed around the restaurant, as they settled into their seats. She had never been here before and was impressed with Richard's choice. It was located nearer Southampton, away from the public gaze of Sixpenny Bissett. Another thoughtful decision. Jenni had spent too long under the inspectorial watch of the village gossips. Her first date with this special man should take place without the news reaching Anna Fletcher's nasty ears. The dreadful woman would probably combust with opinions.

Richard's choice carried Jenni's approval.

Antonio's bistro was simply decorated, but classy. White, painted walls were adorned with simple seascapes. Pristine white tablecloths adorned the tables, with a small glass jar of flowers and a plain, white candle burning. Music was playing softly in the background, adding to the romantic ambiance. There were only a couple of other diners, spaced across differing parts of the room, which made it feel more private; ideal for a first date.

It had been a week since that kiss.

Jenni had been floating on air, figuratively speaking, since the kiss. Full of excitement for what might be ahead, but at the same time, trying to remain grounded in case she was reading too much into it. Being the good friend she was, Kate had tried her hardest to encourage caution. She was worried that Jenni was desperate for this relationship to work and may even try too hard. Jenni had wanted this to happen since she had moved into the village and, despite her setbacks, seemed to think it was her destiny. Kate was fearful that Jenni might be pinning too much hope on the evening.

Jenni had listened to her best mate, nodding in all the right places, but not really paying attention. She didn't want to hear words of caution. She was convinced that this could be the start of something special and was not prepared to hold back. That wasn't her way. She gave 100% commitment to everything she did and a relationship would be nothing different.

Jenni trusted Richard.

He had said all the right things the week before. She wanted to believe him. She wanted to throw herself, full on, into a relationship with this man. She desired him. She fancied him. Try as she might to not jump too far into the future, she could see this man as her life partner. He could fill that 'Reggie shaped hole' in her heart.

The human mind can be cruel sometimes. It casts doubt where there should be none. A little voice in her head kept reminding her of how wrong she had got it before. Despite Richard telling her what he wanted, could he really be ready to move on? Had he been caught up in the moment? It had been a romantic day and anyone could get carried away, when the excitement got too much.

She desperately wanted to believe him.

That kiss had sealed his promise to try; surely?

The waiter broke into Jenni's thoughts as he asked for their orders.

Richard took control ordering the wine. She liked that. It was a task which Reggie had always taken responsibility for. Reggie had been a true alpha male. Ordering wine, going to the bar, holding her chair out for her. Something Jenni had got so used to over the course of their marriage and missed desperately since his death. She was an old-fashioned girl who loved being looked after.

Jenni silently rebuked herself.

Tonight, she shouldn't be thinking about her past love. Her attention should be firmly fixed on the future. She was determined that she would be totally open with Richard, this evening. She did not want to fall even more deeply for this man, if the future wasn't certain. She had secrets, which she was not ashamed of, but if they were going to commit to each other, honesty in a relationship was vital. If he struggled to accept her past, she wanted to know that now. Her heart was too fragile to allow her to fall for this man if he could not accept her completely. Warts and all.

And that honesty had to be on both sides. Richard had said that she wouldn't play second fiddle to Nicola and she needed to know that he was certain of that.

Tonight was a crucial step forward for both of them.

Jenni waited for their orders to be taken, before she broached the conversation. If she didn't do this straight away, she might chicken out later. It was better to crash and burn at the start of the evening than enjoy their night together and fall at the last hurdle.

"Richard, I need to tell you something," she paused, frantically thinking about how to frame her words. She didn't want to make out that this was a 'big thing', but it was important to her.

Richard stared at her, confusion on his face. Jenni looked worried. Had she changed her mind, already? "What's troubling you, Jenni?"

She swallowed, taking a sip of wine for courage. "I believe in total honesty in a relationship, Richard. So if we are going to make a go of this, I need to tell you something."

"OK?" There was a slight tremble in his voice as his mind ran in circles, imagining the worst.

"I had a bit of a thing going on with Henrique." She watched his face intently, looking for any signs, which were not forthcoming. "Nothing serious. Just, well, just a bit of fun. I want you to know. I don't want to keep secrets from you."

Richard was silent, simply looking into her eyes. He was trying to establish how he felt. Should it bother him? Not really. That was the past. Before him. At a time when all he was giving her were signs of rejection. And it had taken her courage to tell him this. She didn't have to. She was not accountable to him for anything. How he responded seemed really important to her. He must get the tone right.

"Right." He took her hand across the table. "Thank you for telling me, Jenni. You honestly didn't have to, but I really appreciate you trusting me with that."

His voice remained calm and light, with no hint of jealousy. What in the hell was she expecting? That Richard would demand satisfaction from his Spanish rival. Perhaps she had built this up in her mind more than it needed to be. The chances of Richard ever finding out were slim, but her principles were such, that she would hate it if he ever found out and she hadn't been completely honest with him.

"I didn't want you to find out from anyone else. Not that it is common knowledge. Kate is the only person who knows about it. And she is very discrete." Jenni smiled, hesitantly.

"You are a dark horse, Jenni Sullivan," he grinned. "Well, good on you. He was an extremely attractive young man. Although I do feel the weight of expectation falling squarely on my shoulders." He squeezed her fingers. "I confess I am a 'born-again virgin'. You may well have to help me out. I might have forgotten what to do." He laughed, breaking the tension of the moment.

"Are you assuming we are going to sleep together tonight?" Jenni grinned, squeezing his hand in return.

"I certainly hope so," he whispered. Raising his glass, he clinked with hers. "Now let's eat. I think I am going to need all my strength to compete with the legacy of young Henrique."

Well, that was one way to break the ice. It could have been a disaster, but Richard seemed to take it in his stride. She hoped he wouldn't judge her. If anything it would make her feel more relaxed when they slept together. Before Henrique, there had only ever been Reggie. She had been pretty naïve. Henrique had helped her grow in confidence, understanding her worth as a sexy woman.

Any perceived tension disappeared as they enjoyed their food. Jenni felt much more relaxed now that she had told Richard about her secret. She hadn't told him to boast about her sexual conquests or to make him feel jealous or uncomfortable. She had done it because she cared about this man. There would be no secrets between them. When she gave herself to him, it would be completely. This wasn't going to be some 'flash in the pan' sexual encounter. She really believed she was falling in love with Richard.

Love and honesty were inextricably linked in her book.

Whilst they were eating, Richard was contemplating Jenni's confession. He would never have guessed it. In fact, he felt quite relieved that this was the big secret she had to tell. His mind had been going down some dark rabbit holes when she started the conversation. Thank goodness.

He decided Jenni and Henrique must have been very circumspect, to keep that one quiet. Richard should feel jealous. But he didn't. Jenni was a beautiful woman. She was a sexy woman, who any man would want. And, if he was totally honest with himself, he had rejected her. Perhaps if he hadn't run away when he did, they might have got together sooner. But you cannot change the past. That was his mistake and he could not blame her for finding solace somewhere else.

Filling up Jenni's glass with wine, he decided that he should be as transparent in this relationship as his new girlfriend. Was she his girlfriend? Do you use such a term at their age? Who knows. In his mind she was and that's probably all that counts.

He had carried a weight of guilt for the way he had treated Jenni that night at Rose Cottage. He had seen the pain on her face as he pulled away from her advances. He had been an absolute shit and she deserved to know why he had been so scared. He had been confused about his emotions at the time. He had wanted Jenni desperately, but the cold ice which had formed around his heart had prevented him. He had been too scared to let go of the past.

But things were different now. He didn't love the memory of Nicola any less, but he was gradually letting her go. Realising that he had many years ahead of him, years of potential happiness with a new partner. A fresh start, with a new woman by his side.

She had trusted him with her secrets. She deserved the same honesty from him. Even if she despised him when she knew how weak he had been.

"Jenni, I need you to understand why I behaved so abominably when you tried to kiss me that fateful night. I honestly don't want to open up old wounds, but as you say, we should be totally honest with each other and not keep any secrets from each other."

"Only if you feel able, Richard. I wouldn't want you to talk of anything which could be too painful for you." Jenni smiled, her expression full of encouragement and support.

God, that's what he adored about this woman, he thought. Even now, she cared more about his feelings than her own. Why had he not trusted her sooner? He regretted that he had wasted far too much time over the last year.

"Nicola was my soul mate. I guess like your Reggie was to you." She nodded without saying a word. "When Nicola died, I wasn't ready. It all happened too quickly. She was desperate to go and I couldn't let her go. Nicola was in pain; so much pain and all I could do was watch. But I let her down and it's that knowledge which has haunted me for years."

His face showed the struggle of emotions. Even after all these years, to speak about that dreadful time was incredibly difficult.

Jenni reached across the table and took his hand in hers, gently stroking his palm with her fingers. "Are you sure you want to tell me this," she whispered.

"More sure than I have ever been," he sighed. "I have never told a soul this. Nicola asked me to help her go. She couldn't take the pain anymore. She knew she was dying and she knew death was taking it's time to carry her off. She pleaded with me to do it, give her pills or a big dose of her morphine to help her. I couldn't do it." Richard lowered his eyes away from Jenni's face, as if to hide his shame .

Jenni remained silent, allowing him to reveal more, if he wanted. She was starting to understand why the death of his wife had broken the man. Trying to put herself in his position was incredibly hard to do. She had heard stories of couples agreeing suicide pacts when one of them had a terminal illness, but to hear about the struggle Richard and Nicola had lived through, brought those stories to life. A decision no-one ever wants to take.

Richard was finding the telling, easier than he expected. It felt incredibly cathartic to do so. "She lived for a further two weeks after that. I made her live through another two weeks of pain, because I was too scared to kill her." He sighed. "And what made it worse was that the police even questioned me after she died, thinking that I had helped her go. I felt such gut-wrenching shame having to admit to the police that she asked me for help and I denied it. I think I went a bit crazy after that."

He fell silent.

Jenni searched for words to comfort him, words which didn't feel sufficient to recognise the hurt and anguish he must have felt. "You must forgive yourself, Richard. You cannot change the past. All we can do is accept what has happened and learn to live with our demons. None of us are perfect. We can only do what we think is right."

He gazed into her eyes. "You don't think anything less of me then?"

"No. What was asked of you; it's impossible for anyone else to judge. How do we know what we would do if placed in the same circumstances? I cannot imagine how you have dealt with this all these years, on your own."

Jenni had loved Reggie with all her heart. What if they had been placed in a similar situation? Could she have helped him? She didn't think she could. Not if she was totally honest. She would have wanted to live every last moment with Reggie; to stretch out those last precious moments. Was that selfish? Was that cowardly? Who could judge that?

Her admiration for Richard had increased immeasurably. She could really understand his pain and why he was haunted by his wife's passing. He had trusted her with his deepest secret. It made her comments about Henrique seem trivial in the extreme.

"Thank you, Jenni. I was in a dark place for such a long time. Meeting you has given me hope. I want to try and move on from the past. With you. If that's what you want?"

"I wanted you before. I want you even more now," she whispered with a seductive tone to her voice.

He smiled. His demeanour was transformed. A huge weight had been lifted from his shoulders. Sharing his past was giving him hope for the future. It had been therapeutic, sharing his perceived guilt with this woman; this woman he was determined to share his bed with tonight.

He knew he was ready.

His heart could be healed. And Jenni could be the person to help him heal. Richard may still have some challenges ahead, letting his guilt over Nicola's death, rest in peace. But he felt that he now had a woman in his life who could help him let go of the past and focus on a happy future together.

"Did you need to be back in Sixpenny Bissett tonight, Jenni? Is Jimmy expecting you home?" He took a sip of wine, smiling at the thought of the night ahead.

"Not particularly. I didn't say anything to Jimmy. He's in charge of Lily tonight and will probably be in bed before I get back." The atmosphere was charged. "What did you have in mind?" she replied, her excitement growing.

"Why don't we go and check into a hotel? See what happens." Richard motioned to the waiter for the bill. He could hardly control his excitement now.

"Sounds the perfect way to end a lovely meal, Richard."

They gazed deeply into each other eyes. No words were spoken. They let their eyes do the talking. Those eyes spoke of desire, of excitement for what was to come. In fact, the couple could not wait to get out of the restaurant and be alone together.

Was this the start of a new special relationship?

Jenni was excited to find out.

CHAPTER THIRTY-NINE
EPILOGUE

What did the future hold for these star-crossed lovers? They had wasted too much time already. Could they grasp the future together in both hands? And jump together.

Richard would be committing himself to much more than a new woman in his life. She came with a ready-made family. How would he fit into the dynamic of the Sullivan household? Being on his own for so long would make the adjustment of joining a bustling home more challenging. Richard and Nicola had never had children together and now he was taking on two grown up men as well as Jenni. Added to that, there was a baby to be considered. Something entirely new for Richard to experience. Could he cope with the adjustments to his solitary life?

There would be bumps in the road ahead, but that's no reason to avoid going on the journey.

And what about the other residents of Sixpenny Bissett. What might the future hold for them?

The Café at Kate's was proving to be a resounding success, much to the delight of Kate Penrose and her family. Kate's financial situation was finally becoming more stable. Slowly and surely, the weight of worry was lifting from her shoulders. Would Kate be able to relax and enjoy the fruits of her labours? Having a new best friend in Jenni was making her life complete. She loved her new neighbour and couldn't remember what life was like before her arrival. Their laughs and companionship at work made the days working together in the shop the best ever, even accounting for the trauma of Rat-Gate. What would the future hold for the Penrose family? Would it be trouble-free now?

Paula and Alaistair were wrapped up in the first bloom of their relationship. They were gradually feeling their way forward as a couple, learning to trust again. With Peter away in Dubai for the next three years, would this new couple finally find peace and happiness together?

The Manor House sat empty. The loss of Herbert Smythe-Jones resonated across the village. His words of wisdom were sorely missed. His calming influence over the community had left a huge gaping hole. What would happen to The Manor House? Who could possibly afford such a huge estate? Would the new owner bring with them exciting possibilities for the village?

Jimmy Sullivan was the most recent newcomer to Sixpenny Bissett. He may have arrived under a cloud, but he had found a place he could call home. His welcoming, friendly personality was a huge draw for the café. The regular clientele loved him, especially the older ladies who simply wanted to mother the lovely chap. What did the future hold for Jimmy and Florence? Could their relationship survive the negativity of Jacky Smith? She wanted something better for her Flo. Could her attitude be changed to see the good in her daughter's boyfriend? Could Jimmy and Charlie work through the custody arrangements for little Lily Rose without damaging both parents and the innocent child? Time would tell.

Jenni Sullivan loved her new life in Sixpenny Bissett. She had found her calling with the success of the café and her catering business. Her two sons were happy, which is all a mother could hope for. The arrival of Lily Rose had filled Jenni's world with joy. She adored her granddaughter and couldn't imagine her life without her. The juggling act Jenni performed on a daily basis to manage her business and family were worth every sacrifice, just to see Lily's beautiful smile when her grandmother walked into a room. Jenni would do everything in her power to navigate the custody challenges with care, balancing the needs of Charlie with the need to provide Lily with a stable family life.

And then there was her relationship with Richard. Jenni loved him. She was sure of that already. Even after two dates. The wait had been worthwhile. However, when it came to relationships Jenni often wore her 'rose-tinted' glasses. She rushed into love head-long, not thinking about the challenges ahead. How would her sons deal with a new man in Jenni's life? Could they warm to the man about to supplant their father in their mother's heart? Jenni wanted her boys to love Richard. But what if they didn't? Could she live with that?

Living with another man, not her Reggie, would take some getting used to.

Not for one minute did Jenni regret her decision to make a new life in Sixpenny Bissett. She had found new friends, new lovers, and an amazing community.

What the future might hold, only time would tell.

The End

For Now

AFTERWORD
A MESSAGE FROM CAROLINE

Thank you for reading The Café at Kate's. I really hope you enjoyed it as much as I loved writing it.

The book is the second in the three part series based on the fictional village of Sixpenny Bissett. Hopefully, you read The Newcomer before following Jenni's journey into the cake business. The series has been inspired by our move to the countryside in Wiltshire. Life in a rural village is very different to our previous life nearer London and the pace of life is much slower. We love it!

I have to reassure my friends and neighbours that my characters are not based on any of our fellow villagers. I pull my characters from a mix of people I have met over the years. Any similarities to residents in our village would be pure coincidence. Funnily enough, I was told by one of my neighbours, who read The Newcomer, that they know who Peter was based upon. Now I am intrigued to discover who that was!

Whilst writing can often be a solo experience, I am indebted to those who support my ambitions. My husband is my firm supporter, giving me the space to be creative and applauding my sales dashboard, even if it's the tenth time I've looked at it in a day. My daughter, Dr Beth Rebisz, is my BETA reader. Her impartial advice and guidance is invaluable. My mother, Pamela, took on the task of proofreading this book. My usual support was unable to help this time. Mum used her previous teaching skills to challenge my grammar and use of words. She doesn't approve of my use of swear words – some have sneaked through, despite that, for impact reasons only.

If you are hooked on the series, the third book should be out later in 2023. A new arrival moves into the village, retired rock star Bernie Beard. He's quite a character and I think you will enjoy following his antics. He agrees to host a music festival to raise much needed funds for the local cricket club. Jenni's relationship with Richard Samuels comes under the spotlight in the final book. Meanwhile, Jenni's best friend, Kate, faces her own struggles with a health worry.

As an independent published author, reviews are really important to help me grow my audience. I would be delighted if you could leave me a review on either Amazon or Goodreads. Your reviews will help me develop my craft and shape my stories as I continue on my writing journey. Thank you. Every review means the world to me.

I would love to hear from you on social media where you will find out more about my books.

Twitter @Carolinerebisz

Facebook www.facebook.com/crebisz

Website www.crebiszauthor.co.uk

ABOUT THE AUTHOR
CAROLINE REBISZ

Caroline lives in Wiltshire with her husband and their cat Elsie. She has two grown up daughters who inspire and support her work. Family is incredibly important to Caroline and features heavily in her books. As do strong female characters. Caroline has plenty of them in her life.

Throughout her career, Caroline worked in high street banking in a variety of roles. Her passion centred around leading teams of staff and using her communication skills to motivate and inspire. Since taking early retirement she has directed her passion towards writing novels.

Caroline doesn't like to restrict herself to a specific genre. Stories come to her and have to be written. All her stories feature strong-minded women and their families. Hopefully that variety of stories keeps the reader interested. Other books in her portfolio include A Mother's Loss and A Mother's Deceit which are both based on the home they lived in Norfolk, a renovated ex-pub. A Costly Affair is a psychological drama which explores the problem of letting a lie grow and grow.

Caroline is currently working on the last book in The Sixpenny Bissett series and has an idea for a new thriller.

Printed in Great Britain
by Amazon